For Your Benefit

Patrick Canning

MONDAY

"Inadequate information, or false information from unknown sources, may have results of enormous importance."

-Edward Bernays

A Non-Threatening Show of Power

Teddy tries to understand what's happening and fails.

For one thing, Tom Hanks is on the client couch of the Lint Detective Agency. You wouldn't think someone as congenial as Hanks would need to employ a P.I., and that if he did, he could do better than one operating out of a strip mall. Yet here he is.

Odd, too, that the coffee pot in the kitchenette of the Lint Detective Agency is empty. The coffee pot in the kitchenette of the Lint Detective Agency is never empty.

Odder still, the door to the office Teddy shares with his brother, Ralph, is closed. Muffled voices inside suggest there's another client being served, one who's apparently significant enough that Tom Hanks has been left to twiddle his thumbs on the couch.

Teddy adjusts his eyepatch. He's just emerged from a small apartment nestled at the rear of his business. It's an uncommon housing solution, to be sure, but with rent in Los Angeles being what it is, and commutes described in hours not minutes, marrying one's residential and commercial starts to look pretty smart.

"Mr. Hanks," Teddy says. "I'm sorry we've kept you waiting. How can I help you?"

"This is a non-threatening show of power."

"Don't try to get him to say anything else. He won't say anything else." Ms. Beauchamp, secretary extraordinaire, waters a rhododendron on her meticulously organized desk. A slight shake in her hand suggests irritation.

Tom Hanks, who up until now has maintained a calm, almost Zen-like forward stare, can't help a sidelong glance at Ms. Beauchamp and the crimson hyphen of lipstick up her right cheek.

While she performs all assigned tasks in a legendarily precise fashion, Irma Beauchamp, a French-Jamaican librarian-cum-secretary well into her golden years, insists on the daily application of make-up while simultaneously refusing to have any regard for the outcome. "I'm no prize pig to be ogled," she'd famously declared in her job interview years before, when her eye shadow had been off by at least two inches to the right.

It's Ms. Beauchamp who's responsible for the coffee pot being 15/16[ths] full and gently steaming every morning, to the point where it's death and taxes, sunrise and sunset; mysteries abound in the wide, weird universe, but cross the Lint Detective Agency coffee pot off the list of things to worry about because it's been taken care of.

Except today.

Today, something Teddy can't yet identify has created a seismic anomaly in the workplace.

"Mr. Hanks, can I offer you some tea?" Teddy says.

Hanks, pleasant as can be, repeats his mantra, "This is a non-threatening show of power."

"I told you he won't say anything else." Ms. Beauchamp shoots a furious glance at the coffee pot, just now showing signs of liquid along its glass bottom. "He showed up with the man in your office, the man who drank all the coffee. And when I made a second pot, the man drank that, too. Pot three is brewing now. I'd like to see him drink *that*, ho yes, I would certainly like to see him try!"

"Who is it?" Teddy asks in a workplace sotto.

Ms. Beauchamp splashes a second cup of water onto the poor rhododendron, flooding the soil. "I don't know, but a third pot is out of the question. I don't care what your name is, the human digestive system has its limits."

Though he's eager to meet the man who's flapped the unflappable Ms. Beauchamp, Teddy tries one final time.

"Mr. Hanks, are you sure there isn't something I can—"

"This is a non-threatening show of power."

Grenade in the Foxhole

Teddy finds his brother seated behind their shared desk wearing a look of acute exasperation. Ralph gets up at dawn every day to do three hundred push-ups and three hundred squats, so it's anyone's guess as to how long he's been dealing with their mysterious visitor. With nothing more than a slight lift of the eyebrows, Ralph conveys to Teddy: Wait until you get a load of this guy.

The man shamelessly poking around the office is so tall, it's safe to assume the textile demands of his angora wool suit wiped out an entire warren of rabbits. Facewise, he's a gaunt Paul Newman, handsome but haunted with a pair of baby blues held captive by unreasonably tan skin. Early sixties would be a reasonable guess, but this is LA, so really, who knows?

A garish purple pocket square and non-denominational prayer bracelet scream 'advertising' to Teddy. The big guns in marketing are aggressive, clever, and loyal to nothing in particular. The well-groomed infiltrator manhandling Ralph's GED certainly looks the part.

Teddy takes his assessment no further.

For one thing, he likes to give everyone he meets the benefit of the doubt, regardless of their appearance. For another, peculiar is something of an assumed baseline in Los Angeles, meaning the brothers have to regularly entertain eccentric walk-ins if they want to keep the lights on.

The stranger studies Teddy's framed degrees for Criminal Justice and Social Work before rifling through pamphlets on sexual assault and domestic abuse. From a multi-sectioned candy dish on the desk, he pockets a handful of low dose aspirin and pastel after-dinner mints. For a grand finale, he lifts onto his toes, achieving a giraffic level of height to squint at the metal rail that winds along the ceiling.

"Christ Almighty! Is this a dry-cleaning track?"

"Mr. Woodbine," Ralph says. "I'd like to introduce my brother, Teddy. Teddy, this is Dixon Woodbine."

Dixon Woodbine slaps Teddy's outstretched hand in a rough handshake. "And so! The other Lint, at last."

On making skin-to-skin contact with the man, Teddy is gripped by the inexplicable sensation he's just stepped onto a trap door above a very deep hole. But, benefit of the doubt and all that, so he only smiles and nods.

"Pleased to meet you, Mr. Woodbine. And you're absolutely correct, this space used to belong to a dry cleaner."

"The décor in here is downright schizophrenic," Woodbine says. "Half considerate, half practical. Now I just need to pinpoint who's which." His finger oscillates between the Lint brothers and stops on Ralph. "You're the pragmatist."

"As needed."

"Ha!" Woodbine swings his finger over to Teddy, "That makes you the softie."

"That's always needed." Teddy gestures to a chintz chair in front of the desk. "Please have a seat, Mr. Woodbine."

Woodbine folds his great height down into the flowery wingback chair, his knees shivering from the stratospheric amount of caffeine found in two pots of coffee. His thin Virginia accent—a teaspoon of Foghorn Leghorn not commonly found in the set Teddy suspects the man hails from—is vaguely charming, taking the edge off an otherwise careless personality.

Teddy nods toward the door. "It's probably not the best advertisement for our services, but I have to admit I'm a bit confused as to what's happening out there."

"Couldn't agree more. Picasso in a bumper car could put makeup on better than that woman."

"I meant Mr. Hanks."

"Oh, good. You've both seen him now."

Returning to his full height, Woodbine leans out the office door.

"Hit the bricks, Hanks. And we're still under an hour, billing-wise."

A final, soft "This is a non-threatening show of power," is followed by the sound of the front door opening and closing.

Woodbine origamis back into the chintz.

"The why of Hanks being here is more or less a matter of height. Skyscraper physique like mine is ill-advised as far as the heart's concerned. I don't mean affection-wise—we love with the best of the horse jockeys—but the human ticker is basically one size fits all, and with this much real estate to service, the lifespan takes a hit."

"I still don't see the connection," Ralph says.

"Hanks is my legitimacy catalyst. Shows I'm not some no-account loony. This way we can get straight to business, because, as discussed, I'm on the clock. The whole thing becomes self-defeating if I have to explain it for too long, so let's move on. You boys were cradle-snatched and raised in a cult."

The Horse's Mouths

"That's right," Teddy answers quickly, knowing Ralph won't be loving Woodbine's brusque manner. "We were fortunate to escape."

"Guy who found you was a grocer, right? Took you in as his own?"

"Yes, we were adopted by a man named Dan Karrr."

"Mmh. And the sonofabitch who ran the cult? What was his name again?"

"Percival Maw."

"Took your eye." Woodbine stares with naked curiosity at Teddy's eyepatch, today's a rich purple. "Lemme guess. Every Christmas morning it's 'Oh great, *another* eyepatch.'" Woodbine crows with laughter, then pivots to Ralph. "And I read you lost your plumbs, son. No joke there, that's just bad luck. Christ, none of us make it out of childhood intact, but the bastard didn't have to take it literally. Still, the Cyclops and the Eunuch. You two should promote that."

Ralph picks up a hand cruncher he uses for grip strength. The padded twist of metal squeaks as it's compressed beyond the manufacturer-recommended PSI. "We're not a circus act."

Teddy, however, isn't put off. He excels at not being put off. "We get by fine on word of mouth, Mr. Woodbine."

"Not to mention good press." Woodbine pulls a folded bit of newspaper from his wool blazer and reads aloud. "Yesterday, Jocular Beef LLC of Solvang, California was accused by a collective of slaughterhouse employees of grossly underreporting injuries sustained by workers in the company's facilities across the state. The class action lawsuit is supported by findings from the Lint Detective Agency out of Los Angeles, which carried out extensive investigations on behalf of the plaintiffs at great personal risk blah blah blah." Woodbine shows the article's photo of Ralph disguised as a calf. "That's one hell of a leather jacket, son."

"I was locked in a veal crate for two days," Ralph says. "Last week we had a couple cow hearts chucked at our front window, so if the reveal here is that you're another sore loser from Big Beef—"

"No, no. Nothing like that. Story caught my eye is all, enough that I asked around. You boys come highly recommended. Reputation good as the one you have has to be earned. One happy customer called you, Mr. Lint, ornery but reliable. And as for you, other Mr. Lint, they swear you're Black Mr. Rogers in an eyepatch."

A ticket zooms in on the ceiling track making Woodbine jolt in surprise.

"Jesus, Mary, and Joseph! What in the hell is that!"

Teddy plucks a message from the clip and reads, "Mr. Hanks has left the building."

"Only just now, huh?" Woodbine chuckles. "Crafty SOB loitered to get the full hour. Well, you don't get to the top doing favors for other people, I suppose. Reminds me of a time I had fondue with Kissinger. The man got a

Nobel Peace Prize for Vietnam, but no, I'm the asshole for double dipping sourdough."

Even the saintly patient Teddy is getting the feeling it would be unwise to keep Woodbine in the office any longer than necessary. For one thing, Ralph looks about ready to toss the rabbit-suited timewaster out by his collar. For another, the man just feels like trouble.

Teddy clears his throat. "Mr. Woodbine, how can we help you today?"

"Okay, okay. Just wanted a little straight from the horse's mouth. Mouths, in this case."

He lights a cigarette and takes a Herculean drag, crumbling an absurdly long hang of ash onto the arm of the chintz.

"You boys ever heard of Royal Jelly?"

Royal Jelly, A History of

Teddy pushes a glass ashtray, already well within Woodbine's reach, a little closer. "Can't say we have."

Woodbine sucks down the last of his cigarette and extinguishes it in the tray. He squiggles deeper into the chair, getting as comfortable as possible before he speaks.

"If one were to mix equal parts of the herbicides 2, 4-D and 2, 4, 5-T, the result is something we call Agent Orange. Agent Orange contains no small amount of 2, 3, 7, 8-tetrachlorodibenzo-p-dioxin, or simply dioxin. Supremely nasty stuff, ranks right up there with Zyklon B and Napalm in the pantheon of god-awful, manmade shit. In the 1960s, the US government commissioned the creation of eleven million gallons of Agent Orange and donated it to the people of Vietnam without even being asked. Operation Ranch Hand. The aim, in short: to defoliate half the god damn country. Fewer places for the Viet Cong to hide, fewer crops to eat. This drives people into the cities, which are easier to control. All very win-win, assuming you aren't Vietnamese or deciduous."

Teddy jots down the info in a playing card-sized note-book.

"Anyway," Woodbine continues, "our beloved chemical factories are churning out these rainbow herbicides as fast as they can make 'em, packaged in 55-gallon barrels shipped across the Gulf of Mexico, through the Panama Canal, and out into the Pacific. A smaller number of barrels take a more direct route across the continental US in shipping containers."

He lights a new cigarette and burns it down in two pulls.

"One of these land route shipping containers arrives in Vietnam and gains something of a reputation. The equipment grunts say it's haunted, some convinced it's retribution from God for our many sins. Whatever the case, it's making people sick."

"Sick how?" Ralph asks.

Woodbine shrugs. "Sick. Pretty soon, nobody will go near the damn thing, save for one brave soul who paints a bright orange ouroboros, that being the snake eating its own tail, along the sides of the container. Apparently, more of that reap-what-we-sow business. Folks get to calling the box Royal Jelly, don't ask me why."

Ralph hand-crunches. Teddy jots. Woodbine continues.

"By 1971, Ranch Hand has fallen out of fashion. A million and a half gallons of left-over Agent Orange, including the Royal Jelly, are destined for incineration on a no-name spit of sand in the middle of the Pacific. All's well that ends well, right?"

"The Royal Jelly never reaches the no-name spit of land," Ralph suggests.

"Correct. The last point of contact for the Royal Jelly is twenty miles south of this very office, at the Port of Long Beach. The container's number is logged on intake and it's loaded into the stacks. But, days later, when a bunch of frantic military types show up looking for the thing, they can't find it. And it's here, gentlemen, we enter the realm of rumor, the most credible of which suggests the container was taken from the port by someone who knew it was going to be there, someone who then buried it in or around Los Angeles, motive and intention unknown. Forty-four hundred gallons of a substance that kills six ways to Sunday, buried in a backyard, stacked in a garage, who can say? Not a particularly nice thought, but anyone who heard the tale could rest easy knowing nothing ever became of it. Until now."

Woodbine leans forward for the climax of his camp-fire ghost story.

"I'm sorry to say, Misters Lint, I believe somebody has finally found the Royal Jelly."

The Dotted Line

"Mr. Woodbine . . ." Teddy says patiently. "Elements of your story . . . it's all very—"

"It sounds like bullshit," Ralph says.

Woodbine nods thoughtfully. "Could be I'm some loose-bolt pedestrian who wandered into the nearest building with AC, right? Hell, I guess the Hanks card doesn't play like it used to. Still, you two are sharp enough to know a cameo like that doesn't come cheap, meaning, at the very least, you're dealing with someone with access to a high-bandwidth line of credit, and even in the unlikely event I'm some goldbricking jerk-off who likes hiring A-listers to toy with one-eyed Black men and Mediterranean beefcakes, well, at least my check won't bounce."

"We start all cases by taking people at their word," Teddy says.

"You, maybe." Woodbine sends a grin in Ralph's direction.

"I just want to make sure I understand," Teddy says. "You think someone found the Royal Jelly, and you want to know who it is. For your own purposes, or on behalf of an organization?"

"That would be private, Mr. Lint."

"I'm sorry, but we make a point of knowing who we work for. Sometimes it matters."

Woodbine temples his fingers and nods. "I read you. Because maybe I'm trying to sniff out the Jelly for myself, right? Next thing you know, Dow's colorful cocktail turns up somewhere like a Congressional mailroom, and that's not exactly the advertisement you want for your business."

"No, it isn't."

Woodbine sighs. "Fellas, I'll be honest, this bristles. As a not unwealthy individual, I'm not quite used to being told what's what."

"Mr. Woodbine, the gentle approach I employ is unconventional in the field of private investigators. This means I can sometimes deliver unconventional results. If you'd like a more traditional approach, one that, say, allows you to retain anonymity, we can, without hard feelings, refer you to a number of reputable firms—"

"Alright, alright. Everybody keep their shirts on." Woodbine's hand knifes into his jacket and reemerges with a business card. "Case Agent Woodbine, CIA."

Ralph takes the card and studies it. "Why would the federal government need to hire private investigators?"

"Mr. Lint, the federal government is a cruise ship. It's big and hard to turn, and it churns a hell of a lot of water. We're keeping a broad eye on the usual channels of disrepute, but I have a few leads that are a touch more intimate.

You two know Los Angeles in granular ways that may escape me and even significant portions of my team. You're also my low-cost wild card so that, God forbid, somebody lets loose with the Jelly and kills a couple thousand people, I have a paper trail of due diligence. Finally, consider my own personal largess. Imagine the man before you walking into any local watering hole and not causing a complete and total exodus. It won't do."

Teddy taps his eyepatch. "I have something of a unique look myself."

"I've done my homework, Mr. Lint, and I do believe your 'gentle approach' solves that problem. I can, and do, talk 'til my tongue gets sunburnt, but it doesn't always win hearts and minds. Your whole, give-a-damn schtick might just be the best Trojan Horse in town."

"My kindness isn't an act, Mr. Woodbine. I try to hear what people are saying and help them if I can."

A pause follows, highlighting the fact that Teddy and Ralph still haven't said "yes" or any derivative thereof.

Out of Woodbine's bountiful angora blazer comes an envelope distended with cash.

"Five today, forty-five on completion of the job. Let's all thank Our Lady of Non-Discretionary Funds. Fifty K to have a look around doesn't sound so bad, does it? I'll even throw in a per diem. Take a break from weepy cuckolds paying in crumpled bus fare."

The taut skin of Woodbine's face softens, and his voice sheds some of its performative quality.

"Help me do some real good. It's important."

Teddy studies the man before him. His face has all the empirical requirements of eyes, nose, and mouth, but everything adds up to less than it should; decades of cosmetic work, Teddy guesses, have averaged together into something voidlike. Still, a true expression shines through, one that says Dixon Woodbine is in real distress. Of that, Teddy is certain.

Teddy looks at Ralph. Ralph looks at Teddy. A conversation passes between them without a word spoken.

Ralph's face says *No*.

The man needs help, says Teddy's. *So we help.*

Ralph's face delivers a reluctant *Fine*.

Teddy produces a standard contract from the desk drawer. "Mr. Woodbine, we'd be happy to take your case."

Woodbine flicks his cigarette ash off the chintz armrest and gleefully scribbles his signature on the dotted line. Then he daintily snatches up his business card and vanishes it back into his jacket.

"We prefer as little documentation as possible, you understand. This is a delicate and somewhat embarrassing situation for the government, so your discretion is firmly requested. Now that we're all wearing the same team jersey, I can tell you we're looking at two groups in particular. One is an artist collective known as The Order. The other is a governmental-reform movement known as Sisters in Sync."

Teddy scribbles the names down in his notebook. "That's it?"

"That's it. I need figures on organizational integrity, ideological viability, membership demographics, asset holdings, historical reputation, outstanding liabilities, and reactive quotient. Whoever dug up the Royal Jelly probably won't sit on it for long, so let's agree to deliverables on Friday. Every hour that passes is a roll of the dice that Sunset Boulevard isn't doused in a rain of lethal herbicide."

Woodbine returns to his full height once more and wrings the Lint brothers' hands. "No need to contact me, I'll contact you. Happy hunting, boys, happy hunting!"

And with tremendous lack of ceremony, he's gone.

"I thought the CIA couldn't operate inside US borders," Teddy says.

Ralph counts the money in the envelope. "He's about as CIA as Ms. Beauchamp. We're barely past the handshake and already the math is off on this guy. The Royal Jelly story feels incomplete." Ralph looks at Teddy. "Fifty thousand will settle quite a few bills, but it may have been cheaper to avoid the whole thing altogether."

"He may be trouble," Teddy says. "But he's in trouble too. I'm sure of it."

"I guess we'll see."

A note from Ms. Beauchamp whisks frantically in on the ceiling track: *He drank the third pot on his way out!*

Everything In Its Place

Ms. Beauchamp scowls at the lobby. She doesn't like having her routine altered, much less blown to smithereens, which is exactly what Hurricane Woodbine's done to it this morning.

Her normal protocol is as follows.

At precisely eight o'clock: unlock the office, put on the coffee, purge the company e-mail inbox. Sometimes a research trip to the library.

At precisely eleven o'clock: eat lunch—usually Jamaican food in a Tupperware brought from home—while watching *The Lighthouse at Providence*, one of the last surviving daytime soap operas.

At precisely twelve o'clock: take an hourlong nap, no dreaming allowed.

At precisely one o'clock: resume the finest clerical work in the city, perhaps the world.

At precisely five o'clock: put the dust cover over her computer, affix a pillbox hat to her head, and take the bus home.

The office's nine-hundred-and-fifty square feet might not be much, but Teddy and Ralph are good boys, and Ms. Beauchamp takes great care to curate a refuge against the endless nonsense that walks through the front door. Efficiency just so happens to be her preferred aesthetic, but there's a practical need for it as well. Teddy has something of a bad habit when it comes to pro bono work, not to mention deferments for cash-light clients. When the IOUs pile up, they can imperil the company's finances, and by extension, the three other businesses in the tenant-owned strip mall. Along with a streamlined budget, a well-organized facility is crucial to the Agency's survival, so Ms. Beauchamp gets to it.

She dusts the freestanding coatrack in the corner, a thoughtful but useless bit of furniture in sunny Los Angeles. She straightens askew pillows on the pair of couches that face one another across a mid-century coffee table. She fans the magazines on said table, giving a tsk of disapproval at the *Better Homes and Gardens* Tom Hanks has torn several coupons from. She double checks a penciled ledger tracking the lifespan of all lobby light bulbs. She straightens a framed illustration of an East Los Angeles grocery store. She polishes her signed headshot of Royce Janus, the actor who plays the easy-on-the-eyes bureaucrat Mayor Becksdale on *The Lighthouse at Providence.* Lastly, the custodian, administrator, and when it comes down to it, backbone of the Lint Detective Agency straightens the floral runner in front of her desk, drains the flooded rhododendron in the kitchenette sink, and refills the coffee pot a fourth and final time.

With anomalies stemming from the morning's client meeting now managed (the rude interloper little more than a dimming memory), order reigns supreme once again in the Lint Detective Agency.

And that's just the way Ms. Beauchamp likes it.

The Denizens of Lorenzo Dunes

Los Angeles may look glitzy on postcards and movie screens, but the meat and potatoes of its landscape is the humble strip mall: an L-shaped building of soulless beige stucco with a Chicano mural on one side if you're lucky. This bland, commercial microcosm usually hugs a cramped parking lot wedged into the corner of a busy intersection. Repeat the model a few thousand times and you have a city, or something that closely resembles one.

Lorenzo Dunes fits the bill exactly, its featureless architecture a passive-aggressive challenge to future archaeologists, daring them to try and guess how we lived, and what for. The inhabitants of Lorenzo Dunes, however, consider it to be something of a house, a home even, and none more so than Teddy Lint. Just now emerging from the Lint Detective Agency for his daily round of "good mornings," Teddy is a believer in the direct application of compassion, an attitude he insists is caught not taught. In other words, kindness ripples.

He heads first to Raoul's Pawn 'n' More, the other business on the strip mall's second level. When he's not lowballing the destitute on heirloom jewelry, Raoul does payday loans, cash for gold, and bail bonds (these being the 'n' More). Raoul has chronic gout and eleven grandchildren, both of which make him ill-tempered. Teddy remarks positively on Raoul's nice red suspenders and tells him he might know a buyer for the Wild West era gun safe that's been taking up space in Pawn 'n' More for going on three years.

Down the stairs then to SUDS!, a coin-op laundromat run by a live-wire named Maggie, a single mother of three high school-age boys. Maggie spells the business name with all caps and an exclamation point in an effort to trick her customers into thinking they're excited about doing laundry. Her other bit of marketing genius involves a ferociously stupid parakeet named Belfast, who's plied with the daily specials over breakfast so he can squawk them at customers throughout the day. Teddy shoots the sympathetic breeze with Maggie, discussing, among other things, strategies for stretching a week's worth of groceries into two, all while Belfast screeches about a new fabric softener branded as smelling like Fiji.

The fourth and final tenant of Lorenzo Dunes, located directly below the Lint Detective Agency, is Chim Chim Donut, run by Phirum and Mony Chim. Like many donut shop owners in LA, the Chims are Cambodian-Americans who traded the Khmer Rouge for pastry sales and never looked back. Both Phirum and Mony work like the dickens, somehow moving a high volume of bright pink donut boxes 24-hours a day, every day, while remaining the most pleasant couple you could ever hope to share a strip mall with. This morning, they're dealing with a price gouging powdered sugar supplier, but what can you do? What Teddy will do is research the fair market price and see if he can't find them an alternate supplier.

The collective mood around Lorenzo Dunes buoys.

Even grumps like Raoul look forward to Teddy's daily emotional welfare check, and Monday morning soon finds everyone in as good of spirits as can be expected. Perfectly timed with Teddy's exit from Chim Chim Donut, a pale green sedan pulls into the parking lot, Ralph behind the wheel.

As Mony and Phirum might say, it's time to make the donuts.

The Celery Express Heads North

As the brothers cruise north on Pacific Coast Highway, Ralph tunes the radio to an easy listening station. The tuner knob fights him more than a tuner knob should, something that might cause a more skittish driver to scramble for the door and sputter "G-g-ghost!"

Ralph, however, remains calm.

The 1999 Ford Crown Victoria was originally property of the FBI's San Diego field office, where it gained the reputation of a bucking bronco. The car that dribbled wiper fluid and burned through brake pads like it had a score to settle was assigned to rookies as a rite of passage until one day someone fresh out of Quantico left it unlocked on the streets of Chula Vista, and it was promptly snapped up by the Sinaloa Cartel.

Details of the Ford's adventures south of the border are unknown, but at some point, it came stateside again, popping up in a police auction in San Pedro where it was bought by one Dan Karrr, a small-time grocer seeking affordable transportation for his then twenty-two-year-old adopted sons who'd just started their own detective business.

Anyone with good sense would've regifted the Crown Vic post haste, or at least shipped it off for an automotive exorcism, but having never received anything more expensive than a matchstick in their lives, Teddy and Ralph were dizzy with gratitude and devoted themselves to taming the vehicle into a force for good.

Out with the smuggling compartments' Saturday Night Specials and tape-swaddled bricks of whatever, in with domestic abuse hotline keychains and vials of Narcan that always went fast. The trunk was stocked with not one, but two sets of jumper cables, along with a zoo of stuffed animals for the traumatized children who inevitably turned up in the course of private investigations. The car's original municipal brown paint job, bleached a diarrheal orange by the Tijuana sunshine, was newly covered with a coat of pale green. Dan Karrr remarked they might as well call it the "Celery Express," and so they did.

So, it's in the Celery Express that Ralph and Teddy are zooming up the literal West Coast, Teddy using the time to decompress from his morning rounds. While he adores the daily custom with his neighbors, inhaling in the carbon dioxide of everyone else's problems and exhaling solutions sometimes leaves him out of breath.

Teddy's probably thirty, though no one knows for sure, not even him. He's got black skin, black hair, and a capsule wardrobe of cardigan sweaters spun from indignantly comfortable cotton. He often color-matches the day's sweater with the day's eyepatch.

Ralph, currently giving the finger to a tailgater, is probably thirty also. He has olive skin, and hair even blacker than Teddy's. He favors short-sleeve dress shirts that Ms. Beauchamp says make him look like a toll booth worker. Occasionally religious, Ralph wears a necklace featuring the ever-popular St. Christopher, patron saint of travelers and religious jewelry manufacturers everywhere.

Teddy's cat-whisker sensitivity and Ralph's vigilance against ill-intentions invited by that sensitivity pair together well. Ralph takes care to wring out his empathetic sponge of a brother now and then, and Teddy ensures his short-fused brother stays out of jail. The dynamic has worked for them as business partners for the last eight years.

"Woodbine," Ralph says.

Teddy nods, as if this is quite the question. "I gotta say, the whole Tom Hanks thing was pretty impressive."

"Sure, but Woodbine's no G-man. So what is he?"

"My guess is advertising. He's charming in that kind of way."

"As an ingrown hair. He has to assume we're going to check his credentials, so why bother with the rouse?"

"I think it's a catalyst," Teddy says. "'Federal government' gets people asking how high to jump. If he can hook us with a three-letter agency, semantics like the truth can be addressed later, if ever. Mercy, that Jocular Beef case really gave us some visibility, didn't it?"

"Maybe too much."

Their phones ding with a text message: a data drop from Ms. Beauchamp.

While the Lints have their cursory, Wikipedia fact finds, Ms. Beauchamp is a former librarian whose proficiency with microfiche is a thing to behold. Her increasingly rare analogue skill set regularly equips the brothers with valuable information, though the updates are not without their quirks, namely that they arrive at random and are usually supplemented with fan theories about *The Lighthouse at Providence*.

> **Irma**: No hits on 'Dixon Woodbine' or 'Royal Jelly' yet. Agent Orange, so-called because of the orange stripes painted on the barrels it was transported in, was an herbicide used in the Vietnam War. Over 5 million acres of upland and mangrove forest and about 500,000 acres of crops were destroyed across Vietnam, a total area approximately the size of Massachusetts. The technocratic strategy was emblematic of the US's failed effort to exert control over a foreign landscape and its inhabitants, who rejected American power until our will ultimately failed. I don't trust Mayor Becksdale's new au pair. Charlotte St. Claire is going to be trouble, I can smell it.

"Massachusetts?" Teddy says. "Mercy. That's a lot of dead plants."

Ralph does a U-turn and parks outside one of the Malibu beach houses that sit dangerously flush with PCH.

"Dad's?" Teddy asks.

"Everything we have on Royal Jelly comes from Woodbine. We need a second opinion."

"Dad doesn't talk about the war. And now that he's sick—"

"So, you admit he's dying."

"I admit he's sick, and he won't get better if we upset him."

"Doctor Scanlan says he won't get better no matter what we do."

"We can't take this to Dad, Ralph. If we need a veteran's perspective, there are plenty of other places to get it."

"Like where?"

Teddy thinks. "That bar up in Ventura. The one by the Navy base."

"The Clove Hitch."

"Right. We can find an enlisted man there, no problem."

"Okay, fine." Ralph opens his door.

"So where are you going?"

"He's our father, Teddy. And he's dying. Whether you admit it or not."

Malibu Marx

Dan Karrr watches the clouds go by from the comfort of a lawn chair in his sandy backyard.

The modest ranch house behind him is the exception in a long line of eight-figure vacation homes sandwiched between the curvy PCH and a ribbon of pristine beach. Bought decades ago with assistance from the Vietnam Era G.I. Bill, Karrr's house has survived earthquakes, mudslides, and an increasing number of wildfires, but to say it has thrived would be a stretch. The scant front lawn is losing a war to crab grass, and the home's rear walls continually shrink in restless drifts of sand. But it's hanging in there, just like Karrr.

His mane of white hair blends seamlessly into the short white beard below. A pair of scratched Aviator sunglasses straddle the bridge of his nose, and a rolled paisley bandana hangs loose around his neck. His favorite Hawaiian shirt—once a vibrant, banana peel yellow—has faded to the yellow of an actual banana, because all-day, every day, Karrr sits out in the sun and watches the clouds go by.

Gone are the days of driving to East Los Angeles to work at Farmer's Delight, the grocery store that had been his entire career. After coming back from the war, he'd stayed at a late aunt's house in Rancho Palos Verdes for a few months. She'd owned a small citrus grove and occasionally sold lemons to Farmer's Delight, who were always looking for good baggers. So began Karrr's trajectory of bagboy, cashier, junior manager, manager, and finally, owner. Forty years of early morning produce deliveries and late-night accounting. He could still smell the black markers he'd used to write sale prices on posters, could still hear the grumble of canned thunder before the fruits and veggies got spritzed. What a ride. Karrr had always enjoyed it well enough. It was certainly simpler than what had come before.

A smoke-colored cat jumps onto Karrr's lap and stretches, her nails pulling threads from his linen shorts. The cat's name is Phù. Karrr always has a cat named Phù. Whenever the current Phù dies, Karrr goes to the shelter and adopts the oldest, ugliest cat they have. Then he names it Phù and tacks on a number. The current incarnation, Phù XIII, has bent whiskers and a frayed tail that suggest she might not be long for this world. Since Karrr understands himself to be in much the same position, he thinks a Phù XIV is unlikely.

Phù XIII glares at a dog being walked by its owners down by the surf. One of the people points toward Karrr's house and mouths "That's Malibu Marx."

The Marx in question isn't a person but a statue, and the statue isn't even of Marx.

The two-ton bust half submerged in the sand near Karrr and Phù XIII is of Karrr himself. The stone monstrosity came into Karrr's possession by way of his sons after one of their clients, a starving artist, offered to pay in trade: solve my case and I'll transform the Volkswagen-size block of low-grade white alabaster in my studio into a likeness of your choosing. Once Teddy and Ralph had finished the job, they picked their father as the subject, and soon learned that some artists are starving for a reason. The resultant carving—wild-haired and heavily bearded—ended up resembling, more than Dan Karrr or anyone else, Karl Marx, the German philosopher loved and hated around the world. Karrr found the whole thing hilarious, and proudly displayed the four-thousand-pound head in his backyard, where Malibu Marx quickly became a local landmark.

"Hey, Dad."

Ralph closes the house's sliding glass door behind him.

"Hiya, Ralph. What's the good news?"

"You're out here too much. I wish you'd at least use an umbrella or something."

"A terminal diagnosis gets one thinking more past than future, and cloud watching is good for reminiscing. Grab a seat, and hand me a drink."

Ralph sits in the flimsy lawn chair next to his father's and digs a tiny bottle of vodka out of a plastic bag dangling from the arm. The sand around Karrr's chair is littered with mini liquor bottles. The aftermath of a Lilliputian Bacchanalia, maybe. That, or Dad's got a drinking problem. Karrr thinks if he can restrict his drinking to the fun-size bottles he won't die a full-blown drunk, an okay theory so long as he doesn't drink five or six a day, which he does.

Karrr drinks down the vodka and tosses the empty with the others. "Thanks. Now what in the hell is your brother up to in there?"

Through the sliding glass door, Teddy can be seen in the kitchen taking mixing bowls and measuring cups out of the cabinet.

"He said he's going to make you some food," Ralph says. "Your fridge is pretty empty, but I'd say it's part of his do-anything-to-keep-from-seeing-you-like-this initiative."

"I look that bad, huh? Ahh, s'okay," Karrr slurs a little, looking back to the clouds. A liquid lunch and heaven-knows how many hours of direct sun have done a number on his lucidity. "Not a bad life I've had. No, not bad at all."

A Cancer by Any Other Name

Ralph watches his father watch the clouds. Karrr's never been one to talk about himself, but these days, especially with the uptick in drinking, bits and pieces of the autobiography have been slipping out.

Ralph glances back at the house. Teddy's busy with whatever he's cooking in the kitchen. They agreed mum's the word on Vietnam and Royal Jelly, but if Karrr just so happens to bring up the war himself . . .

"Tell me about that not bad life of yours, Dad."

"I managed a grocery store." Karrr shrugs. "Not exactly inventing the wheel but so what? I think I did good by people. Fed them. Nourished them. That means something."

Phù XIII slides out of his lap and bats the little bottles around in the sand.

"Nearly had a wife once," Karrr says. "Did you know that?"

"I didn't."

"She wanted to have kids. I couldn't give her that. *Wouldn't,* if you want to be pedantic. I told her it wasn't a good idea considering everything I'd been through. Told her adoption's a damn fine thing. She said no. She said there's a species of snake that tricks birds into keeping its eggs warm. Then the baby snakes hatch and eat the bird. She thought it was quite the analogy. How in the hell do you argue with a mind like that? Oh well. Bon voyage, Gladys. Keep an eye out for those snake eggs! I certainly did okay by the ones I found."

He lands a heavy hand on Ralph's arm.

"Sorry, Ralphie. Shouldn't talk about the damn cult like it was good luck."

"You got us out, Dad. Talk about it however you want."

An off-leash schnauzer trots up and lets Malibu Marx have it right between the eyes, hinging its face all the way down to the sand to do it. Karrr lets the dog be until it growls at Phù XIII, at which point he sprays it with a hose lying next to his chair.

He laughs, then coughs.

"Terminal lung cancer, Ralphie, the last hurrah by definition. A cancer by any other name would kill just as quick, only shame's in pretending otherwise. Things certainly could've turned out worse."

"And they're not over yet."

"No. Not quite. That's enough about me. Let's have something from your life. New cases. Anything."

"We picked up a new one just this morning. Guy named Woodbine. Very odd."

"Yeah, and what's this Woodbine want?" Karrr's head sags toward his chest in the beginnings of an afternoon nap.

Ralph hesitates. He wants to ask about the Royal Jelly, but Teddy said not to. It's more or less a matter of the heart, and in matters of the heart, Ralph defers to Teddy.

"Nothing worth mentioning. Sweet dreams, Dad."

The Metabolic Blues

Karrr's pantry is far from stocked, but like the good grocer he is, he's got a few bits of fresh produce for Teddy to work with.

Teddy searches high and low before zeroing in on an unlikely hero abandoned at the back of the vegetable crisper. For most, the lowly stalk of celery (4 cal.) would be a non-starter. For the calorie-restricted Teddy, it's a godsend.

During the first thirteen years of their lives, Teddy and Ralph subsisted almost exclusively on water and a tasteless nutrient mash. Such was the menu in Percival Maw's cult. Once the boys were out, deprogramming counselors told them and the five other rescued children cautionary tales about castaways who, having had their prayers answered by an eagle-eyed Cessna pilot, returned to the land of plenty only to eat themselves to death. "Take it slow" was good advice, but the food landscape in twenty-first century America is a sensory minefield, and the mammal brain loses to the lizard one more often than we'd like to admit. So, despite the pleas for moderation, young Teddy embarked on a three-year, high-calorie bender that was truly something to behold.

Snacks and candy had their charms, but for Teddy, the name of the game was fast food. If it had a cartoon logo, hard plastic seating, and more preservatives than military field rations, he was in. It didn't take long for the once-scrawny cult survivor to find himself dangerously over-weight, chronically ashamed, and entirely incapable of changing his behavior.

Ralph, whose initial circumstances were identical to Teddy's, avoided a similar fate only by fortune of discovering a passion for exercise that dovetailed perfectly with early-bloomer puberty. He did his best to help Teddy, as did their new adoptive father, who brought home ripe fruits and vegetables seven days a week.

Still, it was no use. Teddy's tailspin continued until obesity-related diseases discussed at checkups began to lose their pre-prefix, meaning if a change didn't come, diabetes and hypertension surely would.

The solution, surprisingly, came from Teddy's own body.

Tired of the fast food abuse, his overworked stomach, intestines, and colon—basically the who's who of the digestive system—decided on tough love for the sake of self-preservation. A firm caloric ceiling was put in place, which, when violated, resulted in uncomfortable side effects. Vertigo, disorientation, jelly legs, ulcers, hallucinations, respiratory strain, heart palpitations, night terrors; Teddy's body pulled every lever it could to get him to stop living like a garbage disposal. At first, the symptoms came if he ate more than two thousand calories a day. Then a thousand. The threshold dropped week after week until finally bottoming out at ninety-nine calories. Ninety-nine calories from which Teddy's body could seemingly extract all the nutrients it needed.

Dieticians, pathologists, and any RN with a passing interest in weird shit would've been fascinated by the teenager who could be laid out by a hoagie (450 cal.), but none ever got the chance. Deathly embarrassed of his condition, Young Teddy would only see Karrr's family doctor,

Doctor Scanlan. Scanlan performed an exhaustive physical examination on Teddy, and while he couldn't pinpoint the disorder's specific mechanics, he confirmed that as long as Teddy stayed at or below ninety-nine calories, it appeared he would enjoy perfectly good health. Scanlan named the bizarre but seemingly harmless condition Post-Traumatic Hypometabolic Magnification Syndrome.

Teddy learned to live with his PTHMS, but it wasn't always easy. Gone were the carefree days of Oreos (53 cal.) and mozzarella sticks (102 cal.). He once got dizzy from looking at a particularly high-resolution picture of a hot dog (145 cal.).

Since even reasonable portions of these foods were calorically costly, Teddy found himself forced into an arranged marriage with the much-maligned, green-haired stepchild of the parsnip family: good old celery. But it wasn't all bad. For four measly calories, celery offered a robust helping of Vitamin A, Vitamin C, and yep—you guessed it—folate. Better nutrient bang for your buck was hard to find, so he accepted the vegetable into his life with open arms.

Teddy reverently removes the stalk of celery from Karrr's refrigerator.

The ribs have some give in the middle and one or two of the leaves show signs of yellowing, but altogether not a bad specimen. With the help of ancillary ingredients and no small amount of culinary daring, Teddy whips up celery soup (163 cal.), celery soda (80 cal.), and most impressive of all, a celery parmigiana (181 cal.) that doesn't smell half bad.

He's putting the last touches on the parmigiana when a text arrives from Ms. Beauchamp.

> **Irma**: Between 1962 and 1971, the U.S. military
> sprayed roughly 11 million gallons of Agent Orange
> in central and southern Vietnam. The herbicide's

dioxin content was abnormally high due to the accelerated pace of wartime production. Dioxin can enter the food supply through the fat of fish and other animals and remain in the soil for generations. Large tracts of land in Vietnam remain unproductive to this day. Dioxin also poses a significant epigenetic hazard: children born from exposed persons may experience debilitating birth defects. How could Mayor Becksdale have put a bomb in Sandra's wedding cake the same weekend he was having an affair in Narragansett? It doesn't add up.

Ralph quietly comes in through the sliding glass door. "You should go see Dad."

"Looks like he's sleeping," Teddy says as he puts the meals into the freezer.

"Teddy. I don't know how much longer—"

"He's sleeping, Ralph." Teddy holds up his phone, showing the message from Ms. Beauchamp. "And we have work to do."

The Seabees Have a Drink

The fertile plains of Oxnard, California, blessed with rich topsoil and a to-die-for climate, come to an abrupt end at the chain-link fences of Port Hueneme, West Coast home of the Navy's famed construction battalion, the Seabees.

Everywhere you look airplane hangars and heavy machinery are painted with a scowling bumble bee who wields a Tommy gun, wrench, and hammer above the adorably optimistic motto: "Can do!" And the Seabees aren't kidding either. They built the flamethrower tanks that char-broiled Axis bunkers, moved literal mountains for airstrips in the Korean War, and were even known to charge NVA positions in fortified bulldozers.

Tales such as these are not uncommon in the Clove Hitch.

The self-proclaimed dive bar sits a quarter-mile north of the base and so close to the ocean its windows are salted opaque with sea spray. There's a pool table but no cues, a pay phone that hasn't worked for years. The life preservers on the walls have a charming reek of brine, and the drinks are all doubles by default. There are worse places to get loaded.

The stools are half-occupied by a gallery of bar flies drinking in the red, tessellated glow of hurricane lamps spaced out along the bar. A trio of firm-faced divorcées up from LA jockey for the worst ex-husband story to an audience of disinterested Hell's Angels, defanged by old age.

At the end of the bar, past an aerospace group down from Vandenburg and a smattering of local farmers, sit two individuals most recently described by one of the Angels as "a five-foot shitstain and his pet She Hulk."

While unkind, this assessment of Mario Pewpee and "Big Sue" Swami, enlistees in the Seabees' Amphibious Construction Battalion, is not necessarily inaccurate.

At four-foot-eleven with a push broom mustache, Mario bears a shocking likeness to his famous videogame namesake. Mario knows this and doesn't like to be reminded. On more than one occasion, he's put a man in the hospital (has had Big Sue put a man in the hospital) for cracking "Where's Luigi?" or similar. Mario has all the conscience of a mousetrap, and the most dangerous position you can find yourself in is between him and a dollar.

Big Sue is far more pleasant. She has curly blonde hair and an innocent smile. When it comes to aggression, she rates somewhere below a butterfly. You wouldn't call her book smart, but she was varsity wrestling captain at Cal Poly and can field strip a backhoe in half an hour. The worst thing you could say about Big Sue is that she regularly associates with Mario.

Anyone wondering why she does this would do well to remember that Big Sue is catastrophically gullible. Mario certainly doesn't forget it and takes care to maintain a steady stream of manipulation in her general direction: put downs to destabilize, compliments to endear, a forever flipping coin as to which might come next. Also relevant is the fact that Big Sue has a beloved and stone-broke uncle with diabetes, that the price of insulin is restless, and that Mario, disreputable as he is—and he *is*—does manage to scheme his way into pockets of money on a semi-regular basis. So, when it comes to the big questions in life, like who to hurt and where to drink, Big Sue defers entirely to Mario.

The unlikely pair of Seabees are swilling blindingly strong mai tais while they wait for well-done skirt steaks. Steaks at the Clove Hitch are pancake thin and more gristle than not, but if you don't eat something, the drinks are liable to knock you clean off your barstool.

Rum dripping from his mustache, Mario side-eyes the two strangers next to him at the bar. One of them has an eyepatch.

Chewing the Fat

The guy with the eyepatch is Black. Mario dislikes Black guys on principle, doubly so when they're buddied up with Italians or Greeks or whatever the Black guy's friend is. The Mediterranean has quite the set of arms on him, though nothing Big Sue couldn't handle. The Black guy has apparently also ordered a steak, because one's just been set on the bar in front of him, and then—and this enrages Mario—the guy just *smells* the meat. After a few deep inhales, he pushes the steak over to the Mediterranean, who eats it in four bites.

Then the Black guy offers the plate's untouched fries to Big Sue.

Faced with the glaring headlights of independent thought, Big Sue looks wide-eyed at Mario. He shrugs.

"Terrific!" the Black guy says.

He slides the fries over, then moves a stool closer himself, as if Mario wouldn't notice. He gives his name, Teddy, and introduces his "brother," Ralph. Right. Mario thinks these two look about as related as him and Cleopatra. Teddy asks for their names, almost like he thinks the four of them are friends all of a sudden. Won over by deep fried potatoes, Big Sue offers up the information all on her own. Mario will have to keep an eye on that.

He's preparing, in no uncertain terms, to tell their new friends to get lost, when Teddy orders everyone another round of mai tais (though he only drinks water himself). Must be on the wagon. Mario can't stand people on the wagon, but if they're giving away mai tais they can stick around, provided they don't put Big Sue's loyalties in flux.

"By chance, have you ever heard of Royal Jelly?" Teddy says.

Mario snorts. "Every grunt from Point Loma to Hunter Liggett's heard of Royal Jelly."

"And?" Ralph says.

Mario stares him down. "Shipping container. Agent Orange from back in the day."

"So, it's actually real?" Teddy says.

"Depends on who you ask, but I'd say so. The military has fuck ups like that all the time."

Big Sue polishes off the plate of french fries, burps, excuses herself.

"How do you mean?" Teddy asks. "If it isn't too much trouble."

Buzzing from his free cocktail, Mario indulges them.

"Way I've heard it, an innocent typo sent one of the shipping containers leaving Dow Chemical to the Nevada National Security Site, the godforsaken patch of desert where we've detonated a couple hundred nuclear bombs. Two months the container sits there, soaking up all sorts of ambient radioactivity before some hump in middle management realizes it's not supposed to be there. Not wanting to take heat for someone else's mistake, the guy just sends the container on its merry way."

Mario swallows another gulp of mai tai. *Free* mai tai, he thinks, reminding himself why he's even giving these assholes the time of day.

"The barrels get a nice tour of the Pacific, make land in Saigon, and are trucked out to a forward operating base, ready for action. Thing is, the munitions techs in charge of the stuff are starting to get a real deep-fried look to their faces, and fingernails are falling out faster than fingernails should. Someone plays hot and cold with a Geiger counter and surprise, the newly arrived payload of Agent Orange is practically glowing. These poor bastards are in possession of a couple thousand gallons of weaponized herbicide so ferociously radioactive they won't even use it on enemy combatants."

Teddy can't help a breathless "Mercy."

"The servicemen take to calling the stuff Royal Jelly, the supremely nutritious and life-giving secretion bees grow their queens in. I guess being forced to kill strangers for eighty bucks a month skews the sense of humor. In any case, the Jelly's scheduled to be incinerated, but by accident or not, ends up back in America instead. Long Beach. Then *poof*: it's off the radar for good. The fairy tale usually ends with someone burying the box in Southern California. Now then. What makes you so curious?"

Curiosity & the Cat

"I could ask you the same thing," Ralph says.

Mario imagines Big Sue kicking the guy's knee sideways out in the parking lot. He smiles.

"What's so funny?" Ralph asks.

"Just thinking," Mario says. "Thinking about what curiosity did to that cat."

"We're . . . military historians," Teddy says. "Yeah."

Teddy is so spectacularly bad at lying that even Big Sue understands this cover story as being zero percent true. He quickly moves on.

"What would happen if somebody got a hold of the stuff?"

Mario swirls the dregs of his mai tai. "Don't know why anyone would give a shit about fifty-year-old weed killer, but if they had half a brain, they'd sell it. Could be valuable to the right *black* market customer, as I'm sure you know."

Ralph gives Mario a look that says he'd love to squash him into a paste, though he seems to decide a bar-leveling brawl with Big Sue is best avoided.

Teddy ignores the comment entirely and lowers his voice. "By chance have you heard any rumblings lately? Like, I don't know, about someone finding the Royal Jelly?"

"As a matter of fact, I haven't," Mario says. "Seems like you know something I don't."

"Oh, we're just curious." Teddy gets up from his stool. "It's been great meeting you two, I hope we run into each other again."

He signs his tab and heads for the door, along with the Mediterranean.

"Hope to run into you again," Mario quietly echoes.

The well-worn machinery of a scheme spins up to speed between his ears. He'll be damned if it doesn't seem like these pricks somehow know where the Royal Jelly is. Not only do they know where it is, they couldn't help but brag about it to two Navy saps minding their own business at a bar.

Mario hurries over to a porthole facing the parking lot. Through the window's salty vignette, he can just make out the plate number of the ugly green sedan driving off into the night.

"I thought they were nice," Big Sue says when Mario returns to the bar.

Mario gives a small chuckle and shakes his head. "Christ, Sue. They thought we were chumps."

"How do you know that?"

"Because I know. Those two have the Royal Jelly or at least know where to find it."

"Do you really think it's worth something?"

"The world's a demented place, and there's an ass for every saddle, even when that saddle is a box of radioactive Agent Orange. This could end up being a nice little payday for us."

Their steaks arrive.

"I thought they were nice." Big Sue saws angrily into her meat. "I can't believe I thought they were nice."

"They're master manipulators, Sue, what do you expect? But something tells me they'll rue the day they tried to trick Big Sue Swami. They've got more dollars than sense if you know what I mean."

Big Sue stops chewing her steak as she tries to solve the riddle.

"Forget it," Mario says. "What do you say? Think we can unburden two loudmouths of their undue fortune and bankroll Uncle Swami's insulin supply forevermore?"

Big Sue's response comes loud and clear through a mouthful of gristle. "Can Do!"

C.S.A.

The brothers' final appointment of the day is a standing one.

With an endless influx of hopeful young transplants and a surplus of locals practiced in storytelling, Los Angeles is a reliable hotbed for cult activity. So, Monday nights at nine o'clock, Teddy and Ralph host a Cult Survivors Anonymous meeting, held in Chim Chim Donut because even if the smell of deep-frying dough doesn't solve emotional trauma outright, it certainly doesn't hurt. Phirum and Mony are happy to offer up their store's seats during the low-volume nighttime hours because a) they're fine people, and b) a regularly scheduled crowd of hungry cult survivors is good for the bottom line.

With every booth at full capacity, the occupants nervously clutching donuts and coffee, a tense silence fills the shop. The Lints give space for anyone to find their tipping point, but after another minute of half-smiles and coffee slurps, it's clear a jump-start is necessary.

"My name is Ralph."

The crowd gives a relieved chorus of "Hi, Ralph."

Ralph thoughtfully sips from his styrofoam cup of decaf. He's not an emotions-on-his-sleeves type, but he and Teddy learned long ago that their unconventional upbringing was too big a thing to repress.

"Thirty or so years ago, seven individuals, including myself and Teddy here, were stolen from maternity wards by a man named Percival Maw. For the first thirteen years of our lives, our world was a six thousand square foot industrial laundromat here in Los Angeles.

"Food didn't come from Papa Maw's weekly trips to the grocery store, he manifested it out of thin air. The booms we heard on the Fourth of July weren't fireworks, they were demons waiting on the other side of doors we weren't allowed to use. The people we saw on TV were colorful genies conjured by Papa Maw's imagination and will alone. Any attempt to connect the dots of what was going on outside was easily confused by The Story.

"It began as a bedtime story, one that chronicled the heroic feats of Papa Maw, every word of it beyond question. That's what we were told, so that's what we believed. The older we got, the more important The Story became. We read it on our own, and eventually performed it as a play.

"Maw loved the stage production of The Story, loved it so much that even the smallest mistake would bring punishment. One of our sisters lost a finger, one of our brothers, a toe. I was chemically castrated. These punishments were for errors in supporting roles. Teddy had to perform the part of Maw himself.

"In the climax of The Story, the Maw character, played by Teddy, was supposed to say to his children, 'You are not enough,' at which point he would provide something the children needed to be whole, something the real Maw changed as he saw fit. But every time we came to the scene, Teddy would go off-script and say instead, 'You're plenty,' rendering The Story's finale completely nonsensical. Even when the rest of us had gotten our parts letter-perfect, this last piece of the puzzle would never fall into place. I think that kept something alive in each of us, something that would have otherwise died. It drove Maw crazy, of course, but he didn't punish Teddy. At least not right away."

While Ralph tells the rest of the tale, Teddy gazes out the window.

Through the cherry haze of the Chim's neon DO-NUTS sign, he sees a sleek white sedan parked on the side of the street. It's a foreign make—Japanese maybe—one Teddy's never seen before. The faces of the two people sitting inside are hidden by a tinted gradient on the windshield. Their clothes, however, can be seen: cream white button downs closed at the top with a large square button.

Maybe because Teddy's been watching, or maybe for no reason at all, the driver starts the engine, and speeds off into the night.

Teddy feels a tickle race up his spine. He's surveilled enough people to know when he's being surveilled himself.

These Modern Delights

"Can I help you?" the Byzantine voice box garbles.

Teddy's in the Celery Express, idling in the McDonald's drive thru across the street from Lorenzo Dunes. The digital clock in the dash reads 1:39 a.m.

Unable to sleep (thanks to thoughts of dioxin and spooky surveillance), he opted for a sorely missed routine, knowing full well he won't be able to enjoy the result.

Apologizing to the innocent McDonald's employee for his coming eccentricity, Teddy begins the art that is his fast food order, gliding around the menu in a frictionless state of flow, marrying otherwise mediocre items into new congresses of flavor. He omits sub-optimal toppings here, specifies a few extra seconds in the fryer there. After a bullseye estimate of condiment needs, he thanks the employee for her professional candor and accuracy. With a vocal quiver betraying tears, his unseen dancing partner manages an awed reply, "I-it was my pleasure, sir."

Parked in the Lorenzo Dunes lot a minute later, Teddy withdraws each item from the bag. Carefully unfolding paper petals, he inhales the mass-produced ambrosias inside. Olfactory calories are a real thing, but about as close to zero as non-zero can get. And anyway, this is fast food, a modern miracle comfortably positioned at the spearhead of food science, its sensations chemically molested until they're better than real, all of it priced so cheap it's financially irresponsible *not* to buy. Practically any amount of the stuff will land Teddy in the hospital, but old habits die hard, especially when they're engineered to be that way. So, here he is.

Teddy's eye sensually roams the contours of a double cheeseburger (437 cal.). He inhales steam from the large order of fries (378 cal.) and allows an ice cube from the Coca-Cola (290 cal.) to melt on his tongue. After a half dozen other menu items receive the same abundance of love, Teddy gets out of the car and approaches a man loitering near the bus stop. The man's name is Blue Joe.

Blue Joe is Lorenzo Dunes' unhoused, resident haunt. He has yellowed eyes and a candy cane posture, but the first thing you'd notice about him is his mouth and the fact that it never stops moving. Blue Joe constantly serves word salads to any pace-quickening citizen within range, though his vitriolic racism and threats of bodily harm make him a poor conversation partner. It doesn't help that he's an ideological glutton, making it hard to pin down who or what he's mad at at any given moment, though he's definitely mad about something. The mix of details Blue Joe has let slip over the years suggests a darkly religious upbringing, military service of some kind, incarceration, addiction, and ironically, a general distaste for words. Teddy suspects a young Blue Joe was flooded with words from an ill-meaning cast of parents, teachers, and drill instructors until, one day, the mental dam finally broke, unleashing a torrent of words that has yet to stop. Whatever the case, Blue Joe's long given up on himself, and so, it seems, has everyone else. Everyone but Teddy.

He holds out the repacked McDonald's bag. "Hi, Joe. How the night going?"

Blue Joe snatches the bag away.

"Out to get me, out to get *you*," he shouts, glazing the bus stop bench with spittle. "They have all the information because they're the ones who *make* the information. What to think is granular. How to think is procedural. That's the one they want to control. How, how, how."

"Who, Joe? Who wants control?"

Probing the McDonald's bag, Blue Joe squishes across the parking lot in his soggy sneakers.

How he heard the word, Teddy would never know; a filament of data, spiderweb-delicate, that floated into his ears after escaping the half-cracked window of a limousine, or a secure phoneline, or honestly who the hell knows. All Teddy gets is the word itself.

"*Lich.*"

TUESDAY

"A desire for a specific reform, however wide-spread, cannot be translated into action until it is made articulate, and until it has exerted sufficient pressure upon the proper law-making bodies."

-Edward Bernays

A Shot in the Arm

The massive, orange snake writhes on a coastline, its tail destroying old-growth jungle with ease. Slipping into the water, the creature swims to an offshore island where a working furnace shimmers the air. The snake slithers inside. Smoke pours out of the oven's flamed mouth as a tinny screech fills the world.

Teddy jolts out of the dream and slaps his alarm clock, nearly hitting his bomb calorimeter by accident. This is far less dramatic than it sounds.

Exact caloric measurements, important to Teddy for obvious reasons, are attained through the accurate-if-anti-quated bomb calorimeter, which looks something like a desktop printer married to an oxygen tank. The device uses electricity to incinerate a piece of food sealed inside a container that's submerged in water. It then measures the change in the water's temperature, with a calorie (technically a kilo calorie) being the amount of heat needed to raise the temperature of a gram of water by one degree Celsius, because sure, why not?

It's not that Teddy doesn't trust food manufacturers—he's sure they work diligently and have the public's best interest at heart—but there's always some funny business once a product enters the packaging stage, omitted ingredients and bogus serving sizes being just two examples. Then there's the marketing, playing ever faster and looser with the truth, which is all well and good to move units, but for sufferers of Post-Traumatic Hypometabolic Magnification Syndrome, for whom the slightest deviation can mean disaster, thermal precision is the only way to go.

Ms. Beauchamp, bless the woman, has brought in a new food this morning, a basket of lychee, one of which, Ralph, bless the man, has thoughtfully placed next to the bomb calorimeter.

Teddy climbs out of his bunkbed and fires up the machine. Then he flips open his little spiral notebook, where he keeps a record of all incinerated foods in between case jottings.

The moment he writes 'lychee,' he's struck with a tuning fork. The word looks a bit like the one Blue Joe said the night before.

A quick Google search before bed told Teddy a lich is "a type of undead creature in fantasy fiction." No problem there, but something about *how* Blue Joe had said the word stuck with Teddy. It hadn't been delivered in the man's usual tone of incoherent rage, but in a hollow whisper, like saying it too loud would invite evil. Strange, because as far as Teddy knows, Blue Joe isn't afraid of anything.

But it's a workday, and there's lots to get done that doesn't involve undead fantasy creatures, so Teddy shakes off his chill, and unleashes scientific hell on the sliver of red and white fruit sealed inside the calorimeter.

After cheerfully documenting the lychee's weenie caloric content (6 cal.), Teddy enjoys the rest of the test-fruit with the confidence it won't trip him into a coma. Riding the resultant wave of sugary energy, he showers and dons a baby blue cardigan and matching eyepatch. Through the apartment's back window, he sees Ralph running wind sprints for an audience of stray cats down in the alley.

Out in the kitchenette, Teddy finds Ms. Beauchamp standing guard over a full coffee pot. She's got a heavy dusting of cobalt eye shadow on the right eyelid but has neglected to do the left.

"Good morning, Ms. Beauchamp," Teddy says. "The lychee was outstanding. Thanks to you I'm starting the day with a full heart and a full stomach."

Ms. Beauchamp is about to respond when her posture suddenly goes ramrod straight. "Trouble," is all she gets out before the front door bangs open.

In waltzes Dixon Woodbine, polishing off the last of a maple glaze from Chim Chim Donut. "Rise and shine, everybody!" It takes only a few long-leg strides for Woodbine to reach the kitchenette, where he downs the scalding pot of coffee and points a jittery finger at Teddy. "Man in the Hathaway Shirt, I'd like a word. Best wrangle your brother, too."

Woodbine disappears into the brothers' office.

Ms. Beauchamp looks about ready to blow a gasket, but her professionalism wins out. She brushes maple-glazed crumbs from Teddy's shirt.

"I'll fetch Ralph, you get started with *him*. The sooner you hear what he has to say, the sooner he'll leave."

Drones!

Woodbine makes himself comfy in the chintz chair. Today's jacket is a maroon and gray houndstooth. Still, the non-specific prayer bracelet. Still, the handsome, troubled face.

Teddy sits behind the desk. "How are you today, Mr. Woodbine?"

"I consider small talk a form of violence. Let's skip it."

"Oh. It's not small talk though, I really want to know."

"I'll tell you soon enough."

Ralph joins them in track pants and a tank top, finger-combing his jet-black hair. "Sorry about my appearance, I didn't expect—"

"You think I give a god damn about personal hygiene?" Woodbine says. "What do you boys have so far?"

"Well, we've undertaken our initial research steps. Obtained third party confirmation of—"

"I'm disappointed in you boys. *Sorely* disappointed." Woodbine crams a handful of the desk's pastel dinner mints into his mouth and grinds them down to a powder. "Perhaps the blame lies with me. I may not have conveyed the importance of haste in our last meeting. It seems this office runs on island time. I demand a continental work ethic!" He coughs out a pink-green cloud of pulverized mints before continuing. "I thought we'd have a few bushes beaten by now. You two appear well-rested and unbloodied. Considering the threats involved, me and my colleagues at the FBI find that a touch concerning."

"Yesterday it was CIA," says Ralph.

"Tomorrow, DMV," Woodbine fires back. "And if you think I'm going to reveal my actual credentials you might just be too naïve for the job."

"Mr. Woodbine," Teddy says, "we've been doing our prep work. Outside research and anecdotal accounts allow us to better approach a case. I think it was President Lincoln who said if he had an hour to chop a tree—"

"I didn't come here for horticulture lectures from a dead Yankee. It's Tuesday. Twenty percent of your time is gone, and you have nothing to show for it."

"The Agent Orange is radioactive," Ralph says.

"Oh." Woodbine sheepishly nibbles on a dinner mint. "You heard about that, huh?"

"That wasn't a detail you thought worth sharing?"

"People get anxious when the big R is involved, I couldn't risk you saying no. And so what? Bananas are radioactive for Christ's sake, you don't hear monkeys complain."

"Is the Royal Jelly still viable?" Teddy asks.

"Say what you will about the morality of A.O., from a manufacturing standpoint, it's absolutely mint, built with one hell of a shelf-life. And on the atomic side of things, the half-life of uranium-238 is 4.5 billion years, so yes, the Jelly'll still take the hair off your chest just fine. But we've got bigger problems."

Teddy blinks. "How is that possible?"

"*Drones*, Mr. Lint! Somebody ordered a boatload of the things to an address in downtown Los Angeles. Three hundred units from a factory in Panama, shipped to an ostensibly abandoned storefront whose every square inch has since been bleached. We took a peek at the paper trail as best we could, but it turned into a shell game of shell companies and the Panamanians aren't playing ball. Someone put the fear of God into them but good."

Ralph gnaws a lychee. "Why would someone order all the drones from the same company? Seems like a pretty noticeable move to make."

"Because, Mr. Lint, it's the only company that offers crop dusting units at scale. Each of those three hundred units is outfitted with a nozzled reservoir capable of aerosolizing fifty fluid ounces, per flight, of any liquid the operator so chooses. Imagine, if you will, a cloud of Panamanian drones canvassing the skies from Redondo to Burbank. Bad news for any Angeleno with a soft spot for respiration. Even with immediate deaths, the real horrors would be yet to come, a fallout ensuring slow, grotesque deaths for generations. We're talking about a town scared stiff by gluten and driving in the rain being doused in a chemical that chews through triple canopy jungle like tracing paper."

"Mercy," Teddy whispers.

"Mercy's got nothing to do with it, son."

Woodbine absently fondles the buttons of his blazer. The lower two buttons are of the standard circle variety. The top button, Teddy notices, is square.

"You'll forgive me if I've been short with you, but our time is less and our objectives are unchanged." Woodbine stands. "*Rapidu knaboj*! Infiltrate the subversives. Get the Royal Jelly."

Two rough handshakes and an expedient exit.

"Rapid what?" Teddy asks.

Ralph shrugs.

Out in the lobby, Ms. Beauchamp cries out in dismay. The second pot of coffee never stood a chance.

The Particulars

While the Lints still don't consider Woodbine trustworthy, his speech lights the fire well enough. Vagaries about what Royal Jelly is or isn't are set aside in favor of focusing on the two leads they have in hand: the governmental reform organization known as Sisters in Sync, and the artist collective known as The Order. When both groups prove impervious to online research, the brothers head out into the field.

Ralph's off in the Celery Express to meet with a well-connected cinematographer he hopes may have some info on The Order. The Lints' only association with the man is that they once served him a subpoena, so no one's getting their hopes up.

On the Sisters in Sync side of things, Teddy's about to check on a lure he cast the day before when Ms. Beauchamp hits him with a stack of can't wait paperwork. She may handle the majority of the Agency's boilerplate bookkeeping, but it's Teddy alone who writes the case summaries, in which he quantifies and organizes the particulars of every completed case, no matter how disparate the elements may have seemed at the outset.

While Teddy toils away in the office, lifetime member of the waste-not-want-not crowd, Ms. Beauchamp, works an ancient machine of painted green metal. With a loud *ka-chunk*, each pull of the appliance's slot-machine-like lever spits a re-formed staple out into a reservoir where it is soon repackaged and recirculated, one of the many tricks that helps keep the agency's office supply budget shockingly low.

At 10:59, after a few hundred *ka-chunks*, Ms. Beauchamp stows the device and gets her lunch out of the minifridge. Back at her desk with a Tupperware of goat stew and some foil-wrapped bammy, she turns on a small television. The screen lights with everyone's favorite 'Small State, Big Drama' soap opera, *The Lighthouse at Providence*.

The opening credits kick off with Princeton Becksdale, mayor of the show's scandal-drenched Providence, Rhode Island. Mayor Becksdale is conniving and lusty and responsible for no less than three comas, but he fixes potholes and eats chowder at photo ops, so the fictional voters keep re-electing him. It doesn't hurt that he's abusively handsome, thanks to the fact that he's played by Royce Janus, a sometimes A-Lister who always hits his marks and eats two-page monologues with ease. Ms. Beauchamp adores Royce Janus and outright refuses to believe the scurrilous rumors. That he's a cannibal. That he's Canadian. Nonsense, all of it. If a piece of undying slander is the price of admission to the A-List, so be it.

A Boy Scout raps his knuckles on the agency's front window.

"Teddy," Ms. Beauchamp calls out, without breaking eye contact with *The Lighthouse at Providence*. "Stinney's Scout."

Teddy emerges from his office and lays his completed case summaries next to Ms. Beauchamp's little TV (careful not to obscure the screen). "This closes all of our cases except Woodbine's."

Her gaze locked on *Providence*, Ms. Beauchamp holds out a sheath of re-formed staples. "I'm adding a line item to the Woodbine case for excessive coffee allotment."

"That's fine. Ms. Beauchamp, have you ever heard of a gynarchy?"

"Some sort of winged dinosaur, I believe. It would be one thing if Mr. Woodbine couldn't afford caffeine, but leaving in a Ghost? Hah."

"A Ghost?"

"Rolls Royce. MSRP starts at three hundred thousand."

The Scout outside the front window taps on the glass again. Teddy holds up a pointer finger and turns back to Ms. Beauchamp. "The gynarchy I'm talking about is a government run exclusively by women. It's one of the leads Woodbine gave us."

"Oh. That kind of gynarchy. Theodore, men have made quite a mess of things over the years. They may be cruel, stupid, and odorous, but I don't see a correlation between genitalia and good governance. My auntie was treasurer of her condo association in Montego Bay. She spent all the residents' dues on a used cigarette boat, went out to sea and never came back. Imagine that on a federal scale. Now leave me be, Princeton's about to cut the ribbon on his love child's memorial gazebo."

Stinney's Scouts

The Boy Scouts of America had (what they considered to be) a major problem. To hear the President of the Greater Los Angeles Council tell it, some bullshit social program had saddled them with six disadvantaged youths in possession of tremendously bad attitudes.

This was the dreaded Troop 85.

The members of Troop 85 had two idols. One was George Stinney, a fourteen-year-old African American boy who was sent to the electric chair in 1944 after a sham trial in Mississippi. George was revered by Troop 85 for the raw deal he got and the eternal youth he retained as a result. Idol number two was, improbably, J. Edgar Hoover, scummy grandfather of the FBI, admired by the boys "'Cause he always got the job done." On one shoulder of their khaki uniform: an unapproved patch of Stinney's face. On the other: Hoover's. Finding "Be Prepared" to be a touch too halcyon and wimpy, the scouts markered a custom slogan over the heart of each shirt that reminded the reader, "You Just . . . You Never Really Know."

Stinney's Scouts, as they came to be known, regularly found themselves in trouble, everything from a lemonade stand price fixing scandal to the flooding of LA's pharmaceutical market with prescription drugs from Vancouver. When a pedophile sting carried out by Troop 85 cost the LA Philharmonic two promising timpanists and a very expensive conductor, BSA administration really started to sweat. Would the revolving door of Den Leaders sacrificed to the troop last long enough for the boys to age out of the program and become the justice system's problem? A great answer to this terrible question came during a fateful Pinewood Derby, when Stinney's Scouts were caught picking the pockets of spectators by a one-eyed man volunteering at the refreshment stand.

They of endless misbehavior had met he of infinite patience.

As the excitement of gravity-fast car races continued, Teddy bought a round of sodas for the boys. They, in turn, enlightened him on the fundamentals of a sound, non-lethal booby trap. When Teddy wrote an impassioned letter to the BSA asking them to let him lead the troop, the administrator in charge signed the papers so fast he sprained his wrist in two places.

The relationship had something of a slow start. Teddy found himself caught in the classic dilemma of wanting to do what was best for the boys, while the boys mostly wanted to superglue doll heads to idling UPS trucks.

The parties discovered a natural symbiosis in detective work.

The Scouts, who found Teddy's investigations kinetic and exciting, knew all the best shortcuts around town, and could talk to people who wouldn't say word one to a private eye. They proved skillful in spycraft, especially make-up and disguises—meaning anytime you saw a middle-aged woman walking down the street in Los Angeles, there was a low percentage chance she was actually two shoulder-stacked ten-year-olds with a gigglingly-assembled bosom. Troop 85's work for the Lint Detective Agency kept them near Lorenzo Dunes, better allowing Teddy to keep an eye on the boys and provide some much needed support. It wasn't uncommon to find a Stinney's Scout asleep on the agency's client couch when they couldn't go home, for reasons shared or not.

To understand the Scouts is to accept their binary nature: at times they're Stinney's avengers, using their talent for mayhem to advance social causes. But when in a J. Edgar mood, they regress into fun-size fascists who despise the homeless, especially Blue Joe, whom the Scouts believe takes advantage of Teddy's generosity.

Teddy follows the window-knocking Scout down to the parking lot where five other tan-shirted boys are throwing bang snaps at Blue Joe.

Putting a stop to the harassment, Teddy passes around a bowl of lychee slices and asks each of the boys how they're doing. As everyone reaches the rinds of their fruit, the conversation moves into a discussion of the latest case. The Scouts have been listening for any blips about The Order, Sisters in Sync, and Royal Jelly. They've got nothing solid on The Order, and although Royal Jelly's come up a few times, it seems to have lots of different definitions.

Sisters in Sync, though?

On that particular front, Stinney's Scouts just so happen to have a lead.

It's in the Way That You Use It

For Teddy, gathering information through computers is . . . fine. Sometimes the answers sought lie nowhere else but in the digital realm, and with a data hound like Ms. Beauchamp on staff, several cases have been solved entirely online. But information filtered through a human being? Colored by context and expertise and seemingly unrelated tangents that come in handy later on? Now you're speaking Teddy's language.

When asked the secret of his highly effective detective abilities, Teddy's answer of "I like people" never seems to satisfy. But it's true. There is no single pill to be swallowed, no philosophy to be absorbed during a paid weekend conference; Teddy genuinely likes people, and consequently, they often like him back. He doesn't just "remember" names, he receives them with gratitude and care. He notices the hard work you're putting in even when no one else does, and he's rooting for you, unconditionally.

This kind of natural affection melts neurosis and suspicion with ease, gifting investigatory gold that other detectives can never hope to reach. Like the proverb about a man who enters the market with a single flower and trades his way up to a horse, Teddy's warm nature ferries him across degrees of separation, person by person, clue by clue, until he arrives where he's headed.

Stinney's Scouts' lead turns out to be a depressed lumber yard cashier who might have a tenuous connection with that whole 'women in government' thing. It's not much, but it's something.

Teddy's got his flower.

He finds the young man in question taking a smoke break in the shadow of some 8/4 Spanish Cedar, stressing about how to break up with his boyfriend. Teddy counsels with honesty, clarity, and concern. "Tell him exactly what you're telling me, Brian. You love him, but you're not *in* love with him. He might resent the truth in the short term, but you owe it to him regardless. And to yourself." When Brian's weepy hiccups recede enough that he can speak in full sentences again, he refers Teddy to a regular customer named Violet who might've mentioned the gynarch-whatchamacallit at some point.

Nearly hysterical with gratitude over having a visitor, the elderly Violet offers Teddy Kool-Aid (110 cal.) and sugar cookies (190 cal.) before he's taken two steps into her Inglewood apartment. Teddy politely accepts tap water instead and they get to talking. Wouldn't you know it? Violet's granddaughter has just made varsity water polo and Violet has the video on her phone to prove it. Teddy watches the video twice, voluntarily. "They have to tread water the entire time? That's like playing a sport on top of a sport. What an accomplishment!" A beaming Violet chats with Teddy a while longer before sending him next door to meet with a woman named Tyronica.

Tyronica turns out to be a meter maid at a breaking point over her profession's endless stresses. Teddy listens, then offers his thoughts. "You deal with people at their lowest and still manage to keep the streets, and society at large, functioning. Your resolve literally makes the modern world possible." A cheered Tyronica thanks Teddy, then mentions that her sister's physical trainer's dog walker's therapist is in that special "ladies club," and that she, Tyronica, would be happy to help. Picking up the phone, she leapfrogs the tenuous connections until she lands on something Teddy can work with: The gynarchists are meeting for lunch in less than an hour, and she's got the name of the restaurant.

Just like that, Teddy's got his horse.

One Must Imagine Lobbie Happy

Lobbie's is a chain restaurant whose B- from the health department doesn't seem to deter too many customers. This is a *fun* place to eat, with servers dumping plastic bags of crab legs, potatoes, and corn cobs onto paper tablecloths for diners to dig at with their bare hands, and if the squares at the health department are too uptight to realize that fun and food safety are sometimes at odds, well, that's their loss.

The Lobbie's logo looms large behind the hostess podium. It features a shades-wearing lobster (the eponymous Lobbie himself) lounging in a steaming pot with one appendage leisurely crooked along the steel rim. He offers no sniffly diatribe on being boiled alive, just a cartoon word bubble that says "Somethin' Smells Good!"

"He seems relaxed, considering," Ralph says.

"One must imagine Lobbie happy," the host monotones as he grabs two laminated menus.

The Lints make sure they're seated close-but-not-too-close to a group of women at the back of the dining room. Conversations at the long table are polite and inconsequential, and if you didn't know what to listen for, you'd have no idea you were in the presence of the most preeminent, gender-focused political revolutionaries on the western seaboard. Lobbie may be content to keep quiet, smile wide, and leave behind the same world he was born into, but the gynarchists have other ideas.

Teddy and Ralph are peeping over their menus at the women when their waiter arrives. Ralph tries to get his order in quick, but it's no use; Teddy strikes up a friendly chat, and they soon learn that when he isn't doing Lobbie's bidding, Nelson dreams of being a jazz pianist.

"Oh, wow," Teddy says. "I can't play jazz piano, but I sure like listening to it. I've heard good things about Thelonious Monk."

Nelson blinks, as if this is the understatement of the century. "Thelonious is a *god*. I mean, you wanna talk about a percussive player—"

"Not to worry, Nelson," Ralph says. "We know you have other tables to get to. The Jambalaya Jamboree, please."

"Right, sure. Excellent choice." Nelson turns to Teddy. "And you, sir?"

"Two un-spiced scallops please, Nelson."

With a look of mild horror on his face at Teddy's order, Nelson gives a professional nod and makes for the kitchen.

"I found Clayton Greene shooting a diaper commercial in the Valley," Ralph says. "He made it very clear he was only talking to me because you followed up with him after the custody case."

"I wanted to make sure there were no hard feelings," Teddy says. "I get why subpoenas exist, but talk about starting off on the wrong foot. If I remember right, his nephew was dealing with a bully taking his fruit snacks. Any idea if—"

"Fruit snacks never came up. When I asked about The Order, though, I could tell he knew something. So I encouraged him a little."

"Ralph."

"I twisted his arm a tiny bit. You may remember he's a cagy son of a bitch, and in any case, it worked. He said the thing we're after is called The *Janusian* Order. Said if I'm interested, I should grab a bite at Endangerously Tasty and admire the décor."

"Endangerously Tasty?"

"Pop-up restaurant on Fairfax. I got us reservations for tonight."

"Perfect."

They're listening for snippets of gynarchist conversation above the lunch din when Nelson arrives with the food.

"Nelson!" Teddy says. "I hope you don't mind but I was thinking about your musical talents, and I had an idea. We did some work for a be-bop conservatory in Toluca Lake last month, and if I remember correctly, they're looking for a skilled pianist. I'd be happy to pass your name along."

"Gosh, that would be amazing! Are you sure I can't get you some seasoning for these? Honestly, dill, coriander? Paprika even."

"All set, Nelson. Thanks just the same."

Shared Indigestion

Teddy savors his unspiced scallops (27 cal.) while Ralph devours his Lobbie's Jambalaya Jamboree (880 cal.).

A text from Ms. Beauchamp arrives.

Irma: Sisters in Sync has no official record, but, as with Dark Matter in the cosmos, we can see its effects and infer backwards. The aide rumor mill in D.C. is rife with off-the-record stories. Significant dark money contributions to numerous pieces of "female-friendly legislation" are likely attributable to SIS (spreadsheet emailed). Forget what I said about the Jamaican speedboat, these gynarchists are alright. I don't want you giving them any trouble. Do the producers really expect us to believe Chantelle LeRoux drowned at Boone Lake when all through season thirteen she was a lifeguard at Providence Public Pool? *A drowned lifeguard?* Please.

The Lints watch as Nelson and several additional servers arrive at the gynarchists' table. There's a plate of scallops for one woman, a Crimson Kipper Lunch Special for another, but most have opted for Lobbie's famous Catch o' the Sea.

Six clear plastic bags of seafood are dumped along the center of the table to much fanfare from the ladies. A tide pool massacre begins in earnest. Crustacean limbs are bent and broken, shells annihilated, exoskeletons sucked clean, all with the unapologetic vigor needed to challenge an inherited standard.

"Think they might have the Jelly?" Teddy whispers below the percussion of claw crackers.

"Reformers looking to cause a stir?" Ralph says. "Sure, the Royal Jelly could be a nice centerpiece. Not sure I buy the optics though. Widespread, unmitigated death is generally a bad look for aspiring political movements."

As consumption gives way to digestion, discourse at the ladies' table becomes more pointed; paradigmal realignment, uterine reckoning, and all sorts of interesting phraseology is tossed around at a tactically low volume. Unfortunately, when it comes to operational specifics, the gynarchists stick to lots of you-know-where and you-know-who type redactions.

Teddy's straining his ears for any mention of ouroboroses, Agent Orange, even Tom Hanks, when a burbling sound complicates his eavesdropping. The sound is coming from his own stomach.

He retraces the day: a lychee for breakfast, a smell of McDonald's pancakes then given to Blue Joe, tap water from Violet the friendly grandmother, a piece of gum from Tyronica the meter maid, two Lobbie's scallops, and . . . that's it. He's still well under ninety-nine calories. But the gurgle comes again—worse this time—and suddenly the cause doesn't matter, only the fuse-lit bomb of indigestion and where best to aim it.

Using the overhurried language of those about to puke, Teddy excuses himself from the table and runs for the first bathroom door he sees. It's his lucky day because the toilet inside is both unoccupied and unguarded by stall doors, allowing him to knee slide up to the porcelain bowl just in time to let loose with the scallops.

"Mercy," he exhales.

Before he can inhale, the door bangs open and a woman runs in.

"Shit! SorrymisterbutIgotta—"

She joins Teddy at the toilet and copies his performance exactly.

"Scallops," she breathes. "God damned scallops."

The inertia of the situation subsides and the two pukers look at one another, their foreheads dewy with sweat.

She's wearing a white jean jacket that reaches just below her ribcage. There's a gap between her two front teeth and a pinky missing on her left hand.

"Andie?"

The woman mirrors Teddy's look of shocked recognition. "Oh my god. Teddy."

A thundering knock sounds on the bathroom door.

The Porcelain Summit

Andie's up in an instant, jamming her turquoise high heel against the bathroom door to keep it from opening.

Teddy takes partial refuge behind the hand dryer, unclear about the exact degree of danger he's in.

"Andie?" a husky female voice asks from outside. "It's Ham. You okay?"

"Yeah girl, everything's peachy, just puked my guts out. Not a pretty sight in here, trust me."

"Okay. As long as you're alright. I'll be at the table." Footsteps fade.

"Sorry," Teddy says. "I'll give you some privacy."

Andie stays by the door. "You don't wanna go out there just yet. The group I'm with wouldn't love a guy coming out of the women's restroom with a woman still in it."

"This is the women's room? Hold on, you're in Sisters in Sync?"

"Yeah. How do you know about SIS?"

"I'm a private investigator. With Ralph."

"Ralph! I knew you guys got scooped up as a package deal, but I had no idea you were still together. And you're *detectives*? That's incredible! Oh, Teddy. I know we were both just on the floor of a public bathroom but—"

She pulls him into a tight hug.

"I can't believe it's you. You look great."

"You, too," Teddy says.

"Glad I look it."

"Is everything okay?"

"Yeah. Well, no, but nothing I can explain in thirty seconds. My ex, the woman who was pounding on the door, will turn you into an accordion if she catches you in here, so we probably shouldn't linger."

"Come to dinner with me and Ralph tonight."

Andie bites her lip. "Does he still hate my guts?"

"What? Of course not."

"Sure he doesn't. Even so, I wouldn't miss it for the world."

As Teddy hands her a Lint Detective Agency card, a muted crash comes from out in the restaurant.

Andie peeks out the door. "Looks like Fortune just tripped a waiter on our behalf. This might be as clear as the coast gets. Teddy, I can't believe this. I've never been so happy to get food poisoning. See you guys tonight."

Teddy watches her go, waits a few seconds, then exits, nearly running into Ralph, who calmly-but-firmly escorts him toward the front door.

"Keep walking," Ralph whispers. "I saw that girl run into the bathroom. One of the gynarchists, a big one, seemed to know something was up. I figured you might be in a jam, so I tripped Nelson."

"Did you—"

"Yes, I left a big tip to make up for it."

"The girl in the bathroom. It was Andie."

"Andie who? *Andie*, Andie?"

"We both had the scallops. And guess what? She's in SIS. I invited her to dinner tonight so we can catch up."

Ralph keeps a poker face. "Ah."

"Is that okay?"

"If she can help the case, I'll change the reservation to three. But I still hate her guts."

Out on the sidewalk, Teddy turns into the alley behind Lobbie's. "I gotta take care of something real quick."

"I'll get the car."

"Great. And Ralph? You shouldn't hate her."

Ralph stands still for a moment, then continues down the sidewalk.

The Scallop Czar

Teddy pushes through the heavy plastic strips hanging in the Lobbie's delivery entrance to find a teenager stacking boxes in a walk-in freezer.

The scrawny kid looks at him in surprise. "This is just for employees, man."

Teddy inspects a thermometer glued to one of the freezer's storage racks. "Do you oversee the food storage temperatures?"

"Yeah," the kid says suspiciously. "So?"

"What's your name?"

At a request for his name, the teenager's bravado shrivels. What if this guy in a cardigan and matching eyepatch is an undercover health inspector in bizarre disguise?

"Mark Acevedo. People call me Ace. I just started here."

"I'm happy to meet you, Ace, my name's Teddy. I don't doubt you're working hard but I think the temperature in here is a few degrees too high for food storage, the scallops in particular."

Ace squints at the thermometer, then at a laminated food safety chart glued to the wall. He lets out a tragic wail.

"Oh Jesus, you're right. Are you gonna report me, man? I'm trying hard, I really am. The Lobbie people are total assholes, they'll fire me on the spot. I'm the one responsible for the scallops, I'm the Scallop Czar!"

A pin on his apron, that of a crown-wearing scallop, confirms this claim.

Ace leans his head against a freezer shelf. The naked lightbulb on the ceiling casts a dynamic glow on his despair, a scene begging to be immortalized with a Renaissance painter's brush.

Teddy's good at noticing these small, profound moments in the unlikeliest of places, and always tries to give them the respect they deserve. After a moment of admiration, it's time to help.

"Ace, I'm not going to report you, but you have to cancel all pending orders and throw out the day's stock. Do you like working with food?"

"I want to be a chef," Ace says, his head still propped against the shelf.

"That's great because you have talent. Aside from the temperature hiccup, my scallops were fantastically prepared. You should be proud of that."

Ace unsticks his head from the frost and looks at Teddy. With line-cook clairvoyance, he says, "You ordered the plain ones, didn't you?"

"That's right, so there were no spices or side dishes for you to hide behind. Don't be discouraged by learning opportunities. A review of food safety practices and a good night's sleep will have the Scallop Czar back in power in no time, I'm sure of it." Teddy holds out a hand.

"Yeah. *Yeah, man.*" And even though it could be some final, health department gotcha designed to add another unsanitary charge, Ace vigorously shakes the offered hand. "Thank you, Teddy."

"You're on your way, Ace. I'll be back again soon to try your latest creation. Until then."

Teddy pushes through the strips of heavy plastic and finds the Celery Express waiting in the alley.

He's about to get in the car when he sees—or at least thinks he sees—the two Seabees from the Clove Hitch, watching him from across the street.

"What's wrong?" Ralph asks.

A bus obscures the small man and the big woman. When it clears Teddy's line of sight, the Seabees, if they were ever there at all, are gone.

"Thought I saw a Seabee."

The Tuesday Laundry Communal

Perched on his gold hoop in the front window of SUDS!, Belfast the parakeet screeches about half-price detergent to a line of Angelenos that ends outside the laundromat.

Inside, near the row of dryers, two pink plastic chairs have been set up facing one another. Seated in one chair is a short, heavyset Mexican woman. Seated in the other is Teddy. Nothing is being said, and the woman doesn't look nervous exactly, but it's clear she's anticipating something.

Teddy patiently takes in the details of her face. Forehead wrinkles creased more tightly near the center. A thin scar through one eyebrow. A semicolon of freckles below the nose. The full cheeks hang into jowls, and the cloud of gray hair has started to admit ribbons of white. It's a kind face, and Teddy likes it very much.

"Consuelo," he says. "You're plenty."

The two-word phrase would be beyond trite embroidered on a pillow, but coming from Teddy, it lands deep, because when it comes to empathy, Teddy's Aretha at the mic, Jordan in the paint, a lifeforce that through effort or fortune has found the exact place it belongs, and lucky are those who bear witness.

The woman lets out an unadorned sob. She needed this. Most people do.

The Tuesday Laundry Communal started casually enough with Teddy offering encouragement to any Lorenzo Dunes patrons who looked like they could use it. He quickly discovered a common denominator of need that could be satisfied by simply reminding the person that they were deserving of love. The service was soon formalized into a regular date and time: Tuesdays, two to four pm, rain or shine.

Everyone's favorite pragmatic spoilsport Ralph had initially balked at a public service that brought in zero money (money the Lint Detective Agency always needed). Teddy had countered with an impassioned speech about the value of service and community. Wanting to avoid hearing the speech every week, Ralph gave in. He spends his Tuesday afternoons up in the office, combing financial records and scrutinizing phone logs because private investigating, like so many other jobs, involves a whole lot of admin work nobody particularly wants to do.

The tearful Mexican woman thanks Teddy and vacates the pink chair. A beefy spot welder in a high-vis vest takes her place.

"Travis."

Participants are asked to say only their name upon sitting down. Lingering is politely discouraged, as are any physical expressions of thanks, like handshakes or hugs. Teddy would, of course, love to participate in each and every one of these tactile exchanges, but he doesn't want the ritual to skew into anything that spotlights him as the cause of the good feelings people walk away with. Every person he sits with *is* plenty, and not because he says so. He simply reminds them of something that's already there.

Ice-chip blue eyes, slightly wide-set. Heavy stubble, thicker on the left cheek than the right. Smile lines ironed into the corners of a big mouth. Droopy earlobes and a closely shaved head that's bald in the middle. The muscles in the neck and shoulders are rigid, showing not just occupational bulk, but an abundance of stress.

After two and a half minutes: "Travis, you're plenty."

Travis loses it. An ugly cry, stale and overdue, fills SUDS!.

The pink chair is vacated again. Someone new sits down. The line steps forward. The Tuesday Laundry Communal continues, person by person, until a small segment of Los Angeles feels lighter than before, ready to face another week at least.

"Downy and Tide!" Belfast screeches at the last participant. "Half-off! Half-off!"

The Leskos

An Uber drops Andie off in front of an absolutely spanking mansion whose waterless fountain and snarls of unkempt wisteria suggest a Condemned Tuscany aesthetic.

After declining the Uber driver's offer to "come hang out at his place later," Andie staggers up the mansion's front path, her footfalls clumsy and wandering. What she calls the "zombie walk" follows almost every dialysis appointment.

She unlocks the front door and the mansion inhales the afternoon air with a vacuous *woosh*. Seventeen rooms in the house, nearly all of them empty. The refrigerator, too, save for a single jar of half-eaten peanut butter. Andie digs a scoop with her finger and heads upstairs.

The main bedroom has a mattress on the floor and not much else, the adjoining bathroom only slightly better stocked with a countertop shrine of perfume bottles and makeup. In a place this empty, even the ashtray of joint stubs by the sink counts as decoration.

Andie starts the shower and sheds her white jean jacket. Her favorite article of clothing could probably be considered an adult security blanket but damned if she cares; it's a pretty neutral coping mechanism considering her pinball adolescence.

Would it be accurate to say life with her adoptive parents was stranger than life in Percival Maw's cult? No. But it came close.

Don Lesko, the father: a successful television producer who amassed a fortune impossible to realize through legitimate means. The glut of Don's wealth came through esoteric financial crimes you needed a master's degree to understand. He had horrifically white teeth, reeked of Barbasol shave cream, and became a basket case around Tax Day because outsmarting the IRS every year tends to make them vengeful.

Sandy Lesko, the mother: a late-stage hippie whose homeopathic cleanses (read: drug benders) in the deserts east of Los Angeles were a semi-regular affair. Sandy had a paralyzing fear of not only red meat, but red food in general. No one ever died of a radish deficiency, but little orphan Andie didn't eat a strawberry until she was nineteen, which is a tragedy any way you look at it.

Andie steps into the shower, enjoying a few seconds of warmth before she cranks the knob to the left. A blast of freezing water is the best way she knows to snap out of a post-dialysis haze.

"Son of a bitch, that's *cold*!"

Sandy and Don. Mother and Father. The only thing they had in common was a devotion to erratic behavior, driving them to do things like adopt a troubled thirteen-year-old girl on a whim. Why? To save their marriage? That ship had sailed so long ago it navigated by astrolabe. To help fill an empty house? Ottomans will do the trick just as well and they don't need unconditional love.

Still, it hadn't been so bad for Andie at first. An expansive home in Bel Air whose doors weren't locked from the inside. Any material want readily provided. The Leskos even employed a full-time Hungarian housekeeper who made goulash so good Andie still dreamed about it.

The cost of these luxuries, it turned out, was having to live in proximity to Sandy and Don.

Sandy was forever fleeing from ghosts, a word she oft-repeated but never defined, the ambiguity of the problem keeping her mania at an almost constant peak. She would run away with Andie at least twice a year, staying in the South Bay, Inland Empire, Nevada even, with men Andie learned not to be alone with. When they ran out of money or places to stay, they'd return to Bel Air with new stories, new scars, and a fifty-fifty chance of whether Don had trashed the mansion in a rage over their absence or failed to notice it at all.

Pathological anomalies aside, Don was a drinker, and when he drank too much, he'd go on long rants about forces at work that Andie wouldn't believe were real even if he told her. He wasn't *going* to tell her, but she wouldn't believe him if he did. Eyes blurry, breath sour with vodka, he certainly wasn't going to tell her about people who spoke in dead languages, who used math of a different logic, who—Christ, he'd said too much already. Best she forget the whole thing.

Sufficiently de-zombified, Andie squirts a jet of frigid water through the gap in her front teeth and shuts off the shower. She towels off, throws in a few jumping jacks to get the blood flowing, and starts to get dressed.

Consistency from the Leskos came only in their deaths. Sandy was killed on one of her spontaneous mis-adventures that Andie fortunately missed out on. Andie could never bring herself to learn the exact details, but had a good enough idea: a generic, extended-stay motel, a strung-out guy put off by something Sandy had said, or done, or maybe nothing at all. Don died four months later on the operating table during his annual, pre-tax season angioplasty.

Andie's postmortem feelings were mixed. Sadness, certainly. Flawed or not, the Leskos had taken her in from the wilds of a cult and weathered all the social confusions and night terrors that had ensued; getting used to a world larger than an industrial laundromat didn't happen over-night. But Andie also had to admit to a therapist, and later to herself, an awesome and enduring relief at the Leskos' near simultaneous departure. The two doomed, unknowable souls had come and gone in a hurry, leaving her with a highlight reel of weird memories, and an absolute albatross of an inheritance.

Pipp the Loyal

Andie spins open a bottle of nail polish and sparks a joint.

People tell her she's pretty and sometimes that's nice to hear. But also, she can't get a cup of coffee without attracting an endless rotation of backwards-hat pests who want to collaborate on vague projects that almost certainly don't exist. And, too, there must be a law she doesn't know about requiring all mildly successful, clearly married men over forty to whisper dirty nothings in her ear every time she has the gall to sit alone in a public bar. In fact, there may be only one man in LA County who hasn't tried to sleep with her, and he's calling her now.

Blowing on the quickdry turquoise polish she's lacquered onto all nine nails, Andie answers her phone.

"Hey, Pipp. How—"

"They've sealed all the exits and dumped kerosene down the air vents. Torchlights encircle, Andie. This could be it!"

This is more or less a standard greeting from Andie's lawyer.

In short, Don Lesko's endlessly creative methods of illegally squirreling away monies have always had to contend with the government's tireless efforts to obtain said monies. Enter Randall J. Pipp, attorney for the Lesko estate, pre-paid by Don for the next thirty years.

Pipp is locked in legal combat with a litany of creditors, plus the State Attorney General who sometimes tags in the Feds, creating a never-ending, free-for-all cage match where fiduciary injunctions fly like folding chairs. Any newly discovered kitties become ensnared in the multi-vector tug-of-war: offshore accounts vs. back taxes, tactical bankruptcy vs. interest garnishment, and so on. The fight is so protracted that all three groups have co-leased an office on Wilshire Boulevard where they can duke it out in the comfort of air conditioning and Italian leather chairs.

At the end of this volatile, monetary tether is Andie, subjected to the endless whiplash of being unthinkably wealthy on Monday, insolvent on Wednesday, and condemned to a lifetime of debt on Friday.

"What's wrong today, Pipp?"

"Oh, nothing, it's just the case I've been building to claim a two-hundred-thousand-dollar account has cratered thanks to the discovery of some incriminating spreadsheets, and you'd better believe that joyless IRS goon Hanrahan never misses a chance to kick us while we're down. We're smooching the sidewalk, Andie, and here comes the jackboot."

Lucky for Andie, the Bel Air mansion is the one asset in perfect Lagrangian equilibrium between all three entities, keeping it safe from liquidation. Anything not nailed down, however, has since been repossessed by, well, who can even keep track anymore? Gone the crystal goblets and sterling silverware. Gone the Benzes and the Rodin. Gone dear old Erzsebet and her heavenly goulash.

It's not like Andie ever needed the finery, and it's not like she'll be around much longer to miss it anyway. For now, she's got her white jean jacket, her Division-I wrestler ex-girlfriend, her jar of half-eaten peanut butter, and Randall J. Pipp's religious devotion to protecting the Lesko fortune.

"The sky is falling, Andie, but not to worry, ol' Pipp's still got a few moves left."

"Pipp, why are you whispering?"

Over the phone, someone in the background says "Turn on three. One, two, three."

"Pipp, where are you?"

"Safety deposit room. Don has a box I haven't been able to get into, so I rented the one below it. Once this nice lady leaves, there she goes, I simply apply a portable arc torch to the roof of my box and let gravity do the rest."

There's a clicking sound followed by the ferocious *whurrrr* of an open flame.

"Pipp, we agreed; no more heists."

Andie has not only tried to dissuade Pipp from grand larceny, she's also implored him to retire outright and keep his entire salary. But Pipp is a widower without friends or hobbies, and loves nothing more than fighting for the Lesko Estate. Andie loves Pipp because he has hair like Einstein, seems to own just a single brown suit, and has not once told her how pretty she is.

"Not to worry, Andie, I've got an exit plan. You'd be surprised how much a writ of habeas corpus rolled up and kinked looks like a gun inside a pocket."

A loud metal *clunk*. Shouts of alarm. Pipp breathing hard.

"Pipp? Pipp?"

No reply. The phone makes rustling sounds, likely from the pocket of a brown suit. No gunshots are heard. The wailing bank alarm fades.

Andie breathes a sigh of relief: Randall J. Pipp has successfully fled the scene.

But whatever Pipp got or didn't get won't much matter, because the thing Andie's after can't be found in a safety deposit box. Her only hope at this point, and it's a faint hope, is that the rare, accept-no-substitute solution she so desperately needs could arrive by the grace of bad scallops and a chance reunion in a public bathroom.

That, and an act of unfathomable generosity.

Generating Awareness

The Celery Express pulls up in front of the Lesko mansion at a quarter to eight. Andie comes out to a warm hug from Teddy and a curt handshake from Ralph.

"It would appear forgiveness remains elusive," she whispers to Teddy as Ralph gets back behind the wheel.

"He's just hungry," Teddy says. "You'll see."

Teddy opens the front door for Andie, hops in back, and the three of them are soon cruising down the pricey stretch of Fairfax Avenue just below Sunset Boulevard.

With the Celery Express parked on a side street to avoid the forty-five dollar(!) valet fees, the trio make their way down the sidewalk, Ralph getting crankier with each step as they pass haute couture stores that offer one rack of clothing, and boutique art galleries stocked with low-hanging, juxtapositional fruit (an Aston Martin kitty-corner from a favela, etc.). Every plant wall in sight is lousy with neon signs done in a handwritten font, most offering platitudes about wine and happiness.

Ralph issues a codgery grunt as he pushes through a line of sneakerheads. "There's gonna be some bullshit with this restaurant, I'm calling it now. Entrées named after emotions. Riddle to get into the bathroom. It's always some bullshit with places like these."

They enter Endangerously Tasty to find the waiters all wearing the mask of an endangered animal and speaking only in haiku.

"See, Ralph," Andie says. "Nothing to worry about. Just your classic meat and potatoes eatery."

"Lint," Ralph says to the koala-masked hostess.

"Lint, party of three. Right this way to your table. Five more syllables."

Despite, or more likely because of, the bullshit Ralph predicted, the place is packed, many of the couples prime fodder for an expert-level game of girlfriend-or-grand-daughter. Most of the diners are scrutinizing their menus with poorly concealed confusion, and Andie and the boys don't fare much better.

It's uncertain if items like Lowland Gorilla Croquettes (650 cal.) and Onion Ring-Tailed Lemur Poutine (780 cal.) are made from those animals or just themed that way (with the actual meat sourced from an un-credited animal more readily available in the supply chain). Absent are any stated links to conservation groups or animal protection agencies, and since nobody in town misses an opportunity to brag about their charity, it can be safely assumed these links do not exist. A vague and unhelpful mission statement in small print below the desserts states the restaurant is meant to "generate awareness and sympathy for the plight of endangered species and poetry." Only one thing's for certain: the Snow Leopard Burger (450 cal.) costs forty bucks and doesn't even come with fries.

An orangutan-masked server ambles up to the table. "Hello and welcome. I'm Earl, I'll be your waiter. Special is scallops."

Omitting articles to fit a haiku isn't the height of the artform, but saddling food service workers with mandatory poetry isn't exactly fair in the first place, so nobody gives Earl a hard time.

"Howdy, Earl," Andie declares. "My brother Teddy and I are going to immediately and enthusiastically pass on the scallops. And thank god you guys have breakfast food. I'll give the Orangutan Omelet a try, no offense, I hope, and a short stack of pancakes, and an orange juice."

"Damnit," Ralph says. "That sounds good. Make it two."

The orangutan shifts his sad gaze to Teddy.

"Chocolate milk. Thanks in advance, Earl."

Earl's eyes roll at the paltry tip an entrée of chocolate milk will bring, then squint in concentration as he haikus the order. "One choc-o-late milk. Two omelets, short stacks, and juice. Thanks for your order."

He collects the menus and shuffles off, narrowly avoiding a waitress in a black rhino mask who's still adjusting to her horn's blind spot.

My Dinner with Andie

"Before we play catchup, you're gonna have to explain that lame, chocolate-milk-for-dinner order," Andie says.

Teddy explains Post-Traumatic Hypometabolic Magnification Syndrome: fast food bender after rescue, digestive circuit breaker tripped, ninety-nine calories, or else. As a perfect example, he's forced to hold his breath when a fragrant plate of Asian Elephant Fajitas (680 cal.) passes close behind his head.

"I have the opposite problem," Andie says. "Metabolism of a supernova. And I guess this isn't a medical condition, but once I got out, I couldn't stop eating breakfast food. Especially for dinner."

"How come?" Teddy asks.

"Dinner has such a terminal feeling. Breakfast food has a certain . . . optimism to it, you know? I could eat breakfast food 'til I die, and even then, room in the casket for hash browns."

Earl the orangutan swings by with the drinks.

Teddy takes bird sips of his chocolate milk (209 cal.) while Andie downs half her orange juice (152 cal.) in one go. Ralph, whether he's aware of it or not, is glaring at her.

"Seems like the first topic should be bygones," Andie says. "Maybe starting with what the hell a bygone even is."

Ralph doesn't smile. "I believe the conventional advice regarding betrayal is to forgive but not forget."

"Sure, but I don't get the feeling you've done either."

"Would you like me to say what I think you deserve instead?"

"C'mon, guys," Teddy says. "Friendly reunion."

Ralph sighs. "Andie. What have you been doing with your life?"

Andie waits a moment to see if it's a trap. "Okay, well, don't laugh, but for a while I tried modeling."

"That's amazing!" Teddy says.

"*Tried* being the key word. Turns out the gap in my teeth is a centimeter too wide to qualify as an endearing quirk. That's a direct quote from a casting director. Plus, now I'm thirty, which is basically Methuselah in that business."

Teddy shakes his head in disbelief. "Well, I'm sorry to say it but those people must be nuts. I think your smile's perfect."

"I appreciate that, Teddy, but since you don't buy *Vogue*, your opinion is worthless, financially speaking. And since money seems to be the only fluency in the modeling industry, and this town, and maybe the world, my smile and pose days are over."

"There are better days on the horizon, I'm sure of it."

Andie looks away from Teddy. "Yeah."

A red panda waiter drops plates off at a nearby table. "Sea Turtle Steak Frites. Fresh ground pepper, miss? Alright then, enjoy."

"Do you guys know what happened to everybody else?" Andie asks.

Teddy takes another sip of chocolate milk. "Shelby and Betsy joined a non-denominational convent that's almost certainly another cult, Robbie moved to Indiana, and Randy's in prison for armed robbery."

"Indiana? Yeesh. What about Karrr? Is he still in Malibu?"

"Still in Malibu," Teddy says. "He's a little sick at the moment—"

"He has lung cancer," Ralph says. "Now that we've strolled down memory lane, how about we do some actual work."

"Sure," Andie says. "How can I help?"

Ralph seems primed to give a non-constructive suggestion, so Teddy speaks quickly.

"'Admire the décor,'" he says. "That's what a source told us. We're looking for any information on something called the Janusian Order, and I'm pretty sure I just figured out where they got the name."

Endangerously Tasty's walls are covered in a gallery of portraits, all of a man Teddy and Ralph easily recognize from their office's daily dose of *The Lighthouse at Providence*. Royce Janus, Mayor Becksdale himself, smiles down on diners from at least thirty different head-shots. The photos are riddled with old graffiti standards: unibrows, Hitler mustaches, blacked out teeth, and lots of speech bubbles filled with words you'd never hear on network TV. The largest photo, maybe eight-feet tall, has been spray painted over with three, neon green masks. Two are the laughing and crying masks commonly used to represent the arts. The third, with its furrowed eye sockets and a yawning trap of sharp teeth, brings to mind not comedy or drama, but something closer to vengeance. The wallpaper behind all the photos is a highly detailed map of Los Angeles. It all makes for an interesting dining atmosphere but yields no immediate clues about the Janusian Order.

Earl arrives with their food. "And so you begin, a culinary odyssey, tips appreciated."

"Terrific," Ralph says. "We need utensils when you get a sec."

What is probably a common complaint earns a rote haiku from the orangutan. "We firmly suggest, a dining experience, technology free."

"A fork is technology, but a plate isn't?"

Earl sighs and tries to think of a unique answer. "The universe—"

"Forget it," Ralph says as he rolls up a pancake and takes a bite. "Bullshit. Always some bullshit."

Just My Type

Teddy takes a precautionary scoot back from the table as his siblings dig into their food, giving little yelps of pain when they pinch a pocket of egg that hasn't cooled yet. Burnt fingers aside, the breakfast food looks to be medicinal for Andie, bringing color back to a face that was looking pretty pale.

"Tell us about SIS," Ralph says at Andie.

"I only joined up recently. My ex, Ham, got me in."

"You dated someone named Ham?"

"Virginia Hamley, most people call her Virginia Ham. I think she's maybe still a little bit in love with me, and she's the jealous type, and she can bench two-fifty, so best keep an eye out. And if you're thinking about messing with SIS, that's not such a good idea either. Felicity's even tougher than Ham."

"Felicity?" Teddy asks, pulling out his notebook and pencil.

"Felicity Ortega. The head honcho. Honchess? She's scary as hell, but in a cool way, you know? She fundraises like you wouldn't believe, SIS has a massive endowment. I know, I know, but it's true."

Teddy pencils "Ortega," "honchess," and "massive endowment" into his notebook.

"Membership is based on sexual orientation?" Ralph asks.

"No."

"But some of them are lesbians."

"Some of everyone is lesbians, Ralph."

Teddy pencils: "some lesbians."

Andie uses her fingers to cut a triple layer bite of pancake. "Why are you guys so interested in SIS anyway?"

"The client in our latest case thinks they might be tangled up in something nefarious," Teddy says.

"It's possible," Andie decides. "But it could also depend on the definition of 'nefarious.' Is your client, by chance, a man?"

Teddy nods.

"Right. So, for some guys, nefarious means an inconvenient opinion, like the idea of more women in politics."

"Have you ever heard the term 'Royal Jelly' at a meeting?" Teddy asks.

Andie thinks, shakes her head. "What is it?"

"We're not totally sure if it's real or not, but the story goes that a shipping container of radioactive Agent Orange went missing after the Vietnam War. Our client says it was recently found by someone who intends to spray it over the city using hundreds of drones. That's what we're working with at the moment."

"Damn. No, I think I'd remember a mass casualty event coming up in a meeting."

"What else can you tell us about Ortega?" Ralph says.

Andie's eyes narrow a touch. "I'm all for helping you guys out, but I also have no interest in selling out my gender. What say we ease into things with another thirty seconds of reminiscing? Give me, hell, I don't know, blood types, favorite breakfast cereals. Anything."

"I'm Type O negative," Teddy says. "Ralph is AB positive."

Ralph looks at him in surprise. "I didn't know that."

"I made sure to look it up after that guy with the box cutter in Encino. Routine background check found us in a magic store," Teddy explains to Andie. "One second the guy's holding a bouquet of flowers, then *poof,* retractable blade misses Ralph's carotid by a hair. As far as cereal goes, Ralph's a Cocoa Pebbles man, and I enjoy a nice Cheerio now and then."

Andie looks down at her plate with an expression that seems excessively sad for a conversation about cereal.

"Andie? Everything okay?"

"Sorry." She works up a smile. "I'm the same as you. I . . . like Cheerios too."

If Walls Could Talk

At the end of the meal, Andie thoughtfully swirls her remaining pinky finger in a pool of syrup. "Do you really think people are in danger?"

"Yes," Ralph says. "Could be, anyway."

Andie looks guardedly at Ralph. If he knew what she was thinking, she'd be in danger too. But no, she hasn't even made a decision about whether she's going to ask or not. Has she?

Part of her is screaming that she should pay for dinner, walk away from her brothers, and die with some dignity intact. But just as some part of Teddy's body insisted on self-preservation with the calorie fiasco, Andie's body does likewise, spouting words that will keep Teddy and Ralph in her orbit long enough for her to make a decision.

"There's a meeting tonight at SIS's headquarters here in LA. Place called the Henhouse."

Teddy and Ralph both raise their eyebrows an amount that suggests intrigue.

"If you guys wanna come sniff around for glowing barrels of poison, I guess that's a noble enough effort. We have to hurry though, it starts at nine, and you'll need costumes."

Andie squints at Ralph.

"What?" he says.

"Move your head a little."

Ralph shakes his head.

"I don't know if you're cooperating or not, but I mean move aside."

Ralph leans, giving Andie and Teddy a clear view of the wallpaper map behind him. At the north end of the Venice Boardwalk, someone's hand drawn the comedy-tragedy-vengeance triptych of masks, along with the message: *Second Weds/mo. 10pm.*

"That's tomorrow," Teddy says. "That's our lead!"

He beams at Andie, then at Ralph.

"She's a natural."

Ralph grunts.

The Amazons, via Mulholland

The bronchial streets of Hollywood Hills, choked with landscaping trailers and delivery trucks in the daytime, breathe easier at night. The Celery Express groans as Ralph coaxes it up the unreasonably steep inclines toward LA's choicest bits of property, where unannounced visits are discouraged by raw gravity alone.

Minutes earlier, down at sea-level, they paid a visit to Harpreet Singh of Harpreet's Hollywood Costume Emporium, whom the Lints once helped sort out a messy probate case. Even with an abundance of student films and sex parties, the local costume business is basically slow eleven months of the year, so Harpreet's been paying the brothers back in free rentals, including the calf costume Ralph used to infiltrate Jocular Beef. Harpreet has a small body and a big mustache. As a Sikh, he's all but commanded by his god to be as kind as Teddy, and the two men have always gotten along swimmingly.

His shop is enchanting but small, so the selection isn't infinite. This means the brothers almost always have to settle for something adjacent to the disguise they're actually looking for (ex: when a case required infiltrating a fake Mennonite Order selling tainted oxycodone, Harpreet combined Huck Finn hats and overalls with Galileo beards).

When Andie told him the night's dress code was toga casual, he came up with a Roman Senator for Teddy, and a Gandhi for Ralph. There was no need for wig loans as the elaborate disguise kit compiled by Stinney's Scouts (always kept in the trunk of the Celery Express) had them covered on the hair front.

"Goddamn wig." Ralph pushes a strand of strawberry blond out of his face as he negotiates the next hairpin turn, narrowly avoiding a G-Wagon bombing down the hill for surely important reasons.

Facing backwards in the front seat, Andie straightens the brown bob wig on Teddy's head. "The commute's a bear, I know. But the higher the house, the better the secrets."

"These chicks must know who killed JFK," Ralph grumbles.

"Honestly, they might. And you probably want to drop the 'chicks' lingo befo—*watchout!*"

They by-inches avoid an Escalade flirting with Mach-2.

"Mercy," Teddy exhales from the backseat. "Nice driving, Ralph."

They continue to gain altitude, the reliably unreliable Celery Express kicking on its windshield wipers and losing power steering at the absolute worst moments. The street eventually whittles down to one lane, making every blind curve an act of faith. Ralph gnaws on his St. Christopher necklace for every last bit of traveler grace. He spits the medallion out in relief when they reach a row of fortress-like properties at the summit of the hills.

"The Henhouse," Andie announces.

She points to the zenith lot: an unimpressive ranch house with a Brutalist, smooth concrete style that's elegant in a mausoleum sort of way. The home is so high up that airplane-warning lights strobe red at each corner of the roof. The thermometer bulge of cul-de-sac is ringed with cars, most displaying a bumper sticker that notes the correlation between well-behaved women and their lack of appearance in the historical record. Ralph finds a narrow spot by a green VW Bug and backs the Celery Express in—standard Lint Detective Agency practice anytime a quick exit might be necessary.

The brothers flip open the sun visor mirrors to finalize their looks. With only one eye to shadow, Teddy finishes first and joins Andie outside the car. She's wearing her SIS tunic, acquired on a quick stop back at the Lesko mansion.

The two of them look out over the LA Basin, its dark geometries twinkling with a million points of light. The otherwise enjoyable scene is dominated by an unavoidable bright spot: North America's largest digital billboard, The Reef. The screen wraps around the top of a building just off the 10 Freeway, where it bombards the surrounding community with bought and paid for photons in an unending slideshow of luxury watch brands, alarmist cable news, and, if the copy is reliable, the loosest slots on the West Coast.

Andie glances back at the car, where Ralph is dusting an entire tray of concealer onto his Adam's apple.

"Will Short Fuse be okay in there tonight? This isn't a place you want to blow your cover."

"Ralph can blend in when he needs to."

"He hates my guts, Teddy."

"He doesn't."

"Teddy."

"Deep down, he doesn't. He's just . . . slow to come around on some things."

"If it weren't for me, you'd still have your eye. I'd hate me too."

"We were kids, Andie. With The Story and every-thing else Maw told us, we never had a chance to read things right."

"You did."

"What matters is that we found each other again. Food poisoning aside, I'm really glad I got the scallops."

Andie can't help a smile. "Me too."

Infiltrating the Henhouse

A woman all of five minutes and already feeling the weaponized insecurity of Big Cosmetics, Ralph grunts an exasperated "good enough" at the mirror and shuts his sun visor.

Andie gives her brothers a final once over: Ralph in Gandhi garb and strawberry blonde shag, Teddy just barely pulling off the Roman Senator in a brown bob. She sighs.

"Can't say I'd buy either of you a drink but stick to low-light areas and we might just pull it off. You'll need one of these."

She clips a metal broach, ovaries attached to an hour-glass, onto all three tunics.

"*Voila*. I now pronounce you gynarchists."

They walk a rose-lined path to the front doors of the Henhouse where Andie pushes the doorbell, unleashing a MIDI rendition of Lesley Gore's "You Don't Own Me".

She suddenly stiffens. "Oh shit."

"What's wrong?" Teddy whispers.

"Herberus, the guard dog. She sniffs for high levels of testosterone."

"Dogs can do that?"

"Apparently. I've never had to worry about it before, so I forgot—"

The doors yawn heavily inward, revealing two women and a dog.

One of the women humorlessly surveys the trio on her doorstep with narrowed eyes. She holds a clipboard whose corners have been worn smooth by years of devotion to bureaucracy. The other woman, a picture of absolute chill, is leaned up against the wall with a rifle at her side. The weapon is strange, thin and metallic with almost no shoulder stock. A pair of small, green dice dangle from the barrel. Behind both women, a gigantic Mastiff snores on a dog bed embroidered with the word 'Herberus.'

"Name?" the woman with the clipboard asks.

"Andie Nightingale. Um, it's Becky right?" Andie looks at the woman leaned up against the wall. "And you're Ruth."

Ignoring the attempt at camaraderie, Becky finds Andie's name on her clipboard. Then she looks at Teddy and Ralph. "And you two?"

Knowing her brothers are each warming up a cover-blowing falsetto, Andie intervenes just in time. "Guests of mine. They don't subscribe to naming conventions. They, um, find the whole practice a touch outdated. Don't you, ladies?"

The Lints quickly nod.

Becky frowns, then snaps her fingers. "Herberus."

The Mastiff doesn't move.

Blushing, Becky frantically taps the dog's butt with one of her loafers. Herberus slowly raises her head but gives zero indication she's going to get up.

"You come to her," Becky says, like that was the plan all along. "Chop, chop!"

Andie starts forward but Ruth, the woman with the rifle, calmly shakes her head.

"One of you," Becky barks at the Lints. "Groin first."

Ralph steps toward the dog bed, hinging at the waist like there's a limbo pole in his path.

Herberus takes a single sniff of his crotch, grunts in the negative, yawns and goes back to sleep.

Looking slightly disappointed, Becky steps aside. "Welcome to the Henhouse, ladies."

XX Marks the Spot

"What just happened?" Andie whispers as they descend a long, curving staircase. "I thought we were toast back there."

"Chemical castration ring a bell?" Ralph says.

"Right. Of course. Sorry. Repression."

The Henhouse, unimpressive on the outside, reveals itself as very much impressive on the inside. The structure is built down into the hill it crowns, bottoming out three stories below in a cavernous living room with a wide, stone-stepped amphitheater at its center.

Positioned around the amphitheater, twelve white marble statues depict heroines of history at three times human size, each engaged in a leisure activity. The ancient poetess Sappho plays ping-pong with Sojourner Truth. Nellie Bly and Angela Davis lounge in a hot tub, while Sacagawea and Marie Curie share a towering pile of nachos (730 cal.).

Mingling between the massive statues are at least two hundred women of the flesh and bone variety, every last one of them wearing a tunic and a pin. The tunic fabrics vary from designer satin to distressed polyester, and even a few patterned bedsheets, providing a visual spectrum of the group's socioeconomic range. Geographic diversity is apparent to the ears instead of the eyes, everything from Texas Twang to Minnesota Nice asking questions like how vulnerable is the treasurer's seat in Calhoun County, how much sugar does it take to kill a congressional staffer's gas tank, and where are the most effective pressure points on the male gonads?

As the newcomers step off the staircase, Teddy gets the last-to-walk-into-a-crowded-room feeling of being scrutinized and loses confidence in his disguise. "Andie, pretend we're talking."

"We are talking."

"Perfect. How's my hair?"

"It's fine, just relax."

"Hey, look at that," Ralph says. "An omelet bar."

"Aw," Andie groans, "I forgot it was omelet night. Oh well, two omelets in one day never hurt anybody. No offense, Teddy. Hey, there's Ham."

Standing in the shadow of Ada Lovelace and Jane Austen frozen in Downward Dog is a woman whose body has the general proportions of a grain silo. Just like a certain Seabee, Virginia Hamley was once a highly skilled collegiate wrestler. Unlike a certain Seabee, she's no one's second fiddle. When her competitors tried to saddle her with what they considered an insult, she emblazoned it across her singlet in sparkly rhinestones. The name Virginia Ham still inspires fear on gym mats across the heartland.

Ham, currently speaking with a red-nosed woman who lets out an explosive sneeze every few seconds, begins to rotate in the trio's direction.

"Eep!" Andie shoos the boys away. "Go mingle. And for god's sake don't try to explain anything you think you know about women *to* women." She heads straight for Ham and her sneezing friend. "Ham, Diane, how we doing tonight, ladies?"

Ralph gives a furtive nod to Teddy and heads for the omelet bar, leaving Teddy to stroll around the edge of the amphitheater.

Patiently slaloming the giant statues (and enjoying the upward breezes a tunic affords), Teddy calms his breathing and brings awareness to his ears, entering an almost meditative state of pure listening. Aside from treating people with dignity, this is his greatest trade secret: be quiet and let people talk. And talk they do.

"My uncle went from touting fiscal responsibility to calling me a 'civilization-ending feminazi' in the span of two Christmases."

"Technically we *are* trying to end the current form of civilization."

"To rebuild it better than before."

"You're saying he's not big on nuance."

"I'm saying no one should drink four rum nogs in an hour and expect eloquence."

And:

"I heard Felicity helped push the 19th Amendment over the finish line."

"Wouldn't that make her like a hundred years old? And wouldn't she have been amending the Constitution as a toddler?"

"Have you met her? Both are possible."

And:

"Gird your toga, girl. I hear Ham's old lay needs a kidney."

"The gap-toothed girl? Abbie? Angie?"

"You ask me, she's got a bum heart to go with it, treating SIS like a captive dating pool, and all in front of poor Ham."

"Ham needs a nice girl. Wrestlers deserve happiness just as much as normal people."

Then Teddy hears it. In between an explosive sneeze and the ambient sizzle of eggs, a word he last heard escaping the chapped lips of Blue Joe. So far as he knows, it's got nothing to do with Royal Jelly, but damned if it doesn't wrangle his attention.

The word is lich.

A Lesson in Lich
The lich-sayer has tangled hair, bright eyes, and no small amount of visible anxiety. Her bored looking

conversation partner is apparently not very interested in the topic because she explains that she, "Um, has to go to the bathroom. Yeah, that's it, the bathroom," before quickly walking over to a nearby discussion.

She of tangled hair and bright eyes is left standing beside Joan of Arc and Lucy Stone doing the Sunday crossword. For being in a room full of people, the woman looks conspicuously alone and deeply sad to boot, meaning Teddy would've tried to cheer her up whether she had said 'lich' or not.

"Hi, I'm Teddy." The name is androgynous enough that Teddy doesn't have to give a fake one, for which he is grateful. Undercover or not, he considers first impressions to be precious things that deserve to be treated as such. "I like your glasses."

"Oh, thanks. My name's Alexandra. Sorry, I'm having a day."

"Anything I can help with?"

"I don't want to be a sob story."

"Sob story nothing. Try me."

"Well, if you really want to know, a nosy cousin of mine got results back from one of those ancestry tests. Turns out our family lineage goes all the way back to Alexander the Great. As in, *the* Alexander the Great."

"That's amazing! Why would that make you sad?"

"Alexander the Great conquered most of the known world before thirty. He brought glory to Macedonian Greece and defeated King Darius the Second, who wasn't exactly a pushover. I, on the other hand, with all the modern advantages of anti-lock brakes, penicillin, and little to no threat from the Persian Empire, have risen to the spectacular heights of working in a Studio City comic book store. I'm Alexandra the Passable at best."

"Nonsense!"

"I don't know why I even came out tonight. I'm all for the cause, but I risked a dozen head-on collisions just to get groin-searched by a Mastiff. Now I've lost my third conversation partner in as many minutes because I have nothing to contribute. I think I'm gonna leave early, maybe microwave some leftover Dominos and fall asleep to any white-noise Netflix that doesn't touch on the Hellenization of the ancient world."

"Okay, that contingency plan doesn't sound half bad," Teddy admits. "But I hope you'll stick around just the same. I'm having a great time talking to you, plus there's an omelet bar and these neat statues."

"I do like eggs," Alexandra reasons.

"And anyway, not all greatness is measured in miles of conquest. I bet your Great Uncle Alex couldn't help me with my problem."

"What's your problem?"

"I need to learn about liches."

Alexandra smiles big. "You heard me talking about them?"

"I did. A friend of mine said the word the other day, but I have to admit I don't know much about it."

"Well listen close, Teddy, because you came to the right person."

Alexandra's posture improves. Her cheeks flush. Everybody, but everybody, likes to feel useful.

"Liches are mythological creatures, usually sorcerers who stuck their nose into necromancy. They live past a natural age, becoming frail and skeletal. If you put a lich in a boxing ring with, well, anything, it would lose in the first round. They're not built for strength or speed. What liches do best is *time*."

Alexandra spreads her hands in a rainbow arc to illustrate the passage of time.

"Let's say a wide-jaw, wavy-haired hero shows up with a broadsword. The lich can just chill in a cave for a few decades and play solitaire until heart disease fells the guy for him. And here's what I think's the coolest part of all. A lich could put an idea out into the world before you're even born, so that by the time you come along, whatever they've done is just a part of the world, and since the lich is in no hurry, its end goal can be set for well after you die. How can you fight something that pre- and post-dates your own existence?" Alexandra's eyes go wide. "Oh my god, I just realized something. The patriarchy is kind of a lich. I have something to contribute after all. I owe you one, Teddy. Come visit my shop sometime?"

"Yeah . . . Of course."

The buoyed Alexandra skips off to share her lich-patriarchy theory with a clump of women from SIS's D.C. chapter.

Now it's Teddy turn to be alone and miserable.

Alexandra said liches are mythological, and Teddy doesn't doubt that's true. But he doesn't think Blue Joe was talking about an aged skeleton in tattered rags.

What about something working so quiet and slow it would be nearly impossible to notice? For some reason, that definition feels right on target.

Sisters Out of Sync

For another hour, women from every corner of the country trickle in through Herberus's olfactory sieve, ready to reshuffle the political deck by any means necessary.

Solemnly, they recount the horrors of the past; angrily, they catalog the horrors of the present. Arranged marriages. Witch trials. An inexplicable lack of pockets. Denial of property ownership, of a vote, of an existence without condition. These things have happened and continue to happen, but won't happen going forward if those gathered in the Henhouse have anything to say about it.

The Lint sisters find each other.

"You have lipstick on your tooth," Ralph says.

"Ooh, thanks."

"I got some info on SIS's goals and strategies. These ladies mean business and make some damn good points, too. Did you know unmarried women under thirty can't check into Qatari hotels? You hear anything interesting?"

Teddy is about to recount his chat with Alexandra, but in a rare omission of the truth, doesn't. The whole lich thing is so inexplicably unnerving that he feels like he'll be endangering Ralph just by saying the word out loud.

He's spared from having to lie when the lights in the Henhouse go out, plunging the gathering into darkness.

Spotlights converge three stories above the amphitheater where a cube-shaped room made of glass hangs from the ceiling. A high-fidelity version of "You Don't Own Me," much more satisfying than the wimpy doorbell rendition, begins to play from unseen speakers. A pair of purple velvet cocoons dangling below the glass cube show signs of movement, one tangle of fabric unwinding in time with the music, elegantly making its way down toward the amphitheater. The second bundle, still in its starting position, shakes but doesn't unfurl.

Becky and Ruth leave their front door post and come halfway down the stairs to watch the show. A dimly lit silhouette in the glass cube also seems to be paying attention to the activity below.

As Lesley Gore reaches the exhilarating 'And don't tell me what to do!' portion of the anthem, the descending acrobat's fabric runs short and she crashes into the stone floor, inviting the bloody nose to end all bloody noses.

Becky drops her clipboard and races down the staircase. She attempts to drag the nose-bleeding aerialist up the amphitheater steps like they're under heavy machine gun fire, but the performer's foot is still caught in the coil of fabric and she keels around in a circle two feet off the floor. The second performer, still stuck in her velvet cocoon three stories up, yells something urgent about oxygen.

The commotion is enough to rouse the unrousable Herberus, who trots down the staircase with her nose held high in a fragrant jet stream of cooking eggs. As the dog nears the omelet bar, Diane, the sneezing woman, lets out an absolute bomb that propels her backwards into Andie, who's hard at work disappearing her second omelet of the day. The piping-hot fold of egg spirals off Andie's plate and lands squarely on Herberus's butt. The Mastiff gives a bark of surprise and takes off in a mad gallop, scattering toga-clad women like Roman bowling pins. A line of women domino down the shallow steps, sending Teddy stumbling into the center of the amphitheater where he slips on the aerialist's blood.

Getting dazedly to his feet, Teddy realizes all noise in the room has suddenly stopped, and again, he feels like all eyes in the room are on him.

This time, it's true.

Did he get all the lipstick off his tooth? Did Alexandra clock his gender and squeal? Hold on . . . his head feels ventilated. *His wig.* It's been catapulted onto the statue of Eudora Welty setting a volleyball for a spike-pose Harriet Tubman.

The stunned silence runs its course, and the crowd goes into a full on townspeople vs. Frankenstein's Monster rage. A pair of powerful hands grab Teddy, and the next thing he knows he's dangling a foot above the ground in a headlock, courtesy of Virginia Ham.

While he can't see what happens next, the sensation is unmistakable: someone has put a hand up his tunic and is holding a knife blade directly against his penis.

The Knife's Edge

Yelps propagate through the crowd as each woman has her hair tugged on, just in case. Andie makes sure she's the one to "tug" on Ralph's wig. He's ready to do a barroom brawl dive down into the amphitheater but Teddy shakes his head "no."

"Is there something there, Diane?" Ham asks, tightening her hold on Teddy's neck.

Diane, the sneeze-prone woman with one arm up Teddy's toga, nods. "Indeed there is, Hamb."

Teddy watches in horror as Diane's face begins to pinch. A sneeze at this moment would be the most consequential of his life.

"*Ham!*" Teddy gurgles into Ham's stony forearm. "*Ham! Shesgonnasneeze.*"

Diane's eyes squeeze shut and her mouth hangs open. This is it.

The mob draws in as if inhaled, knowing this is probably the closest they'll ever get to seeing a guillotine in action. Lips mumble creeds of unity and retribution that have been marinating for millennia. Even the superlatively clerical Becky has a Christmas-morning look in her eyes. The Henhouse buzzes with shared energy; if you weren't a gynarchist when you walked in, you might be now.

Focused on Teddy's groin as they are, nobody expects the gunshot.

The thunderclap of a fifty caliber round fills the amphitheater. Everyone but Herberus (busily devouring the rogue omelet) covers their ears and looks up.

A woman of advanced age stands at the top of the staircase, a gigantic silver revolver smoking in her right hand. Particulate from the gun-shot ceiling settles gently atop her salt and pepper hair as she waits for the magnified echo to play itself out.

"Diane, kindly lower your knife." Her voice is sonorous with a faint rasp. A smoker's voice.

Diane does as she's told. As the shock of the interruption ebbs, her delayed sneeze finally arrives, sending her knife-arm slicing upward in precisely the way every-one had hoped or feared.

"Maria's nose is likely broken," the woman on the staircase says, indicating the aerial performer who crashed into the floor. "Becky, I want you to carefully untangle her from the fabric and take her to urgent care. Diane, you'll please get Shailene out of her knot and help her up onto the catwalk."

Becky and Diane spring into action.

"Virginia."

Ham just about capsizes with glee at hearing her name come from the woman's pleated lips.

"Release the man."

Ham sets Teddy down.

The woman on the stairs beckons Teddy with a curl of her finger.

An irresistible gravitas, not to mention the portable canon in the woman's right hand, prompts Teddy to com-ply. He's rewarded with a firm handshake.

"My name is Felicity Ortega. Let's have a drink."

A Nightcap with the Head Honchess

Teddy follows Felicity Ortega up the stairs and out onto a catwalk that leads to the suspended glass cube.

"Thanks, Felicity," the woman being helped out of her cocoon gasps.

Ortega nods and continues into the hanging room, its plate glass walls, ceiling, and floor set against steel gird-ers spaced six feet apart. The room contains two egg-looking chairs, a silver bar cart, a large porcelain globe, and a female mannequin dressed in some kind of tactical gear.

Unlike sociopaths and tarantulas, heights don't crack Teddy's top five fears, but a glass floor with a three-story drop is a touch unnerving regardless. Among the tiny party guests milling far below, he notices Andie and Ralph keeping a close eye on him and their gun-toting hostess.

Ortega strides over to the bar cart and grabs two highball glasses. Her skin is a wrinkled golden brown, her lipstick a violent fuchsia. She's the only one in the mansion not wearing a tunic, dressed instead in a drab pantsuit so utilitarian it could hardly be anything other than stolen from the dressing room of a North Korean newscaster. While she smells surprisingly like rosewater, her energy is pure jaguar.

She pours bourbon (64 cal.) from a crystalline decanter into the glasses, adds a cross-section of orange (5 cal.), then a few drops of clear liquid from an unlabeled brown vial (?? cal.).

Despite Teddy's superlative manners, when Ortega offers him one of the cocktails, he hesitates. That last ingredient worries him, and not just because of unknown calories. When is an unlabeled brown vial anything other than poison?

Ortega seems amused by his hesitation. "Estrogen floater. I find it tunes a conversation to a more copacetic frequency. Especially with mixed company." She gives her a pinky a phallic wiggle. "Don't make me call Virginia to pinch your nose and pour it down your throat."

Teddy accepts the glass.

Ortega takes a gulp from her own and sits in an egg chair.

"What's your name?"

"Teddy."

"Okay, Teddy the Man. We've introduced ourselves. We each have a drink. Time for a conversation."

Teddy takes the chair opposite her and sips his cocktail. The citrus lily pad tickles his nose, and the overall flavor is nothing to brag about, but it doesn't kill him, so that's nice. The cartoonishly large revolver Ortega has placed atop the nearby globe, however, does concern him, and his eye lingers.

"No need for last rites just yet," Ortega says. "That was only crowd control down there."

"I think you might need a ballistics team to dig your crowd control out of the ceiling."

Ortega throws her head back and laughs, showcasing a small fortune in silver molars. "Good. A sense of humor is worth a lot, though we still have to color the rest of you in, and fast. Because here's the thing, we get a lot of devotees to the Old Guard coming around looking to gate-crash and stir up trouble. Could be you're some run of the mill misogynist from the internet who got brave and decided to stir shit up in real life. Worse, you could be a red-pill journo wired for sound, salivating at the prospect of an out-of-context soundbite. Worse still, you could be one of those Janusian pests looking to play an oh-so-funny prank."

Teddy would love to inquire about that last possibility, but Ortega doesn't slow down.

"So, Teddy the Man, answer me carefully. Which one are you?"

"None of the above, ma'am. I'd like to say more, but I'm not at liberty to do so."

"'Not at liberty.' Huh. Okay, let's start with something easier. How'd you get past Herberus?"

"I'd rather not say."

"You already played that card."

Teddy gulps. "I came here with my brother. He's a eunuch, and the dog checked him instead of me."

"A eunuch? My kind of man, but why'd he go and do a thing like that?"

"He didn't, it was done to him. We grew up in a cult."

Ortega squints. An amused look of recognition spreads on her face.

"Those kids that got pulled out of a bowling alley years back."

"An industrial laundromat, but yes."

"There was something about it recently, too . . . Jocular Beef. Ah, so, you're detectives."

Ortega strikes a match and lights a cigarette.

"Well, credit where it's due, I suppose, you two have successfully infiltrated the Henhouse. But there end the accolades because you've also been found out. Take a look out on the gangplank. The woman holding the small-bore rifle is Ruth Dice. Ruth was an Olympian. Bronze in the ten-meter, Gold in the fifty, meaning she can put a bullet wherever I want a bullet to be put. So, at liberty or not, you're going to tell me why you're spying on my girls, or you and your ball-less brother can become fertilizer for my well-manicured lawn."

Teddy looks below his feet at Ralph and Andie, well within Ruth Dice's Olympic-level range.

"We were hired to look into the whereabouts of a dangerous substance," Teddy says. "Your organization came up."

"It usually does," Ortega says flatly. "Who's signing the checks?"

"I can't tell you that."

She points her cigarette at the revolver. "Even if I, say, shoot your other eye out?"

"Yes, ma'am. Even if that."

Ortega exhales a patient plume of smoke. "Okay. Tell me something else instead. What do you think about feminism?"

Under the Gun

"Feminism?" Teddy gives another involuntary glance at the revolver. "No complaints."

Ortega chuckles. "There's a lot happening in this mean old world, and I don't penalize someone for failing to prioritize a cause personally precious to me. However, you're also a schmuck of the highest order if you view half the planet's population as anything less than full-fledged human beings. The fact this even needs to be said in an age of atom smashing and robotic food delivery is not a great look for the species. So, answer fast and true, feminism is . . ."

"A worthwhile pursuit."

Ortega claps her hands gunshot-loud, making Teddy jump. "Spectacular. A basal level of agreement. Now we can get into it."

She grabs ahold of Teddy's egg and drags it closer to hers with surprising strength.

"Rule by men may have helped put some distance between us and the primordial ooze but god damn if it wasn't a circus of misery for untold millions along the way." Ortega's voice is raspy but full, the words coming easy. "Even if physiological differences contributed to hierarchies of the distant past, at some point women were artificially excluded through societal means. Notice, for instance, there are no clubs moonshotting for rule by men, because that's largely what we have already. There is a gathering in this very city that celebrates that status quo, an explicitly mercantile take on Bohemian Grove in which men transact sums of money that would make a Rothschild blush. I don't know when it takes place and I don't know where, but when I do, there will be hell to pay."

Teddy appraises the female mannequin posed near his egg chair. It sports a gas mask, shin guards, shoulder pads, a bandolier of tear gas, a winged Valkyrie helmet, and a clear plastic riot shield laser-etched with SIS's ovaried hourglass. Each component looks mass produced, suggesting an absolute motherlode of riot gear could be taking up space elsewhere in the Henhouse.

The Sisters in Sync are obviously much more than omelets and aerial workouts, and Teddy wonders if a fleet of drones and a certain shipping container might not be hidden somewhere on the property as well.

"Royal Jelly," he floats.

Ortega gives him a predatory glare.

"Come again?"

"I'm wondering if you've ever heard of the Royal Jelly?"

"Have I heard of the Royal Jelly?" Ortega muses to herself. "An interesting question."

She stands and paces the square perimeter of the room.

"Here are some other interesting questions. Why are women boxed out of sovereign leadership roles? Why, when we're more cooperative, more empathetic, more nurturing, more disposed to a wealth of traits that lend themselves to quality governance, are we excluded? *How* are we excluded? Now that may be the most interesting question of all."

She raps a knuckle on the glass above a steel truss.

"We're put in a cage and told the bars aren't there; a daisy chain of lies stretching back centuries, designed to maintain a structure of oppression. *That's* how it happens. This is the challenge I was presented with. My response was to build something in opposition, a breath of fresh air. The Sisters in Sync is a noble cause stifled by Royal Jelly at every turn."

"I don't understand."

"Royal Jelly is what we call the unseen forces that wound our strides for equality. Forces that change shape or evaporate anytime we get close." Ortega grits her teeth so hard Teddy can hear the silver fillings squeak as they try to stay put. "I've come to accept it as a player in the game. One that will never leave. One that, apparently, now sends its emissaries to taunt me."

"Wait, no. I think—"

"What the Jelly doesn't know, is that I'm going to use it against itself, and you, Teddy the man, are going to help me do it."

The Glass Floor

"Ms. Ortega," Teddy says. "I think some wires may have gotten crossed here—"

"Quite the opposite. Things have never been clearer, and that's good, because focus has been a real issue around here lately."

She stomps her foot on the glass floor a little harder than Teddy would like.

"Some of the women down there . . . I've seen more resolve in a ping pong ball. They want selfies by my statues, a tryst with a *cause de jour,* an opportunity to hold up a sign in a crowd of people that already agree with them. Then they move on, and how can I blame them? The hot commodity these days is attention, and the daily chores of democracy do little to entertain. These women have the cause in their hearts, but they need a magnetic center around which to rally. I saw it briefly, down there in the amphitheater when you were held at knifepoint. That was a moment. I've never seen that kind of focus in them, the kind of the focus we need to overcome Royal Jelly."

"Er, where exactly do I come in?"

"You and I are going to tell a story. A story that started when I extracted you from danger and showed benevolent mercy. A story that took a tragic turn once you identified yourself as an agent provocateur in the service of Royal Jelly, dedicated to the destruction of our enterprise."

"But, Ms. Ortega, I don't—"

She picks up the revolver.

"The tree of liberty isn't watered with the blood of patriots; it's watered with showmanship! You came here an adversary, you will leave an ally. Your sacrifice will be remembered."

When she points the gun at Teddy's face, he automatically hurls his cocktail, shouting an apology as he does it.

His aim is good not great: the glass goes wide of Ortega, but the estrogen-infused bourbon sluices straight into her eyes. Blinded by the alcohol, she lets off a wild shot, hitting the biggest target available: a tempered pane of glass that wasn't designed to withstand high caliber rounds at point blank range.

The glass floor shatters.

Down goes the bar cart, and the egg chairs, and the globe, and the mannequin dressed for battle, and Teddy. Ortega alone has the good fortune to be standing directly above a steel girder, and even with an orange slice covering one eye she manages to stumble her way to the catwalk. In a panic, she grabs the railing with both hands, so down goes the gun, joining everything else already in freefall.

Acting on pure instinct, Teddy reaches out.

His hands find the unfurled tongue of fabric still dangling from the disastrous aerial workout. Friction burns his palms. He manages to get his legs around the fabric. Friction burns his thighs. The glass cube's décor smashes loudly on the ground below. Teddy squeezes as hard as he can and waits for his own crash.

It never comes.

Opening his eye, he finds he's slowed to a stop a foot above the marble floor.

The revolver, last to join the race down to the amphitheater, is snatched out of the air by Ralph, who never took his eyes off the scene above. He traces a wide arc with the gun's barrel, sending two hundred riled up

Sisters in Sync running for cover. Even the great Ruth Dice is caught off guard and forced to lay her sporty rifle down on the gangplank.

Under Ralph's provided cover, Andie helps Teddy down from the aerial silk and the three of them sprint up the staircase. Once they're outside, Ralph jams the revolver between the door handles to create a barricade that, judging by the sound of hundreds of angry footsteps stampeding up the staircase, is unlikely to hold for long.

Parking the Celery Express face-out will have been time well spent.

Definition Unknown

"Holy *smokes*!" Andie gushes as she watches the Henhouse shrink in the rear-view mirror. "Is this what your job is like?"

"Rarely," Ralph says. "Teddy? You okay back there?"

"Yeah," Teddy pants.

"What the hell happened?"

"We were talking about feminism, and robots, and a Bohemian Grove in LA. Then I mentioned the Royal Jelly and it was like an activation phrase. Ortega went crazy."

"She knew about it?"

"She had her own definition. Stinney's Scouts warned me about that, said when they asked around, people seemed to have different ideas about what it is. Ortega thought I was trying to destroy SIS."

Teddy tries to calm the overload of questions ricocheting around his skull. His already high levels of empathy, supercharged by Ortega's estrogen cocktail, have him giving everything she said serious thought, particularly her definition of Royal Jelly: an invisible mode of attitude control, odorless and colorless as carbon dioxide. It sounds an awful lot like Alexandra's eternal lich.

But that wasn't the only interesting thing he overheard in the Henhouse, and when the Celery Express pulls up to the Lesko mansion a few minutes later, Teddy opens his door.

"I'll walk you up, Andie."

"Oh, okay," she says. "Thanks for letting me tag along, Ralph. Nice work with that six-shooter tonight."

Ralph only grunts, but it's not an entirely unfriendly one.

As they walk up to the mansion, Andie excitedly pokes Teddy's arm. "Did you hear that grunt? Talk about progress. I don't know if you guys are in the market for a third investigator, but—"

Teddy stops at the front door. "Andie, what's your blood type?"

Andie's enthusiasm dissolves. She suddenly gets very busy pulling a set of house keys out of her pocket. "My uh . . . I don't . . ."

"Andie."

She abandons the housekey charade. "O negative."

"So it's me. I'm the candidate."

"How did you know?"

"I heard some of the Sisters whispering that you need a kidney. Is it true?"

"Yes."

"And that's why you were so eager to have dinner tonight? Rekindle some memories, build some rapport, and then comes the big ask because you think I won't say no?"

"Teddy, that's not what happened."

"You asked us our blood types."

"I know. It just came out. I . . . I'm nearing the fatal part of a fatal disease, one that can only be cured by kindness. And out of nowhere, I'm sharing a bathroom with the kindest person I've ever known." She meets his eye.

"I haven't asked you for anything, Teddy. I honestly don't know if I was going to."

Teddy looks back at the car. "If we talk for too long, Ralph's going to want to know what it was about. And I don't like to lie. Goodnight, Andie."

Grocer, Hero

Virginia Ham pounds on the front door of the Lesko mansion a little past midnight. No response, but the door's unlocked, so Ham's coming in.

She heads straight for the main bedroom and finds Andie sitting in an empty bathtub, eating from a jar of peanut butter.

"Why aren't you answering your phone? What the hell was that tonight?"

Andie looks up as if she's only just noticed Ham. "Hi, Ham."

Ham's rage breaks. "What's wrong?" She looks at Andie with hesitant concern. "Dialysis?"

"Do you want to hear a sad story?"

Ham sits on the rim of the tub and waits for Andie to begin.

"Once upon a time, a man named Dan Karrr owned a grocery store in East Los Angeles called Farmer's Delight. Dan smoked a pack a day, a bad habit he'd picked up in the Army. On one of his many smoke breaks, he sees a guy with a full grocery bag leave the store and head into—what Dan thought was—a condemned building down the street. The guy with the grocery bag is maybe five feet tall. Skinny, comb over, thick glasses. A grocer knows about how much food sustains about how many people, so it strikes Dan as a little strange that this relatively insubstantial man is carrying what he estimates to be enough groceries for five adults, or seven children, into what used to be an industrial laundromat bordering the garment district. Still, it's not exactly sound-the-alarm strange, so Dan decides to just keep an eye on things.

"Now that he's looking for it, he notices the little man with the big bag every week. The little man gets his groceries, walks down the street, looks around until he thinks no one's watching, and disappears into the supposedly condemned building. The next time the little man comes in, Dan makes sure he's working the register. Oats, salt, powdered milk, and the biggest bottle of Vitamin D supplements they sell. The shopping list does nothing to dissuade Dan's curiosity.

"The next time the little man comes into Farmer's Delight, Dan walks down the street for a closer look at the old building. *No Trespassing* signs all over the place, every door soundly locked, and way too many security cameras for an abandoned laundromat. Dan is liking the whole situation less and less. He's walking away from the building when something unusual happens.

"One of the locked doors opens, and a malnourished kid staggers out onto the sidewalk, squinting at daylight like he's never seen the stuff before.

"Dan asks him if he's okay. The boy isn't sure what he means. Dan asks if he's being kept against his will. The boy has to think about this one, but decides, yes, that sounds right, he *is* being kept against his will in there, and so are six others.

"Dan tries to get the kid to come with him, but the kid says he won't leave his siblings who are all still inside. Dan tells him to go back in and get them ready. He runs back to Farmer's Delight faster than he thought possible. He tells one of the employees to call the cops, then scours the aisles for that little bastard. No sign of him in meat or produce. Nothing in baked goods. Dear god, he must've missed him somewhere. He describes the little man to one of the cashiers. Yeah, sure, he just checked out.

"The boy on the sidewalk is named Teddy. Teddy goes back inside and tells his brothers and sisters that they're about to be rescued. When the little man comes back from the grocery store—his name is Percival Maw— one of the girls—her name is Andie—tells Papa Maw that Teddy was talking to a stranger, and that the stranger is going to take them away.

"Percival Maw doesn't waste any time. He grabs some anesthetic and a nasty piece of silverware called an evisceration spoon, and he goes looking for Teddy. Little Andie is even more frightened now, 'cause Papa Maw is acting strange, and when he asks her where Teddy is, she points to the dryer room. She knows Teddy likes to hide there sometimes.

"By now, Dan Karrr's pounding on the outside door so hard he breaks a finger. He's been to war and knows what people are capable of, especially when the walls are coming down. A boy named Ralph opens the door. Dan sticks his apron in the jamb to keep the door from closing, tells Ralph to let the cops in, and runs toward the screaming.

"By the time he finds them, Maw's gotten one of Teddy's eyes out. Dan socks him in the jaw before he can take the second. The two men try to strangle each other until a few bag boys from the store arrive and help turn Maw into a human pretzel. The cops come soon after. It's all over.

"The kids are confused, but the girl named Andie knows she's done something she regrets. She runs up to the ambulance they're putting Teddy in. She says she's sorry and he tells her, even then, even in that moment, even after what she did, that it's not her fault.

"She sees lots and lots of people who try to help. She was a child in a cult. She didn't know better; she *couldn't* know better. Maybe. But the worst is yet to come.

"The kids go their separate ways. Andie never finds the courage to contact Teddy, she can't bear the thought of having to face him. Eighteen years later she runs into him on the floor of a public bathroom. And after all that time, after all she did to him, she does something truly unforgivable."

Ham can barely manage the question. "What?"

Andie looks at her with a pained smile. "She asks him for a favor."

WEDNESDAY

"No matter how sophisticated, how cynical the public may become about publicity methods, it must respond to the basic appeals, because it will always need food, crave amusement, long for beauty, respond to leadership."

-Edward Bernays

Folgers Fort Knox

Insectile larvae writhe in royal jelly, the beehive kind of royal jelly, except then it's the other kind, Woodbine's kind, and the baby bees disintegrate, and the Jelly eats through the hive, and the tree it hangs from, and the surrounding jungle. Forest melts into desert a moment before the all-white of a nuclear explosion. An impossible volume of sand inhales skyward in elegant curves of inertia, a column of white fire at its core reaching for the stratosphere. A flock of birds that want nothing to do with the spreading poison take flight, transforming one by one into drones that climb over the Santa Monica Mountains before diving down into LA proper. The drones strafe one another in a computer-perfect pattern as they blanket streets, cars, buildings, trees, people, in a patina of fatal rain.

LA's dawn chorus of leaf blowers puts an end to Teddy's nightmare. He sits up in the bottom bunk, tangled in his sheets.

"Just a dream," he says. "Just a bad dream."

After a shower to wash off the nightmare sweat, he dons a fresh cardigan and eyepatch—red—and braces for another round of Mr. Woodbine's Wild Ride. He finds Ms. Beauchamp consolidating pen ink at her desk.

"Good morning, Teddy." Her voice loses a bit of its warmth. "Alright, young man, that's five minutes past eight."

A Stinney's Scout, previously fast asleep on the couch, rolls over and moans.

Though Ms. Beauchamp is far from the Scouts' biggest fan, she isn't so heartless as to turn away a bedless child. Her policy on the lobby couches is that they're fair game during off hours, but checkout time is eight o'clock (with a five-minute grace period if she's in a good mood).

"Let me get some cereal in him first," Teddy says.

He backtracks to the kitchenette and finds something like a naval mine sitting on the counter.

Ms. Beauchamp has brewed the morning coffee as usual, but has also added defensive measures, sealing the top of the pot with a quiltwork of duct tape penetrated by stirrer straws. Anyone attempting to take more than their fair share of coffee (Ms. Beauchamp has perhaps, a certain, exceptionally tall client in mind) will be forced to pour through a small hole in the duct tape at a sane, governed rate.

Steering clear of the coffee pot, Teddy pours a bowl of Cheerios and makes a phone call.

"Hello?" Andie says.

"Hey, I hope I didn't wake you up."

"Are you kidding? I was up all night. Teddy. I'm sorry. I'm so fucking sorry I don't even know what to say."

"It's alright. Your news took me by surprise, and I didn't handle the moment so well. You're the one who's sick, and I thought about myself instead."

"If this call turns into you apologizing to me, the world is beyond saving."

"Oh, that's never true no matter what." Teddy munches a Cheerio (.2 cal.). "How are you feeling?"

"Late-stage renal failure is no picnic, but dialysis helps slow the collapse. Good days and bad days."

"I want to help you, Andie, I do. It's just, with my condition . . ."

"You don't have to say no, Teddy, because I'm not asking the question. Really. I'm just glad to have you guys in my life one last time. It's more than I could've asked for."

"We're not giving up yet. I'm going to ask my family doctor, he's a man who feels . . . unencumbered by conventional laws. Maybe he'll have a solution, though I can't promise it'll be above board."

"So long as it filters urine and controls blood pressure, I won't ask for a backstory." Andie pauses. "Did you tell Ralph?"

Teddy delivers the bowl of cereal to the crusty-eyed Scout and looks out the Agency's front window. He sees Ralph down in the parking lot talking to a huge man he doesn't recognize.

"I haven't told him yet, but I'll have to eventually. First things first. Let's see if we can't get you a good day and go from there. I'll let you know what the doctor says."

"No one deserves you, Teddy. Me included. Bye."

Teddy hangs up. "Ms. Beauchamp, who's Ralph talking to?"

"An associate of Mr. Woodbine's, though you wouldn't know it by his disposition. Impeccable manners. Said 'No, thank you, ma'am,' when I offered him coffee."

Ms. Beauchamp shoots a harried glance at her fortified coffee pot. It's unlikely Woodbine has managed to pull off an elaborate caffeine heist, but as the sleepy Scout finishing his Cheerios might say, "You just . . . you never really know."

Another Square Button

Teddy joins his brother down in the parking lot. Ralph's body language indicates that the guy he's talking to is, so far, alright.

The stranger is bald and very dark skinned. A pair of tiny, brass-rim sunglasses pinch his nose. His bulky body strains a cream linen dress shirt whose top button, like Woodbine's the day before (and the mysterious, surveilling couple in the car the night before that), is square. He and Ralph are standing beside the plum-colored Rolls Royce Ms. Beauchamp previously identified as a Ghost, though the custom badge on the car's trunk reads '*Fantomo*'.

"Good morning, my name's Teddy."

"Good morning. I am Ousmane Ba, an associate of Mr. Woodbine's. Please call me Ousmane if you like."

"I'd love to. May I ask if you're from Senegal?"

"I am indeed."

Teddy's knowledge of accents has obvious value in the world of private investigations. The Case of the Missing Dane, for instance, ended when the heavily disguised suspect used a 'v' sound in place of 'w' ("The chocolate factory man? That's easy, Villy Vonka. Oh."). But Teddy mainly studies accents so he can ask new friends about their life without a clumsy, "So, where are you from?" To the expat and refugee alike, a correct guess almost always elicits surprised joy. Ousmane Ba is no exception, though he limits his elation to a nod of approval.

One of the *Fantomo*'s heavily tinted windows lowers an inch, revealing a counterfeit smile inside.

"*Bonvenon*, boys," Woodbine says. "What say we have a chat while Mr. Ba takes the odometer for a stroll."

Teddy and Ralph exchange shrugs and join Woodbine in the absurdly roomy backseat.

The car's axis tilts as Ousmane Ba gets behind the wheel and the Rolls Royce departs Lorenzo Dunes, receiving a catlike hiss from Blue Joe as it goes.

Dixon Does Los Angeles

"Tell me, boys," Woodbine smooths his jacket, today a professorial tweed. "Is Los Angeles on the precipice of becoming a freak-populated wasteland—more so, I mean—or have you two finally dug up something of interest?"

Despite his request for a report at the end of the week, it seems Woodbine is intent on a daily dose of micromanagement. At least today's visit comes with moving scenery.

"We got into a SIS meeting last night," Teddy says.

"Did you really?" Woodbine claps his hands in excitement. "That's more like it! And?"

"Their leader, Felicity Ortega, has a Royal Jelly, but it isn't the same as yours. I think their organization could have the potential to carry out a large-scale attack, but we saw no evidence linking them to drones or Agent Orange specifically."

"What else?"

"Their Denver omelet could use some work," Ralph says.

Woodbine shakes his head. "You boys claim to be doing a whole lot of choppin', but I don't see the chips flyin'!"

He begins lecturing Ralph on the merits of a strong work ethic, allowing Teddy to study the rest of the *Fantomo*.

There's something off about the car's dashboard, but it takes Teddy a second to realize what it is: a total lack of the number nine. The speedometer's markings go from eighty-eight to one hundred, and when the odometer ticks up, it goes from eight directly to zero. Teddy's attention goes next to Ousmane Ba, specifically a tattoo bunched up in the accordion of skin on the back of his neck. The letters are unreadable until the gods of expectoration, so fixated on Teddy's destruction the night before, choose today to bless him. Ousmane sneezes, hinging his head forward enough to reveal the tattoo in full.

La lupo protektas la ŝafojn de si mem.

Ousmane's head returns to its normal position a moment later, reencoding the tattoo.

Teddy wonders what the language could be. Wolof? French? He doesn't know offhand, but it's clear that even people tangentially connected to Woodbine are strange. Their best chance at progress might come through investigating Woodbine himself.

They know who he isn't (few government employees own a bespoke Rolls Royce), which leaves the riddle of who he is. A bored billionaire? A high-functioning psychotic? Some unrelated, second thing? Why the allergy to nines? Why the cryptically tattooed chauffeur?

". . . and the ant learned a valuable lesson." Woodbine checks his watch and jolts. "Good lord, is that the time? I'll be late for class. Mr. Ba, let's drop these two back where we found them, changed for the better."

Ousmane drives back to Lorenzo Dunes, the *Fantomo* coming to a heavenly-smooth stop in the parking lot.

"Remember," Woodbine cheerleads as they climb out of the car. "You're men of action. Kick over the rocks! Rattle the cages! Do what you have to do to get results. So long, boys."

The second the Rolls is gone Teddy runs for the Celery Express.

"What's up?" Ralph yells.

"Time to investigate Woodbine."

Ralph gives a whoop of agreement.

Follow that Fantomo

With the heater refusing to turn off, and the turn signals refusing to turn on, the Celery Express is feeling especially sassy that day, but the cop engine plays nice, and Ralph catches up to their elegant target in less than two blocks.

After a hearty sampling of LA traffic, Ousmane slows the *Fantomo* outside a corporate campus on the Miracle Mile. The property is centered by a high rise of black glass without any kind of signage. On one side of the building is a parking lot, on the other, a rock and sand Zen Garden, all of it enclosed by a classy and impenetrable wrought iron fence. The *Fantomo* is immediately waved past a guard gate and into the choicest of parking spots.

Ralph circles the block. At the rear of the property, he and Teddy see a service entrance with a security guard who looks as grimly professional as the one up front.

"Mercy," Teddy says. "What is this place?"

Ralph finishes the lap and street parks across from the front gate. Ousmane Ba and Woodbine have since disappeared into the building.

"Well," Ralph says. "Seems about all we can learn from a distance."

"Distraction?" Teddy says.

"Distraction. We get the rear guard up here and infiltrate through the service entrance."

Teddy nods.

In sensitive cases like this one, a distraction has to be Goldilocks perfect: big enough to draw attention, but not so big as to break the semblance of a normal day. When a brief spitball session between the brothers yields nothing quite right, Teddy texts Andie.

> **Teddy**: Hi, Andie! ☺ How's it going?
> **Andie**: having a ball at Club Dialysis. you?
> **Teddy**: Trying to get into a building. Need a distraction. Ideas?
> **Andie**: i know a man BORN to do the job. send me the address

"Hey, neat. She knows someone for the job."

"Tell me you're kidding."

"C'mon, she did great last night."

Ralph neither confirms nor denies. "Let's get ready."

The trunk latch wants to play games but Ralph brute forces it open. Per usual, the Stinney's Scouts' disguise kit inside has everything they need.

Ralph stretches a bald cap onto his head. "This doesn't mean she's going to become a regular fixture around the office."

Teddy puts on a dress shirt padded with a fake gut and love handles, then pulls on a shiny black beard. "I'm not saying she will, just that I liked having her around, and I don't think you hated it as much as you're pretending you did. She could be going through more than we know. People usually are."

Ralph draws himself Scorsese-heavy eyebrows and a pencil thin mustache. "We can't trust her."

"She's our sister, Ralph." Teddy slips lifts into his shoes and replaces his eyepatch with a pair of extra dark Ray Bans. He's debating dropping the kidney bomb when he notices a man with a head of wild, white hair, running toward them from a city bus.

"Randall J. Pipp, attorney for the Lesko estate," the man in a brown suit yells over frenzied handshakes. "Friends of Andie's are friends of mine. I'm at your service, up to and including death."

"I'm pretty sure it won't come to that, Mr. Pipp," Teddy says. "Are you feeling alright?"

"How's that? Who's alright?"

"He's asking how many drugs you're on," Ralph says.

"Drugs? Goodness, I never touch the stuff, though I did eat a teaspoon of powdered caffeine on the bus ride over. Couple long nights at the office."

"Terrific. We need to get inside this building. There's a guard here, and another in back. We were thinking—"

"Leave it to your old pal Pipp!"

Pipp sprints toward the front gate guard like a sicced dog.

"He's not gonna kill the guy, is he?" Teddy says.

Ralph tucks a last bit of hair under his bald cap. "Probably not. Let's get into position."

Pipp fortunately doesn't commit manslaughter but proves to have more enthusiasm than cunning. His first plan is to tell the guard that there's been a zoo escape, but he doesn't have an answer when the guy asks what kind of animal got out. When the guard tells him to get lost, Pipp tries a spin move, but his feet tangle up and he falls. When the guard leans down to help him, Pipp snatches his badge and barrel rolls into the parking lot. At this, the exasperated guard keys his walkie and says the magic words: "Frank, you'd better c'mere a sec. Whack job's got my badge."

Frank—formerly known as the guard watching the service entrance—hustles around the building, passing a chubby man in sunglasses and a mustachioed bald guy walking oh so casually down the sidewalk.

Teddy looks over his shoulder to see Pipp feign surrender before snatching Frank's badge too. Their patience artfully thinned, the security guards chase Pipp through the pristine gravel of the Zen Garden.

Concern for Pipp's safety nearly compels Teddy to turn back, but Ralph tugs him along to the Frank-less service entrance. They're in.

Walk with Purpose

The Lints walk quickly but calmly down a hallway until they reach a chic, high-ceilinged lobby. A team of receptionists rolls calls at a horseshoe desk in front of a massive, free-standing plate of black glass etched with gold lettering that spells out *The West Company*. Opposite the receptionists, a network of fine leather chairs plays host to a dozen or so well-dressed business types who sit with the impatient air of high-paying clients.

Teddy and Ralph watch as an employee escorts one of them to a bright green door with its own security guard. The pair enter a smaller room on the other side, a kind of privacy airlock, before the green door closes behind them.

"What do you think they have in there?" Teddy asks. "Chocolate river?"

"We'd have to ask Mr. Vonka."

Ralph doesn't like the look the green-door security guard is giving him and Teddy. He nudges his brother toward the constellation of leather chairs, and they pretend to look busy.

"Business, business, business," Ralph wallas. Then, in a whisper: "Check out the receptionist, third from the right. It's the guy we helped out of that email scam. Complete asshole, remember?"

Teddy squints at the receptionist in question: a red-haired man armed with a cheap haircut and almost comic scowl.

"Oh, Gerry Weinstein," Teddy says. "He was a nice enough guy . . . in his own way."

"That's Teddy-speak for complete asshole."

Gerry Weinstein's case had been simple. Gerry himself, had not.

As a less than sunny person, Gerry had taken Teddy's above-average compassion as a personal insult and retaliated by constantly trying to trip Teddy up with unwinnable, ethical dilemmas. A school bus of nuns is going to crash into a fund raiser for special needs kids, while, all the way across town, a bomb has been planted in the penguin exhibit at the zoo, and today's the day the kids from the school of photographic memory are visiting, and you only have time to stop one bad thing from happening, etc., etc. Teddy always took each 'what if' tragically seriously, giving Gerry perverse satisfaction as Teddy ultimately condemned an imaginary flock of birds to a fiery end.

Ralph pulls out a little notebook like Teddy's, and flips through a list of names until he locates Weinstein, Gerry. Unlike some of the other names, there is no check mark next to Gerry's. "Perfect. He still owes us."

"I think he'd help either way."

"Right."

Then, disaster. Perhaps angling for employee of the month, the suspicious security guard is heading straight for the Lints.

Ralph acts fast.

"Get to Gerry," is his parting directive before he goes the way of Randall J. Pipp, sacrificing himself for the mission by walking straight into an employee carrying a stack of lidded containers.

Both men fall to the floor and the plastic tubs do likewise, spilling a wealth of shredded documents. A good disruption becomes a great one when the building's over-zealous AC kicks on, transforming the lobby into a snow globe of partially annihilated information.

The inbound security guard goes for Ralph, and Teddy goes for the receptionists' desk, making sure he's helped by the least friendly-looking one.

St. Gerry the Generous

Unconcerned with the clerical snowstorm blanketing the lobby, Gerry 'No Relation' Weinstein gives Teddy a bland, professional smile.

"Yes, sir. How can I help you?"

"Gerry, it's Teddy."

"Oh, hey. Teddy. Didn't recognize you at first."

"I'm sporting something of a different look today."

"Yeah, listen, I know I still owe you guys payment for—"

"Don't worry about it, Gerry."

"*You* say that, but I bet your brother's still got my name in his little book."

"I'm not here to collect," Teddy says. "I'm working a case."

The AC shuts off, settling the flurry of paper as Ralph is dragged out the front door.

Teddy lowers his voice. "What is this place?"

Gerry jerks a thumb at the black glass behind him. "The West Company, in case you didn't notice."

"Right, but what does the West Company do?"

"It's an ad agency," Gerry says. "Marketing. Public relations. Whatever a paying client wants."

So, Woodbine *is* in advertising. Interesting.

"A man walked in here a few minutes ago, he was wearing a tweed suit."

"Mr. West."

"A tall guy. Arrived in a Rolls Royce."

"Like I said, that's David West. He founded the damn company."

So, Dixon Woodbine's real name is David West. Interesting.

Teddy nods at the green door. "And what's through there?"

"Oh, that?" Gerry cops a shit eating grin. "That's the dream factory."

The other secretaries absorbing the never-ending flow of calls shoot annoyed looks at Gerry and his lengthening personal conversation.

"Think you could get me in?" Teddy whispers.

Gerry gives a humorless laugh. "I know I owe you guys a few bucks, but my main function here is not letting in riff raff, and I hate job hunting. I'm not throwing away a regular paycheck just so one of your scuzzy clients can bilk an exec for child support or whatever it is you're doing here."

"This is bigger than that kind of thing, Gerry. People could get hurt."

Gerry shrugs.

Teddy looks out the front windows of the building where Ralph and Randall J. Pipp, both thoroughly roughed up by West Company security, are limping their way back to the Celery Express. Like a team of selfless speed-skaters, they've forgone personal glory (and personal safety) to catapult Teddy forward in the race. Failure is not an option.

Teddy sighs. "How about one of your riddles? If I answer right, you let me in."

Gerry leans back in his swivel chair, intrigued. Then his face lights up, something wildly cruel in the hopper.

"A witch walks into your office. She'll give you the power to stop one major bus crash a year, for the next ten years. You'll save hundreds of lives, easy. In exchange, you have to send a telegram to an animal rescue across town that houses blind kittens. The telegram message contains a specific sequence of letters and numbers whose printing friction will melt the receiving unit and start a structure fire, killing all three hundred helpless little kitties. And you have to do it on your birthday."

"*Mercy.*"

"You have five seconds."

Teddy wrestles with the abstract.

"I'll give you a hint," Gerry says. "The right answer is taking the deal. Taking the deal gets you through the green door. C'mon, Teddy, cook the cats."

Teddy slumps. "I can't."

"No deal, no door." Gerry holds his hands up. "Can't say I didn't try."

Teddy turns to leave, a failed speed skater. Then he stops.

"Gerry. Something's just occurred to me. I think you're having a bad day and I think I might know why."

"I can't wait to hear this."

"Today's your birthday."

Gerry's sadistic grin withers. "How did you know that?"

"I remember it from your case file. It's a crummy thing when everyone forgets your birthday. Is that what happened?"

Gerry's face threatens a sob but he swallows it down. Glaring at Teddy, he unlocks a small safe and hands over an ID card.

"You're João."

"I'm what?"

"João Alvarez, textiles rep from Lisbon who missed his connecting flight at JFK this morning. Take it or leave it."

Teddy looks at the badge's picture. João's on the heavy side, which is a good match for the fat suit, but he's definitely not Black. Worse yet, he has two eyes. With some help from his friends at the Sharpie corporation, Teddy markers a pair of sunglasses onto João's ID, and courtesy of the fine folks at Ticonderoga Pencils, shades the skin enough to complete a casual resemblance.

"St. Gerry the Generous," Teddy proclaims. "Happy Birthday, Gerry. I promise you'll have a proper card next year. And don't give up on the people in your life just yet, the day is far from over."

Without looking Teddy in the eye, Gerry gives a small nod and goes back to the phones.

Armed with João's badge, Teddy approaches the security guard by the green door. She takes a break from pulling strips of paper out of her hair and checks Teddy's ID badge.

"Welcome, Mr. Alvarez."

Teddy steps through the green door and into the small privacy room beyond. Another green door awaits, this one printed with the words: *The Plaza Of Midnight Oil.*

Teddy opens the door and skates on in.

The Plaza of Midnight Oil

It feels a bit like stepping into a cathedral, a suddenly vacuous space that humbles the entrant without debate. An atrium ceiling glints with sunshine seven stories above a busy plaza whose perimeter is lined with glass-walled offices too numerous to count.

Not wanting to look like a wide-eyed tourist, Teddy lets himself be pulled into the churn of employees hurrying around with storyboards, look-books, market analyses, and it's-your-ass-if-you're-wrong lunch orders.

Riding the outermost arm of the galactic swirl, he gets brief vignettes into the perimeter offices where art directors scream themselves the perfect shade of red, and data brokers, those day traders of consumer attention, lounge with their feet up on desks, confident in their domination of the zeitgeist. In offices higher up, clients awaiting their pre-purchased PR miracles ooh and aah at a network of pneumatic tubes that shoop canisters of documents too sensitive to be digitized into a departing artery marked *TO SHREDDER.*

Spiraling gradually inward, Teddy passes isolated kiosks that part the flow of employees like rocks in water. The sushi bars, each dressed with arrangements of illegally-sourced orchids, don't have a single open stool. Towering espresso machines, brass monstrosities the size of church organs, regularly spew plumes of caffeinated steam into the crowd. Teddy takes a humid blast of Ethiopian Arabica to the face and gets a contact high that almost knocks him off his feet.

He's closing in on the center of the plaza now, where a circular, glass-walled office plays spoke to the wheel of activity. But the thing that draws the eye is on the roof of the office: a tower made of TV screens that reaches three stories high, like a spinal column ripped from some undying media god. The screens are busy with spots for prescription drugs and class-action litigation against drug companies. Spots for fast food and diet shakes. For hair plugs and razor blades. Products to solve problems that don't exist. Products to solve the problems those products create. Greenwashing. Pinkwashing. Celebrity endorsements and installment plans for toaster ovens. A double helix of smartphones wind their way up the column, displaying real-time social media posts from noteworthy influencers. The churning mosaic of image and sound is so horribly captivating that Teddy momentarily forgets to keep up with the plaza's flow of traffic. He's about to be pancaked by the inertia of commerce when someone yanks him out of harm's way.

His savior is a young man dressed in a black t-shirt and black jeans. He's got blonde-white hair buzzed down to the scalp, and beady eyes framed in a pair of lensless glasses.

"I'm Eddie Mannheim, I'm an entrepreneur," he shouts, shaking Teddy's hand without asking.

The two of them stand with their backs flat against the glass of the central office.

"The Plaza of Midnight Oil," Eddie announces wistfully. "Can't believe I'm finally seeing it in person. This here's the West Company's heart of hearts, or *koro de koroj* as they might say, wink, wink."

"Right, yeah, hi, I'm Teddy, er, João."

"Teddy Zhou. Is that a Chinese name?"

"Um, yep. Chinese."

"Right on. I love the Chinese market. I'm here for the new employee orientation. I'll go ahead and say you have the same look."

"Yes, the orientation."

"Trying to get some face time in with Teach before class, eh? Nice try, but I had the same idea. Office door's locked."

Teddy looks through the glass behind him and gets a glimpse at the core of it all: David West née Dixon Woodbine, sitting in a chair, staring catatonically into space. Before Teddy can decide if his client is meditating or comatose, Eddie Mannheim yanks him back into the churn of foot traffic.

"C'mon, we don't want to be late to class."

The Braintrust

They enter one of the larger glass-walled rooms lining the plaza. Inside is a classroom, thirty desks lined up in a neat grid before an empty teacher's desk.

Most of the seats are already filled by well-groomed twentysomethings whose shiny teeth and picture-day hair give them a fresh out of the carwash look. After a cursory interest in the newcomers, they go back to their conversations already in progress.

Nearly every Ivy League school is mentioned by name, ditto summer homes and Wall Street internships. The students alternate between bragging and waiting to brag, taking care not to appear impressed while someone else lists pedigrees and accomplishments nearly identical to their own. While there isn't an academic lightweight in the bunch, actual wisdom seems to be in short supply.

Eddie finds a pair of seats near the middle of the pack, and Teddy soon learns a great deal about his new friend, all without ever asking a single question.

Unlike most of the student body, Eddie Mannheim started from zero. Inventively ambitious, he claims he escaped poverty by selling his plasma, bone marrow, and any other piece of himself he could find a buyer for.

Eddie just turned twenty-six. He has no real ideas of his own but can sell the absolute pants off any that come within earshot. Even at a young age, he has a growing track record of successfully removing the 'potential' modifier from potential multi-million-dollar ventures. He avoids inflammatory foods, "complainers," and above all else, psychiatrists (though were he to trip and fall onto a chaise lounge, the attending doctor would likely identify him as a sociopath). He's maintained a six-pack since the fourth grade and uses words like 'grindset' in earnest. Every morning, with the aid of coconut oil and a diligent assistant to massage his throat, he swallows an equine vitamin pill in the hopes of living past a hundred and thirty (at least).

His wardrobe is all black to remove a daily decision that could be better spent elsewhere. His head is shaved for the same reason. He's always willing to pick up and burn out on a new hobby, forever failing to grasp the fact that one essential component of mastery is denial of all that is not that thing. He overestimates the accuracy of his conversational Japanese and thinks the set of Russian nesting dolls in his guest bathroom make him an authority on Soviet Era economics. Back when he still flew commercial, he raised his hand when the infamous "Is anyone here a doctor?" call came for a stroke victim, and nearly performed a tracheotomy with a Bic pen before he was subdued by the flight team.

At his core, Eddie believes he's clued into some asset-and-debit truth of the world wherein everything, from The Law of Conservation of Mass to musical chairs, is inescapably zero-sum. In his view, the only available positions are accepting this fact, or welcoming exploitation from those who have.

His hero, idol, no-but's-about-it god isn't Henry Ford or Tony Robbins (though he has posters of both above his bed), it's David West, and wouldn't you know it, the man himself has just walked through the door.

Weeding

With a few strides of his absurdly long legs, Professor West reaches the teacher's desk, where he sets down a stack of books and a jar half-filled with what might be kernels of white corn.

"Who here is impervious to advertising?"

The class, buzzing with confident energy only a moment before, goes completely silent. A few students risk unsure glances at a neighbor, but no hands go up.

West assumes a casual, cool-teacher seat on the edge of his desk and wet-noodles his arms.

"Okay, everyone relax. Give your arms a shake, like this."

The class obediently mimics him.

"This classroom has been carefully stocked with the best minds, from the best institutions in the country. Some of you *must* be impervious to advertising. So, let's try this again. Who here is impervious to advertising?"

This time, about a third of the class raises their hands.

Knowing how unpredictable the man in the tweed suit can be, Teddy keeps his hand down.

"That's better. Keep 'em up." West scans the room. "Alright, identified and noted, all eight of you. Now get out."

An awkward silence is followed by awkward laughter.

"It's not a joke," West says. "Your enrollment in this course has ended. You may go."

Still, no one moves.

West bull rushes a sleek MBA in the front row. *"Get out of my classroom!"*

The young woman flinches, then lets out a sob and flees. One by one, the other hand-raisers follow suit.

All except one.

West looks oddly pleased as he strides over to the young man's desk. "Not gonna leave, huh?"

Eddie Mannheim shakes his head. "No, sir."

West smiles, then punches Eddie in the mouth.

Teddy gasps as several of Eddie's teeth click across the floor like dice.

"This is not a research project! This is not a cushy internship! This is going to war and burning the ships behind us because we have no use for non-believers!"

West grabs Eddie's collar, intending on dragging him out the door, but Eddie holds onto his seat. After a few hearty tugs that stutter the legs of Eddie's desk, West stops.

"So. You want to stay?"

Glasses askew, Eddie nods.

"What's your name?"

Blood burbles between Eddie's split lips. "Edey Bannheimbh."

"I can tolerate a crisis of faith provided it's followed by resolve. But you have to pay the heretic's toll."

West walks to the teacher's desk and shakes the glass jar. With the help of context clues, Teddy realizes its contents aren't corn at all, but teeth. It seems West has used this syllabus before.

Shakily, Eddie gets up from his desk, collects his scattered teeth, and drops them into the jar.

"Good." Professor West faces the class. "Let's begin."

Propaganda 101

"There was a time in my life when I was betrayed by someone I trusted, and the little I had was taken away from me. In the deepest depths of my personal nadir, I discovered my superpower. I discovered that if I said the right words in the right way, I could get people to believe whatever I wanted. Not only could I have a vote in what they did, I could influence how they *thought*."

West begins a slow circuit around the classroom, his already imposing height exacerbated by the standing-sitting imbalance.

"The democratic El Dorado is impossible in a modern mass society. Your neighbors, your friends, and your family are driven by herd instincts and prejudice. They are frequently disoriented by external stimuli, making them incapable of lucid thought and clear perception. Expecting them to make decisions or engage in rational discourse would be a mistake. Democracy, therefore, requires a supra-governmental body of detached professionals to sift the data and think things through. To keep the entire national enterprise from grinding to a halt, major issues must be framed, and crucial choices made by the responsible administrator."

West gestures to himself in a 'yours truly' fashion, then reverses the gesture to include everyone present.

"But you're not there yet. Make no mistake, your minds are still molded, your tastes still formed, your ideas still suggested, by men and women you have never heard of. With the right guidance however, it may be possible for you to join our benign elite of rational manipulators who win gradual impression through patient research and sober planning."

The collective mood in the room boomerangs from fear back to eagerness, the trivial matter of graphic violence already forgotten.

"We never sell," West says. "What we do is bring questions into the public consciousness, questions *we* have the answers to, so that when we speak, we're expressing the demands of a public already keyed to the issue. Ignorance of our values is friction. Your job is to remove those frictions by appealing to emotion over intellect, bias over information."

His face damp with oratorical sweat, West returns to the front of the room. He slaps the stack of books sitting on the teacher's desk.

"This, my friends, is your Bible, your deepest keel, your most beloved teddy bear. Keep it close, welcome its teachings into your heart, and remember, always, that those who manipulate the organized habits and opinions of society constitute an invisible government which is its true ruling power."

Every student around Teddy, even the actively-bleeding Eddie Mannheim, is hyper focused on West, their minds gift-wrapped for anyone who can speak with this much fluidity and conviction.

"Welcome to that invisible government," West announces triumphantly. "Welcome to . . ."

At what should be a triumphant finish, his voice trails off. His gaze goes unfocused, and he looks like he might be sick right there in the classroom.

"Welcome to . . . Welcome to the West Company," he finishes in an uncertain whisper.

Then he snaps back into a smile that almost convinces.

The look on David West's face reminds Teddy of another he saw recently. That of Lobbie the Lobster, grinning inside a pot as he's boiled alive.

Burn Before Reading

Half an hour later, Teddy, Ralph, and Eddie Mannheim are seated in a waiting room with a diverse clientele.

The moans of a man with a toothache are interspersed by the squeaks of a queasy hedgehog. A PSA poster on one wall offers tips on how to avoid the common cold, another, on how to spot signs of Equine Streptococcus ('Healthy as a Horse? Don't be so Sure'). An unsupervised ferret gnaws on the shirtsleeve of a receptionist who, judging by her lack of reaction, has seen it all before.

There's nothing remotely legal about a combination doctor-veterinarian office, but no one waiting for medical attention seems to mind.

Teddy made an appointment with Doctor Scanlan that morning under the guise of a Post-Traumatic Hypometabolic Magnification Syndrome checkup, but his actual aim is to inquire about any loose kidneys that might be lying around. This means he's going to have to tell Ralph about Andie's predicament sooner rather than later, and he still isn't sure about the best way to do it.

Despite delirium from blood loss, Eddie Mannheim is dutifully trying to read the book West gave out to the class. He's making good progress, but every now and then, he slumps into Ralph, who's carefully placing strips of paper on the waiting room's coffee table.

During his apprehension in the West Company lobby, Ralph managed to pocket a clump of shredded paper, and even though he knows the odds of pulling anything meaningful out of the mauled documents are wildly low, it's the shameful private investigator who lets even the smallest clue go to waste. Lucky for the Lints, someone in the West Company cheaped out and didn't spring for crosscut shredders, so there's a chance.

"David West, huh?" Ralph says as he peels a strand from the ball of paper and lays it out between issues of *People* and *Dog Fancy*.

"I'm telling you, Ralph," Teddy says, "it was something to see. He gave one heck of a lecture before he, I don't know, fell apart at the last second. I'm worried about him."

"And what's our new friend reading?"

"*Propaganda* by Edward Bernays. I took a peek on the ride here. Woodbine, I mean West, plagiarized most of his lesson from it. It's basically a playbook on mass manipulation."

"Oh, goody."

Eddie adjusts his empty glasses and studies the Lints. "Didn't you used to have a beard? And weren't you bald in the car?"

"Go back to your book," Ralph says.

"Okay."

Ralph checks his watch. "Our rendezvous in Venice Beach is at ten tonight. If we get outta here quick, we can beat traffic, maybe get a snow cone or two on the Boardwalk. So let's get your vitals, get this guy some triage, and hit the road. You feeling okay?"

"What? Oh, right the checkup. Um, to be honest, I mostly came to ask about something for Andie."

Ralph's mouth tightens. "What about Andie?"

"She's sick. Renal failure."

"That's the kidneys, right?" Ralph's anti-Andie demeanor eases. "Jesus, that's awful."

Teddy hopes against hope that his brother won't connect the dots, but Ralph suddenly goes rigid and stops his paper sorting.

"She asked for our blood types. *Did she ask you for a kidney?*"

"Lint," the receptionist calls out.

"She didn't."

"Teddy, I swear to god if she—"

"She didn't ask me, Ralph. Not outright, anyway."

The receptionist whistles for their attention, sending an incontinent macaw into hysterics. "The vet will—oh, you've got a human with you—the doctor will see you now."

Bert Scanlan, Improbable M.D.

Teddy, Ralph, and Eddie enter an exam room to find a goateed man wrestling with a monitor lizard.

Dr. Bertrand Scanlan is a licensed physician in the state of California. He's got a wall's worth of diplomas, though if one were to read the small print, they might notice half of the degrees are in the veterinary sciences. When questioned about this hybrid model, Scanlan is always quick to point out that humans are in essence and in scientific fact animals themselves, so all doctors are veterinarians by default, whether they admit it or not.

Despite all indications to the contrary, Scanlan is a phenomenal general practitioner and absolutely the first call you want to make if you've ingested pills of unknown identity. He can usually diagnose the offending agent based purely on what color seahorses the patient is seeing swim around her kitchen wallpaper.

He served as a field medic in Vietnam where he met a young intelligence officer named Dan Karrr. For the next forty years, Scanlan treated Karrr's scrapes and bruises in Los Angeles, eventually caring for Karrr's adopted sons as well, making him the first and only medical professional to study Teddy's caloric anomaly. Were he to publish on the matter, he could likely get the condition named Bert's Disease or similar, but Scanlan honors Teddy's wish to keep the whole thing under wraps.

The monitor lizard's girthy tail sends a container of tongue depressors flying across the room before Scanlan finally gets it in a headlock and administers a mystery tincture that calms it down.

"God damned dinosaurs, pure and simple." Scanlan peels a teal latex glove off with his teeth and spits it into the trash. "Nothing like a good wrastle to get the blood flowing though. Not that I have to tell you," he says to Eddie. "You try to kiss a freight train, Sport?"

"He had a bad day at school," Teddy says. "We were hoping you could take a look."

"Okie dokie. Lay him down."

The Lints help Eddie onto a padded exam table lined with a strip of tissue paper. A large-bellied chihuahua lying on a tiny, stainless steel exam table nearby, hiccups.

Scanlan gives the dog a squirt from the tincture, then indulges in one himself. "Anybody else?"

Both Lints politely decline, and Eddie's busy reading *Propaganda*. Scanlan shrugs and helps himself to a second drop before getting down to business.

"Let's have a looksie." He flips on a dental light, startling a cage of yellow canaries. "Yeesh, kid. Cuspids are all cracked to hell, and someone's done a thorough job of removing the upper incisors. Where'd they end up?"

"Jar," Eddie mumbles, still reading the book even with a stranger's hands in his mouth. "Heretic's toll. I deserved it."

"If you say so. I can throw together some dentures but I'm short on human teeth at the moment. Might have to mix and match from outside the species. Okay by you, Sport?"

Eddie loopily nods.

"Alrighty, here come the dreams." Scanlan straps a mask over Eddie's mouth and ballparks a few spins of the valve on a tank of anesthetic.

Iron-willed to the end, Eddie gets in one more paragraph before the gas takes hold and the book falls from his hands.

"Let's let him marinate a second and tend to you," Scanlan says to Teddy. "What seems to be the problem?"

"Oh, I'm actually feeling fine." Teddy gives a sheepish look at Ralph. "I wanted to ask you about something else."

Lupine Liver

"Kidney, ay?" Scanlan says as he sifts through a junk drawer of animal teeth.

"Have you ever performed a transplant?" Teddy asks.

"Sure, I have. Both planned and improvised, and of the two, I have to say, improvised is the more fun."

"Someone I know needs a transplant. I was wondering if you had any . . . unconventional suppliers."

"Afraid not. Your friend should've gotten sick a year ago. They clamped down on black market organs ever since the thing with Senator What's-His-Name."

"What thing?"

"Some prick state senator up in Sacramento fell in love with his escort, who, as it turned out, was in desperate need of a new liver. Took some doing, but he found her one. Later testing showed the organ to be lupine in origin. The senator had it tested after the girl nearly bit off his nose. Now he's got the Justice Department lasered in on the black market organ trade."

"Could I be a candidate?" Teddy asks. "To donate?"

Scanlan laughs so hard he almost falls out of his chair. "Chronic malnourishment in your adolescence, a non-clinical enucleation procedure, and a metabolic house of cards to boot. Teddy, I don't recommend you cough unless it's absolutely necessary. An organ transplant is major trauma, even in the best of cases. No self-respecting practice in the country would risk it on someone with your history."

"Would you?"

"Well sure, but my official recommendation is a no-go. Odd things, organ transplants. I've seen a number of rejections, mutations." Scanlan goes wrist-deep into Eddie's mouth and begins to tinker. "Even seen traits of the donor manifest in the recipient. I don't buy the wolf liver story wholesale, but rabies, asthma, eczema, it can all travel. Speaking of travel, I went up to see your dad last week."

Teddy's response is reflexive: "He looks good, right?"

"I don't know about good, but his spirits seemed high enough. Gave him a few new prescriptions."

"To fix him."

"Fix him?"

Scanlan looks at Ralph, then back to Teddy.

"I'm talking about the kind of drugs you find in hospice. The emphasis is on comfort, understand?"

"Comfort is good."

Scanlan takes his hands out of Eddie's mouth. "Teddy, I visited your father to say goodbye."

The chihuahua hiccups. Eddie Mannheim recites *Propaganda* in his sleep. Teddy says nothing.

The Coastal Bazaar

A college student in an unventilated cow costume hands out coupons for Jocular Beef on the Venice Beach Boardwalk. Herds of the happy mascots have been dispatched across the state to counter bad press from a recent exposé, and so far, sales are up six percent.

The coastal breezes yank a flier out of the cow's felt hoof and send it sailing over the heads of disoriented tourists and world-class skateboarders. Like a magic carpet on a mission, the coupon flutters through clouds of marijuana smoke and deep fryer exhaust before dive bombing straight into Ralph's forehead.

Ralph grabs the flier, reads it, and tosses it into the nearest trash can.

The clue on the wall of Endangerously Tasty wasn't very precise, so he and Teddy walk slow, keeping an eye out for anything Janusian Order-related. Ralph disappears two cherry snow cones while Teddy catches up with any old clients they recognize. Nearly everyone's heard about Royal Jelly, and recently, too, but there's zero consensus on a definition. A few know the Agent Orange version, others have heard it used as slang for a PCP and cold syrup cocktail, a euphemism for the female pleasure center, or a sourceless feeling of existential dread.

Ralph and Teddy are strolling with the evasive grace of locals, but a short guy in a fishing hat bumps roughly into Teddy anyway. Ralph's about to Frisbee the guy's hat onto the beach, but Teddy pulls him along.

As they near the northern border of the boardwalk, Teddy points to a palm tree on a grass embankment.

"Look at that."

A faint carving in the trunk shows the trio of masks last seen on the wall of Endangerously Tasty.

The Lints sit in the grass and watch shadows grow long in the rusty sunlight. Ralph idly picks at his ball of shredded West Company papers while Teddy sends a text.

> **Teddy:** Doc would do the operation in theory, but no luck just yet on the kidney. We'll figure something out.
> **Andie:** thank you x 1000000 for trying. i have no expectations
> **Teddy:** I told Ralph. He said 'That's horrible.'
> **Andie:** that warms my little heart, I'll win him over yet. you guys find the venice thing?
> **Teddy:** Working on it now.

"Giving Organ Hunter the bad news?" Ralph asks.

"I'm telling her Scanlan can do the procedure. It's not the update I was hoping to give, but it's something."

"Teddy, I hope I don't have to say this, but you're not giving Andie a kidney."

"Well, I'm not going to let her die either."

Ralph waves away a seagull nipping at his ball of paper. "Almost twenty years we don't hear from her and the first thing out of her mouth is 'Hi, what's your blood type?'"

"We didn't reach out to her either. You and I were already together, but I don't think any of us were eager to stir up memories with a reunion."

"You should hate her for what she did."

"Well I don't. And I want you to stop hating her on my behalf."

"What I don't understand is why you'll go through all this trouble for Andie, but you can't even look at Dad."

"I don't want to talk about that."

"That's the problem."

An ugly silence follows, and both brothers are relieved when a series of messages pour in from Ms. Beauchamp. They're preceded by a disclaimer noting portions of the summary were provided by Stinney's Scouts, since much of the Order's lore is word-of-mouth only.

Irma: Hollywood, McCarthy era: creatives tired of being pushed around band together to combine art with anarchy. They call themselves the Bacallian Order, at the time operating under the purview of Golden Age Silver Screen star, Lauren Bacall (I'm a fan).

Irma: An early stunt sees the Bacallians mail H.U.A.C. a stack of papers listing the names of hundreds of (invented) subversives. Instead of black ink, they use black mold, carefully grown on the paper by a playwright who dabbled in microbiology. The Bacallians are about to claim responsibility when the daughter of a H.U.A.C. clerk who brought his work home with him dies after a severe allergic reaction to the mold.

Irma: Sen. McCarthy and his goons eventually go by the wayside, but the Order, now underground, persists. They plant Cannabis in front of LA City Hall. They spike the biggest, oldest trees in the San Gabriel Mountains. They arson the headquarters of an anti-integration bowling league in Toluca Lake. You get the idea. In my opinion, releasing H-bomb-irradiated Agent Orange—two uniquely American pieces of warfare—would be in lockstep with their lethally-mischievous past. The Order is rumored to have a safehouse somewhere in Hollywood, but the Scouts couldn't get a specific address.

Irma: I'm 99% sure that Mayor Becksdale's wunderkind love child, Jasper, is the one suing him (under the pseudonym Bryce Kayke) because A) Jasper passed the bar when he was 9 years old, B) his favorite snack is rice cakes, and C) he's a little sh*t.

The Mnemonic Magicians

Night falls. The mood is laid back but dangerous: a sloth holding a flare gun.

Shops shutter and possession-laden wheelchairs are pulled under tarps. Tourists who've had their fill retreat back to their hotels, overstimulated and eager for a shower.

Foot traffic on the boardwalk thins, but a smattering of people who have presumably solved the Endangerously Tasty riddle linger in the grass with the Lints, trading unsure glances with one another as they await . . . whatever the Order has in store.

The clock strikes ten.

"Look," Ralph says.

A group of masked performers gather below a street-lamp whose light is tainted a sickly blue to dissuade intravenous drug use.

"The Mnemonic Magicians," they say in toneless unison.

One can guess the quality of the Mnemonic Magicians by their attempt at alliteration that's spoiled the moment it's said aloud. Wearing either a laughing or crying mask, they take turns stepping into the sapphire spotlight, delivering short bursts of improvised poetry loaded with droll observations and overburdened metaphors.

It's physically painful to listen to, but the Lints have their notebooks and pencils in hand, dutifully copying an onslaught of words that doesn't slow down and somehow keeps getting gets worse.

Ralph scours his transcript, hoping for a rogue acrostic or anagram to jump out at him. No such luck. A headache takes root as the auditory equivalent of chewing tin foil continues.

The hopefuls sitting around Teddy and Ralph fight tears and clutch the grass like gravity's about to turn off. Some do great impressions of the Hear No Evil monkey, while others revert to the fetal position. The audience quality arcs from common iron to hardened steel.

Teddy squints at his notebook. "I don't think there's anything to be found in this mess," he says. "Ralph, this isn't a test of cryptography, it's a test of endurance."

Ralph watches as someone runs off with an honest-to-god poetry-induced bloody nose. "I think you might be right."

When it becomes clear no one else is quitting, the Mnemonic Magicians stand aside. A figure wearing the third mask from the Order's icon, the scary one with sharp teeth and malicious eyes, steps into the lozenge of blue light. The glow-in-the-dark mask gives off an eerie, ghoulish glow.

The Ghoul clears its throat and addresses the ten or so holdouts still sitting in the grass.

"The chaff is now gone. Presently, the wheat remains. Off to the Safehouse."

The Transit

A shifting amoeba of cyclists, scooter-riders, skateboarders, and joggers follow the Ghoul eastward through the streets of Los Angeles.

The tour snakes nonsensically through Culver City, Crenshaw, Koreatown, and Chavez Ravine, garbage-choked aqueducts offering smells not soon forgotten, thundering freeway overpasses frying auditory nerves with ease. Riders wipe out on dead palm branches or are sent sprawling by potholes. Someone goes right when they should've gone left and ends up at a quinceañera. Another is lured away by a pair of well-dressed Scientologists and never seen again.

Scooter batteries die. Bike tires puncture. A passing car paints a straggler with the last sips of a strawberry milkshake. The challenges are many, but this group didn't sit through a full set from the Mnemonic Magicians for nothing. They wipe ice cream from their eyes and tenaciously hermit crab from old rides to new without slowing down.

The Ghoul ditches its bike and starts a frantic footrace up the steep grades of Griffith Park. After a few hysterical altitude changes, they plunge back down into the Basin, sprinting across lanes of traffic whose cars don't slow down.

Up parking garages, down fire escapes. Through playgrounds, over fences. Shin splints and an urgently needed tetanus shot.

The Ghoul enters the subway system via a loose manhole cover.

Climbing down the service ladder into a world of absolute darkness, Teddy and Ralph realize they're the only ones left. Still, the glow-in-the-dark mask beckons ever forward, through warm puddles of sewer water and over the crunchy bones of long-dead rats.

Then the Ghoul stops.

"Are you devoted to your art?"

A faint light appears in the tunnel ahead.

"Are you sure?"

The light begins to grow, accompanied by the rumble of an approaching train.

"Um, Ralph?" Teddy whispers.

Ralph doesn't move from where he's standing in the middle of the tracks. "Bullshit."

The train's light reveals an abandoned subway stop on the right side of the tunnel. Teddy starts to flee, but Ralph grabs his sleeve.

"Bullshit," he repeats. "It's always some bullshit with people like this."

The headlight blooms sun bright. A blaring horn fills the tunnel. Teddy prepares for annihilation, but the light passes harmlessly overhead.

"G-ghost train," he stammers.

Navigating by feel through an abandoned subway tunnel will make most anyone superstitious, but Ralph remains pragmatic. He calmly points to the tunnel ceiling where a pale burgundy ballast stamped with the words *Mole-Richardson* dangles from a track. The movie-grade light is mounted to a powerful speaker that plays the diminishing clack of a train that never came.

"Okay," the Ghoul says.

It climbs a service ladder and vanishes in a disc of white light.

"All those people from Venice," Teddy says. "They tried so hard to make it."

"They'll be fine."

"Ralph, we just did a marathon-length obstacle course and they left with nothing."

"They weren't looking for a cache of Agent Orange. We are. Climb the ladder."

Frowning, Teddy climbs, passing through another manhole into a windowless room of white subway tile.

The room's only door has been spray painted with the now-familiar comedy-tragedy-vengeance masks of the Janusian Order. Presumably, the Ghoul went through this door because there's only one other person in the room and it definitely isn't the Ghoul. He's short, dumpy, and staring at his phone.

Ralph gives a titanic sigh. "Hello, Vaughn."

The man looks up from his phone.

"'Ello, me septic tanks."

Waldo Vaughn

Waldo Vaughn was a nasty little cretin from day one.

He stole milk from the other London kiddies the second he got the hang of his opposable thumbs. He nicked favorite toys and asthma inhalers, every theft a thrill. One day, when a boy wouldn't hand over a lolly, Vaughn pushed him down. *Wow,* what a feeling! Instantly, his fling with thievery ended, and a lifelong romance with violence began.

Like Jesus, Vaughn's story doesn't get really good until his thirties, but other than flipping over tables and desecrating a fig tree, there end the similarities.

At thirty, Vaughn left London for California because he hated rain and heard the LA punk scene was halfway decent. He had no interest in music, punk or otherwise, but the genre's high-energy, underground shows gave him plenty of opportunities to explore his passion for hurting others. When someone fell in the pit, he'd stomp on their fingers. When someone was alone at the urinals, he'd punch them in the back of the head and run. Following the 'do what you love and never work a day in your life' adage, Vaughn took jobs as a bouncer, allowing him to not only hurt people on a regular basis, but to collect a check for doing it.

He'd been working a basement club downtown—dealing drugs and daydreaming about manslaughter—when he first met Teddy and Ralph, who'd been investigating the club's owner for PPP loan fraud.

Standing in the white-tile room, Vaughn is forty but looks fifty. His paunch hangs over skinny legs, and his moist forehead is plastered with glyphs of greasy hair. He wears a ratty leather jacket, the sleeves held on with safety pins. He's watching a snuff film on his phone with the subtitles on, the frequent appearances 'oof' and 'ack' making it look like a banned episode of Adam West era Batman.

"Hi, Waldo." Teddy says. "Good to see you again."

"Pitch 'n' toss says let in you two come up the apples. 'Spose ya want t'ave a butcher's."

Possibly the worst thing about Vaughn (worse even than broken fingers and stolen milk) is his custom abomination of Scottish-Cockney slang. Regular Cockney slang—replacing words with a rhyming counterpart, e.g., dickie dirt for shirt—already violates a core tenet of communication that it not be needlessly complicated. Vaughn further bewilders things by tinting his Cockney with bastardized Scottish English because it makes Americans work even harder to figure out what the hell he's saying.

"Can we go in?" Teddy asks.

"A bit like our Buster Keaton at the downtown, innit? I was kind enough to let you in, and what did you do? Got the gaffer pinched for half-inching a bit of Covid bees an'."

"He spent the money on escorts and a dinosaur skull," Ralph says.

"Sure, but when you put the bluebottle onto 'im they found a 'ole 'ost of irregularities, didn't they? Facing twelve years a' bird lime, what does 'e do? Flees to bloody Moldova, 'e does. Now I spend me days in this dank 'elter-Skelter."

Ralph takes a step closer to Vaughn. "One way or the other, we need to get through that door."

One of Vaughn's hands is inching toward the inside of his jacket when Teddy speaks up.

"Waldo, that club owner was planning on having you paralyzed for fooling around with his wife, remember? The loss of a job is a traumatic thing, but in this case, I think it was probably better than the alternative."

Vaughn thinks this over, tocking his head from side to side. Finally, he taps the masked door with a combat boot and goes back to his snuff film.

"In ya go then."

The Safehouse

The dim stairwell is rank with subway fumes and patchouli. Somewhere up above, the dulled sounds of a party thrum.

"Another few seconds and I would've had him."

"Not everything is a test of strength, Ralph."

"It is with guys like Vaughn."

The Lints climb the stairs to the second floor and find a room scattered with mattresses and sleeping bags. On many of the mismatched pillows, bolt cutters and crowbars are nestled like teddy bears. A stopped-up toilet, unshielded from the rest of the room, hosts a basket of cards for bail bondsman on top of the tank (including one from Lorenzo Dunes' own Raoul). The windows are soaped, the walls ornamented with rat-gnawed molding and peeling wallpaper. It's all fairly gross, but not without a palpable feeling of long-use, as in this place would probably get historical landmark status in a flash, if only the city knew about it.

Teddy and Ralph snoop around, but don't say much. They're both exhausted from the journey. Their shoes are wet. Things have been left unsaid and unresolved.

They head up to the next floor and Ralph stops on the top step.

"Whoa."

The third floor, also a single room, is home to hundreds of mannequins, each affixed with a comedy or tragedy mask of the Order. The fanged Ghoul mask glows menacingly from the middle of the inanimate crowd.

The Lints stand still, maybe waiting for one of the mannequins to move. None do, save for a general vibration brought on by the music above.

"I just don't see why talking to people like they're human beings can't be step one."

"I'm not sure Waldo Vaughn is human."

"I'm serious, Ralph."

"Teddy, there are unpleasant realities in life."

"I grew up in the same cult you did."

"I'm not talking about that. I'm talking about a dangerous line of work filled with people who don't give your well-being a second thought."

"I don't believe that."

"It might be true anyway. Dad always said—"

"I don't want to talk about Dad."

"Talk? You can't even look at him."

"Knock it off, Ralph."

"And when he's dead it'll be too late—"

"*Stop.*"

The echo spreads, then dies among the mannequins.

Teddy takes a breath. "I'm trying."

"I know."

"Just, let's do this job. Let's finish this case and then . . . I'll find a way."

Ralph nods.

Climbing yet more stairs, they come at last to a lively party where, by appearance or activity, every guest is identifiable as an artist. There's a very life-is-but-a-dream attitude swimming around the room, but the mood isn't exactly toothless either.

Teddy and Ralph have reached the Janusian Order.

The Art of Artistry

The temperature in the room must be well above a hundred degrees, and it's humid too, owing to a makeshift sauna someone's built using paint cans of rocks hung over butane flames.

Teddy wipes sweat from his brow. "*Mercy.*"

"Yeah, let's get to it. Mingle?"

"Mingle."

They part, Ralph heading for a powder blue grand piano whose guts have been packed with dry ice and beer. He grabs a longneck from around E flat and holds it against his forehead. His Mnemonic Magician-induced headache is still hanging around and the heat isn't helping.

A freckled woman in orange overalls smiles at him from the higher octaves.

Ralph smiles back, despite the fact she's got a deck of Tarot cards spread out on the piano bench. Fortune telling and the like rarely help his mood, but he takes a cue from Teddy and gives kindness a shot.

"Hi. I'm Ralph."

"I had a feeling. Would you like your palm read, Ralph?"

"Why not?"

"My name is Vivian Mojica. Your name is Ralph."

"I just told you that."

"With your eyes."

"And my mouth."

She slides her hands into his.

"Mmh. You look like a new recruit, Ralph. How'd you like the commute?"

"It had its moments."

Vivian inspects the lines of his palms. "And where are you in your soul's commute?"

"I don't know."

"That could be a problem."

"What's the deal with this room? What's everyone doing?"

"It's a testing ground," Vivian says dreamily.

"For what?"

"For the Order's projects. That quartet of baritones over there is seeing if they can reach a decibel low enough to induce loss of bowel control."

"I thought that was a myth."

"Doesn't hurt to double check. They're going to try it at Disney Concert Hall next week."

"How about her?" Ralph indicates an old woman wailing on a water heater with a sledgehammer.

"Practice for the LA Auto Show. She's going to dent as many fenders and egos as she can."

A salsa dancer walking past the paint cans tosses on a half glass of white wine, drawing a ferocious hiss from the rocks.

"And the sauna is because?"

"Annual meeting for a multi-level marketing cosmetics company tomorrow at the Beverly Hills Hilton. We're going to hijack the thermostat and have Wilshire Boulevard running black with rivers of overpriced mascara."

"I'm still coming up short on the point of all this."

"It's art, Ralph. Art delivered with explanation is self-defeating."

In the span of their short conversation, the beer in Ralph's hand has hurtled from cold to hot. Fortunately, drops of water—probably condensation from the sauna—drip from the concrete ceiling onto his head.

Refreshed, he tries again with Vivian. "I like the orange overalls. I've heard a few people here mention Agent Orange tonight."

Segue of the year it isn't, but the thoroughly stoned Vivian Mojica doesn't seem to care.

"Agent Orange?"

"Yeah, but everyone here's been calling it Royal Jelly."

"Royal Jelly? Oh, I know Royal Jelly."

"You do?"

"The pansexual DJ from Dublin who's addicted to painkillers."

"Uh, sure, but I was talking about the Agent Orange version, as in the chemical weapon from the Vietnam War."

"Ralph, I'm worried about your soul's commute."

"I'm just wondering if the Royal—"

"What do you want out of life?"

"Ten seconds off my mile time would be great."

"The body is important, but you've seen to that already. It's your soul that's at risk."

"Why?" Ralph says, growing increasingly unnerved at this personal conversation with a stranger. "What's the difference?"

"For your benefit, and for ours."

Vivian presses her thumbs, yellow from cigarette smoke, hard into his palms, searching for something.

"There's a soul in here somewhere," she says. "I can feel it. Tell me where you are in your commute."

"I'm . . . trying to get better. At forgiveness."

"Yes, that's it."

"You can feel that?"

Vivian's big-pupiled eyes lock onto Ralph's.

"Each of us has a lesson to learn over and over. It can't be avoided, only accepted. That's what I call Royal Jelly."

"Oh."

A Meeting of Black Hearts

Mario Pewpee, perched on Big Sue's shoulders, appears to levitate out of the subway manhole in the white-tile room.

It was only too easy for him to bump into Teddy on the Venice Boardwalk and drop a transponder into his pocket, but by god, was watching the signal beacon bounce around Los Angeles nauseating. Mario worried that Teddy had found the bug and tossed it onto a bus, but given the secret subway tunnel and this weird room at the top of a ladder, he's thinking they're on the right track after all.

Big Sue sets Mario down in front of a gargoyle of a man standing next to the room's only door.

Mario ignores the man and tries the door. It's locked.

"Ye din come with the flock, yer naw gettin' in. Too bad," Vaughn opines, though it's clear he's ambivalent at best.

"What's in there?" Mario asks.

"Somefin' yer naw gon see, tha's wha'. On your bike, then."

Mario nods to Big Sue. She steps close to Vaughn like they're in an overcrowded elevator, a positioning that almost always elicits fearful compliance.

Vaughn finally looks up from his phone. He calmly scans the beltlines and pockets of the new arrivals. Seeing no holsters or gun bulges, he slides a large hunting knife from his jacket.

"Right, Burks. Allow me to introduce the WASP knife. Weapon a choice fer divers in all seven seas 'cos Davey Jones don' allow for fas' movement. Yer enjoyin' a coral reef an' you cop a flower pot: big in an' ou' pokes ou' a the fisherman's daugh'er. What do?"

Mario can't tell if he's being made fun of, and defaults to indignant rage. "Listen here you Limey fuck—"

"Shark starin' ya down and you've got no harpoon, naw cage. Wha' then? This is wha'."

Vaughn articulates the knife like he's hocking it on an infomercial, gracefully drawing attention to a small hole in the blade.

"Right 'eres the fun. Compressed CO2 cozied up in the 'andle. Good fer sharks an' Hampton Wicks think they're tough. Ya stick 'em in the jam tart if ya like, push this button, an' 'ere comes eight 'undred PSI a CO2. Slush yer organs, it will. Tested it on a watermelon in me backyard. Foun' seeds three blocks away, no pork."

Mario still doesn't know what the hell this guy is saying, but the door is still locked and the knife looks sharp. Big Sue is tough, but she has the same weakness for stab wounds as everyone else. Mario doesn't want to risk damaging his heavy.

The wheels of schemery turn in his head.

The gibberish-spewing bouncer with the dive knife has a quick-to-violence air about him. Those types can be useful. Mario doesn't like the idea of bringing someone else in on the Royal Jelly score, but a third of something is bigger than half of nothing, and one never knows when a human shield will come in handy.

"Here's the rub, Bob. I could give two shits what's on the other side of this door, except for the two jamokes who recently went through it."

Vaughn resheaths the knife, an indication for Mario to continue.

"Those Boy Wonders may very well be in possession of something valuable, something I seek to relieve them of. Maybe we can discu—"

"Fifty percent."

The Cockney gibberish is gone.

Mario scowls. "Twenty."

"Forty."

"Twenty-five."

"Hold on. I've just come down ten percentage points. You've done five."

"You started with an unreasonable number. I factored that into my bid."

"T'hell with your factor *and* your bid, choke on 'em for all I care."

"My number is based on the value, not your inflated starting point."

"A negotiation's about finding the bloody value you consummate fuckwit!"

"Try halving your dogshit evaluation," Mario says.

"Fifteen," says Vaughn.

"That's more like it."

"That's fifteen for *you*, Jack."

"Not in this lifetime."

Big Sue yawns.

It goes on like this for a while until both men get confused and agree on a should've-been-obvious-at-the-outset thirty-three percent for everyone, mainly so they can stop doing math.

Tense handshakes are exchanged, unwholesome laughter shared; an unholy alliance has been wrought.

Poolside with the Janusians

Despite the fun of being fully clothed inside a sauna, Teddy climbs the building's last set of stairs. He's half hoping to stumble onto a trove of orange-striped barrels, but he'll settle for a reprieve from the heat.

His effort is rewarded in part. No barrels, but the building's top floor is about thirty degrees cooler, and the background music is Vivaldi. The teal rectangle of a swimming pool built into the exposed concrete floor glows at the center of the dark room, the water's surface littered with debris from clusters of poolside artists.

Teddy wanders past a bar cart where a troupe of beefy male ballerinas in leotards are serving each other Singapore Slings and indulging in the occasional *grand jeté* as the mood strikes them.

He tunes his high gain antennae to the conversations around the pool.

From a pair sharing a roach while they practice calligraphy:

"Hear about Hansen? Excommunicated."

"What? Why?"

"Interacted with a brand on social media."

"Excommunication's too good."

From a trio using pinhole photography to capture a wilting flower:

"PRC dissidents basically get prefab careers. A narrative of resistance is built in from the get-go."

"Some of them get black bagged and tossed into re-education camps."

"Ugh, state-sponsored oppression is my favorite aesthetic."

From a sextet sculpting nudes out of cigarette ash and bubble gum:

"Anyone seen the big man tonight?"

"He's around here somewhere."

"Silence is Golden should be starting any minute now."

"He's got that look in his eye tonight."

"Low blood sugar."

"Best steer clear."

Teddy's phone dings with a text from Ms. Beauchamp:

> **Irma**: ~37mm American adults have a chronic kidney disease. ~90k are on a list for a transplant. ~5k die while waiting each year. Dialysis patients produce hardly any urine at all (not sure if useful, but I found that interesting). One of the leading causes of death resulting from kidney disease is heart failure. Mayor Becksdale's invalid mother is almost certainly the one who brought down the clocktower; her explosive-making skills previously established in season sixteen's Troubles arc.

Teddy puts his phone away. He looks longingly at the diving board over the pool's deep end: a nice, quiet place to think things over.

Taking off his socks and shoes, he scoots carefully out on the flimsy board. Just below his toes, zigzags of crushed cigarettes float alongside Granny Smith apples bobbing like pale green buoys. There's a loud splash in the shallow end as one of the ballerinas tosses in an empty wine bottle. The bottle takes on water and sinks through a phantasmic layer of eerily floating newspapers and bathrobes, coming to rest at last on a bed of wishing coins scattered below. Through random gaps in the coins,

Teddy can see the pool floor has been tagged with generations of overlapping graffiti.

There are proclamations of ART FOR THE ART GOD and ARS GRATIA fARTIS. Political time capsules of I LIKE IKE and I GOD DAMN DON'T. Kilroy was apparently here and someone thinks England should get the hell out of the Falklands. Every yacht should be sunk, every man is in possession of his own stylo, and ONLY YOU CAN PREVENT FORESTS.

Teddy recognizes the last phrase as a snarky slogan for Agent Orange. Is it random discontent, or does someone in the Order have herbicides on the brain?

The diving board wobbles.

Teddy looks over his shoulder to find a man scooting up behind him. He's got perfectly white teeth, perfectly golden hair, and a glowing aura normally reserved for the pregnant.

"Royce Janus," he says with a velvety voice last heard on the Venice Boardwalk. "I know you know, but it's rude not to say."

Silence is Golden

It takes Teddy a moment to adjust to a version of Mayor Becksdale that's not six inches tall and partially occluded by Ms. Beauchamp's head.

"Pleased to meet you, Mr. Janus. I'm Teddy Lint."

"Hey, that's great." Royce smiles and Teddy is momentarily under his spell.

Those who decry the ultra-famous as talentless children of happenstance and careful marketing may have a point when it comes to some popular actors, but not Movie Stars, and Royce Janus is a Movie Star.

His charming features become more pronounced by the year, keeping him on the short list for leading roles at nearly sixty years old. He's a film legend, a daytime TV institution, and now, apparently, an anarchic figurehead of sorts.

Teddy tries to recall the rumors that Ms. Beauchamp always downplays or denies outright. Something about Royce being Canadian. That's not so bad. But there's something else, something involving . . . cannibalism. Teddy doesn't go in for celebrity gossip, but the exit-blocked diving board suddenly feels a bit more like a plank.

"You're one of the guys who kept up with me to-night," Royce says. "Bully for you. A race like that after a heaping scoop of the Mnemonic Magicians is no small thing, but of course, that's the whole point."

A splash in the pool makes Teddy jump. The ballerinas have lobbed another wine bottle into the flotsam.

"Artists may be fuck ups, Freddy, but they're valuable fuck ups." Royce gazes at the overserved dancers with admiration. "I'm not saying I want them building my bridges or measuring my anesthesia, but art makes life worth enduring. If I can provide a place to crash, a target to aim at, maybe just the latitude to be drunk for an evening, well, then I'll have done my duty. These boys have just returned from a very important mission."

"They have?"

Royce checks his platinum wristwatch and trills his eyebrows. "A drone-assisted miracle is on its way, Freddy, unlike any you've seen before."

Teddy grips the coarse surface of the diving board so hard it draws pinpricks of blood. LA's demise is going to arrive on a Wednesday of all days, which feels somehow anti-climactic.

"Did you know there's a positive correlation between billboards and fatal accident rates?" Royce says.

Briefly lost in visions of toxic clouds and mass panic, Teddy's focus comes back to the diving board. "What?"

"Billboards. Government's known about the link since the '80s. Now they're letting companies stick digital ones on cars and offshore barges because why let perfectly good ad space go to waste? Money for the money god, I suppose."

Whoever's controlling the music in the room ditches the feathery touch of Vivaldi for something more fatalistic, possibly Wagner.

Without removing them from around his neck, Royce presses a pair of binoculars into Teddy's hands and nods toward a grimy window.

Teddy hesitantly raises the binoculars to his eye, pulling Royce awkwardly close. Royce helps himself to the binoculars' other eyepiece and directs their view to The Reef.

The digital billboard glares as bright as ever, its colossal screens pushing sugar water and rabid legal representation.

"Money for the money god, eh?" Royce repeats. "How about gold instead?"

Cheek to cheek, they watch—Royce with ecstasy, Teddy with horror—as a dozen black rectangles rise like insects from the street below The Reef. The drones space themselves out along the top of the screens and begin to emit faint vectors of paint. A layer of metallic gold oozes down the ads. The drones slowly descend, killing the unsolicited messages with a thick topcoat that lets nothing through.

"Death to organized graffiti," Royce calls out.

"Death!" the artists around the pool reply.

"Death to vulgar pollution!"

"Death!"

"Death to attacks on confidence in what we have and who we are."

"Death!"

When The Reef is fully opaque, a roar of triumph fills the room, then someone jumps into the water, starting a chain of cannon balls and belly flops.

Teddy cries a tear of joy, earning a hearty back slap from Royce.

"I knew you'd see the beauty, Freddy."

Teddy says nothing as he savors the relief of someone certain the world was about to end, only to watch it escape ruin one more time at least.

Caged No More

Down on the sauna level, a shout of "Silence is Golden!" brings raucous cheers.

Ralph searches the piano's dry ice for another beer and finds they're all gone. Looking beyond the piano, he sees something else, something he missed before: a pair of cages wedged into the room's inactive fireplace. One contains a dog, the other, a gamecock.

"Vivian. *Vivian.*"

Vivian snaps out of a peyote stupor. "Wha?"

Ralph points at the fireplace. "What's going on with those two?"

"Oh. They got rescued from fighting pits. Someone's doing a piece where they'll be euthanized on the governor's lawn."

"Euthanized? Why?"

"Awareness."

"Awareness of what?"

"I don't actually know. Supposedly someone here has a potassium chloride connection. I said why don't we just dip a banana in the pool and be done with it, but—"

Ralph walks over to the fireplace and kneels by the animals. He hates, even more than pseudoscience and lactic acid buildup, the sight of a caged animal. Growing up in a cult can do that to a man.

The dog's breed looks to be that of an unspecified mutt, the scrappy kind that gets found in the cargo hold of some transatlantic ship after years of misadventure abroad, where songs and folklore have been written about the dog's legendary exploits, but it moves on just as mysteriously as it came, meeting a president or two before riding the rails west, subsisting the entire time on fish heads and literal garbage without ever losing the luster in its fur, and while it's not a fighter in size or bite, it's got spirit aplenty. The chicken looks basically like a chicken, but Ralph sees no reason why either should meet their end on the governor's front lawn.

He drags the cages out of the fireplace until they're under a leaky spot in the ceiling. The animals eagerly drink the dripping water. The doors on both cages are held closed by thick twists of bailing wire. Ralph crouches down and sets himself to the chicken's cage first. Unwinding the wire with his fingers is slow and painful but it needs doing, so he does it.

"Let's see beyond the palm," a voice says.

Ralph feels the gentle pressure of Tarot cards being laid on his back, followed by Vivian Mojica's breathy gasps.

"A flight of fancy kind of man, yes, that's clear. Ah, you will bear many children."

A troupe of drunk ballerinas thunders down the stairs, one drinking straight from a bottle of crème de menthe, suggesting the liquor's run dry on the upper floor as well. The burly dancers paw dry ice smoke away from the piano and wail when they discover the dearth of beer.

Ralph's fingers start to bleed.

Someone dumps water on the sauna rocks.

The string quartet won't let the low note go.

Vivian Mojica lays a final card on Ralph's back.

"Danger," she shrieks. "Danger all around!"

Freddy Walks the Plank

Royce lets the binoculars hang slack around his neck. "Fifty gallons of gold paint, eighteen gallons of molasses, and four pints of superglue for that perfect, go-to-hell viscosity. The ballerinas mixed it themselves."

Teddy's living-to-see-another-day high dissipates. This is strike two on finding the Royal Jelly, and he's on the wrong end of a diving board with a possible cannibal.

"I feel like I can trust you, Freddy."

"Well sure, but my name is Te—"

"Heavy lies the crown, Freddy. And if that sounds bad, consider the fact that these people think I'm a god. Just imagine *that* kind of headwear."

"Why do they think you're a god?"

"They worship whoever's in charge of the Order. I tried to talk 'em out of it when my turn at the helm came, but they weren't interested, and artists don't often take rejection lightly. Consider the fact that a big chunk of twentieth century suffering could've been avoided if a Viennese art school hadn't been quite so picky."

"Everyone here seems happy enough."

"That's the point of the Order. The members are freshly fed and exercised, but it won't last forever. This town's a logjam of untapped talent and all that energy's got to go somewhere." Royce gestures expansively at the artists splashing around in the pool. "Look at them. Riding diminishing-returns from their favorite stimulants as the tightrope frays a little more with each job and audition that doesn't call back."

"I still don't see why that makes you a god."

"Los Angeles is a godless town by design, Freddy, and you can't take away God without replacing it with something else. Stellar Mexican food and a to-die-for climate aren't gonna cut it. This is a city-shaped game of Three Card Monte that inhales rubes from the flyovers, bleeds 'em dry, and dumps whatever's left on the county line. These people need a Mother Hen. Right now, that's me."

"Sure but—"

"Every generation, one of us rare fortunates is asked to take up the mantle. It's an honor and an obligation. The Bacallians, the Wellsians, the LeGuinsians, the Hanksonians . . ."

"Like Tom Hanks? I know him. Well, I offered him coffee once."

"No doubt a core memory of his. But now it's the Janusians, and I'm Royce Janus. At some point people are forced to admit their gods as mortal, which tends to make them furious, meaning its best for the god to not be around when it happens. The people gathered here tonight are wise in one way at least: they know they can't go west to solve their problems. The buck stops with me, Freddy. I need the next hit, and I'm all out of ideas."

There's a ribbon of desperation in Royce's normally sublime voice and he's looking increasingly pale and sweaty. Recalling a comment about low blood sugar, Teddy tries to paddle over a Granny Smith.

"Mr. Janus if you'll wait just a second—"

"Royal Jelly," Royce mumbles.

Teddy's heart considers skipping a beat, but by now he knows to wait for the definition.

"Royal Jelly?"

"When my blood sugar gets low . . . my mind wanders into fantasy. Do you want to know what that fantasy is?"

Teddy risks a nod.

Royce leans close, dipping the diving board a worrying amount. "I've heard tell that if you fry the pituitary gland of a grown man in full fat butter, add a sprig of rosemary, some sea salt . . . the result is a culinary ambrosia unlike any other. They call it Royal Jelly."

Teddy's not sure if he should be relieved or not. Apparently, Royce isn't planning a terrorist attack using

Agent Orange, but his personal definition of Royal Jelly doesn't exactly set the mind at ease. The apple is almost within reach when Royce begins to shout.

"Royal Jelly. *Royal Jelly*! I've waited long enough!"

He lunges forward and the diving board snaps in half, spilling Teddy and a drooling Mayor Becksdale into the deep end.

The Janusian Colonic

Sweat stinging his eyes, fingers slick with blood, Ralph finally gets the chicken's cage open. Without taking a break, he moves onto the dog's cage.

Vivian Mojica has abandoned her portends of doom and taken to running around on her tippy-toes, tracing surplus gold paint onto the ceiling.

The biggest ballerina is jawing with the string quartet, saying if they don't drop their attempt at sonic incontinence and liven things up with a little Stravinsky, he's going to [hiccup] knock their [hiccup] god damn blocks off. Fortunately, the musicians take requests, especially when they're phrased as threats, and the quartet switches to a spirited piece from Stravinsky.

Euphoric with crème de menthe and a live rendition of his favorite composer, the big ballerina begins to twirl, using the old woman's sledgehammer as a dancing partner. He spins faster and faster, becoming a complex physics equation to the applause of sauna-delirious artists who fail to realize how close they're repeatedly coming to decapitation.

The sweat's really pouring into Ralph's eyes now, so much so that for a second he thinks he sees those asshole Seabees from the Clove Hitch standing at the top of the stairs with Waldo Vaughn.

A loud crack sounds as the ballerina's sledgehammer nicks a leg of the grand piano. The instrument keels over in an explosion of splintered wood, spilling chunks of dry ice across the floor. One steaming block sends the chicken fluttering into the air. When the two-inch spur still attached to the bird's leg accidentally lops off a woman's ponytail, she claps, and the other artists join her. They love a bit of chaos and seem to sense a generous helping of the stuff is on its way.

The other ballerinas flood onto the dance floor, one of them picking up Vivian Mojica on a whim. As he does, he inadvertently steps on a chunk of dry ice and the pair begin to spin in place, turning the still-painting Vivian into a human Spirograph. As the spin tightens, Vivian's brush leaves a golden circle on the leakiest crack in the ceiling.

This catches the big ballerina's attention, probably because it looks a lot like a Midas-touched bullseye, and what hammer-wielding drunk could possibly resist that? Licking his lips, he strides to the middle of the dance floor, winds up, and delivers the sledge straight into the target.

This is how the party ends.

It's also how Ralph learns there is a pool on the floor above.

He's just about got the dog's cage open when twenty thousand gallons of water pour through the ceiling, carrying Teddy, that actor from Ms. Beauchamp's soap, and a bunch of drunk artists down in a frothy whirlpool that siphons everyone down the staircase in a mandatory water slide.

Ralph is desperately pulling at the dog's submerged cage when it smashes into a stairwell wall and busts open. The freed mutt surfaces, and the gamecock flaps harmlessly up onto its back.

The four-story colonic ferries everyone toward ground level in a violent vortex of mannequin limbs, dry ice, and an illegally-augmented chicken using a dog as a life raft. The wave crashes into the white tile room, draining through the manhole into the pitch black of the subway tunnel below.

It's a soft landing for no one, but the army of mannequins gets the worst of it. The Janusians, bruised but elated at their generous helping of chaos, chatter excitedly.

Ralph picks up the Ghoul mask, and by its faint light locates the freed animals. He pushes the chicken into Teddy's arms, scoops up the dog, and the four of them rush off into the darkness.

On the Merits of Showers

The cramped but cozy shower in Teddy and Ralph's apartment is one of the best-stocked showers in Los Angeles County. A good rinse has revitalized the brothers' constitutions after many a day spent poking around the city's various underworlds. The setup in Percival Maw's cult—a hose above a floor drain, the water cold, the soap powdered—likely factors into the brothers' love of a good shower as well.

Standing with the mutt between his legs, Ralph pulls out all the stops. He squirts a salon-grade, lemon sage shampoo onto the dog's side where a number has been spray-painted like a car in a demolition derby. The number slides off the dog's fur in a creepy, Halloween font. Next comes a conditioner so silky it could turn sandpaper into peach fuzz with a single wash. Soaking wet, the mutt's skin-and-bones physique plainly shows, making it all but certain he was used as a bait dog to train bigger dogs to fight.

That was then.

Now he's being dried with a low-twist, double loop, Turkish cotton towel and a hair dryer set to low. At the end of it all, he still looks a bit like a cartoon who's had a stick of dynamite blow up in his face, but at least he smells nice.

Not one for frills, Ralph gives the rescued animals the names of Chicken and Dog. Simple, maybe, but effective.

With some distance from their near-drowning ordeal, both animals have become a little wary of each other, leaving Ralph to juggle them such that Dog isn't left alone long enough to pee under Ms. Beauchamp's desk, Chicken isn't left alone long enough to peck the couch pillows to smithereens, and both aren't left together for a fight that hasn't quite left their blood yet.

Ralph makes a quick pencil sketch of a bone—good enough to convey the general idea—attaches it to the dry cleaning track, and sets it to loop. The distraction works like a charm on Dog, allowing Ralph to bring Chicken into the bathroom.

After carefully removing Chicken's leg spur, Ralph gives him the same luxurious rinse and lather, the bird's feathers proving a handsome green and purple below the layers of grime.

A wonderfully high-sodium dinner of leftover Thai food finds the rescuees well-fed and sleepy. Abandoning any lingering thoughts of bloodlust, they snuggle up on the client couch next to an exhausted Ralph as he calls Teddy, who hopped a bus to Venice Beach half an hour ago.

"Hey," Ralph says. "Get the Express okay?"

"Yeah. We got a parking ticket, but it's here. How are the animals?"

"Fat and dreaming."

"Good. I'm sorry I yelled earlier."

"You should yell more often, but Teddy . . . I'm wondering if it's time we pull the rip cord on this thing. Every time we follow a lead, we barely make it back alive. I'm not even sure if the Jelly is real. I say we give

Woodbine—West, whoever—his money back, and dump the case on the cops."

There's a pause on Teddy's end.

"I need to understand West," he says at last.

"Why?"

"Because I still think he's in trouble."

"That's a David West problem."

"But he hired us, Ralph, people hire us to make their problems ours."

"I know, but nothing adds up. Why put us onto SIS and the Janusian Order? Why even give us the Royal Jelly case in the first place?"

"I don't know, but I feel like there's a false bottom to all of this, something bigger than West wasting our time. It might even be bigger than the Royal Jelly."

Ralph looks at his ball of paper on the coffee table. The shredded documents from the West Company, congealed after their dip in pool water, might yet have something interesting hidden inside. The same could be true for West himself.

"Alright," he says. "We'll see it through."

One Coke Over the Line

Much is made of the freeways in Los Angeles. How big. How many. Local naming conventions and surefire shortcuts and a whole lot else. Teddy's never found them to be anything other than common roads.

Except at night.

At night, the snarls of daytime traffic mostly vanish, leaving behind infinite stretches of pavement that will take you wherever you want to go.

Problem is, Teddy isn't sure where he wants to go.

With the heat on low and the dull, repeating ambiance of tires on pavement, the Celery Express becomes a mute button on all the noise of late, allowing Teddy to string a few thoughts together without being interrupted by a hungry Royce Janus, for example.

Ralph agreed to see things through, mostly due to Teddy's assertion that there's something underneath it all. So, what's the something?

SIS and the Janusian Order. Felicity Ortega and Royce Janus. Both resorting to false narratives to further worthy causes? Maybe. But why is an all-powerful ad magnate tinkering with either? And if the Royal Jelly is real—and that's a Pacific Ocean-sized *if*—where is it, who has it, and why does West even want it? His errands have had just enough intrigue to keep from smelling like total bullshit; nothing is patently true or wholly false, and that's what makes things so tricky.

There are other concerns too, like Andie's kidneys, Karrr's lungs.

The charm of a nighttime freeway fades and Teddy is hit with the sudden panic that he's going to be stuck on the road forever. No progress. No destination. Just miles of asphalt stretching forever outward on a Mobius Strip too big to escape.

The next thing Teddy knows, he's in the drive thru of the McDonald's across from Lorenzo Dunes.

"Can I help you?"

"Oh, uh. One Coca-Cola, please. Large."

Over three hundred calories is insanity. But what about a sip? Maybe if he breaks the calorie barrier just a tiny bit, he can numb his troubles for a few hours.

Teddy parks at Lorenzo Dunes and shuts off the engine.

He admires the delicate beads of condensation on the outside of the cup, listens to the siren song of carbonation bubbling within. The promise of unnatural sweetness would be honored, a guaranteed experience.

Teddy unwraps the straw. He's about to put the barrel in his mouth when a knock at the window makes him jump.

"Oh. Hi, Joe."

Blue Joe makes a gimme motion with his hands.

Senses regained, Teddy passes his Coke through the window.

"Joe, what's Lich?"

"No food? *No food*?"

"Please, Joe. Tell me what Lich is."

Upset at the liquid-only offering, Blue Joe throws the McDonald's cup onto the sidewalk and shuffles off.

Teddy studies the ink blot of cola, unwisely trying to find meaning in the random pattern.

There: the macho bumble of the Seabees. There: the smiling-as-he-dies Lobbie. That bit might be the taunting masks of the Janusians, or the ovaried-hourglass of SIS. How about Malibu Marx twisted with an ouroboros over a scatter of kidney beans?

Teddy tries to see the confederacy of malice all at once; the edge of the spill, the shape of it all. He almost makes out the skeletal face of a lich before the pooled Coke bleeds apart into nothingness.

Ralph offered him an out and he didn't take it.

Maybe he should have.

THURSDAY

"We are governed, our minds molded, our tastes formed, our ideas suggested, largely by men we have never heard of. These 'invisible governors' are a heroic elite, who coolly keep it all together, thereby 'organizing chaos,' as God did in the Beginning. It is they who pull the wires which control the public mind, who harness old social forces and contrive new ways to bind and guide the world."

-Edward Bernays

Good Morning, Malibu

"Mr. Karrr?"

Karrr grunts awake, wrapped in a coarse blanket. The sky shows hints of dawn, but no actual sun.

"Time is it?"

"It's early."

"Jesus my back hurts."

"You slept in a lawn chair."

"Fair point. Who are you?"

"My name's Andie."

Karrr sits up.

"My god. Andie."

"It's good to see you again, Mr. Karrr."

"Look at you, all grown up."

"I have you to thank for that."

Karrr shakes his head. "I've been thanked enough." He gestures to the empty chair. "What brings you to Malibu at this lovely hour?"

Andie sits.

"I ran into Teddy and Ralph this week. I hadn't seen them since you rescued us. They mentioned you're sick. I'm really sorry to hear that."

"These things happen."

"I'm . . . sick, too."

Karrr studies her. "Terminal?"

"Looks that way. Knowing death is coming, not someday but soon. I don't always know how to deal with that. And I don't know if healthy people understand."

Phù XIII emerges from her sleeping spot under Malibu Marx's chin and slinks up to Karrr. He brushes a coating of cold sand from her back.

"Ever since I got my diagnosis, I've used it as an excuse to stop living," Karrr says. "I sit by my statue, I drink, I pet my cat, and I wait to die. Funny thing is, it hasn't happened yet. For some reason, I keep waking up again. Like you said, a healthy person might not understand, but I'm starting to think it means something. And if that's true for an old fart like me, why not for you? We're sick, but we're here. Our job is the same as always: to find out why."

Phù XIII shivers off the remaining sand and jumps onto Andie's lap.

"That's good advice," she says, petting the cat.

"Maybe. Don't know if it's worth getting up before dawn and coming to Malibu for."

"No, it's . . . I haven't been sleeping much anyway. When I saw Teddy, I did something I shouldn't have. Something I'm ashamed of."

Karrr waits to see if more details will come but doesn't seem to mind when they don't. "Regret is unavoidable."

"Yeah. Yeah, probably it is. What do you do about yours?"

Karrr gives a strange laugh. "I've chased a few different destinies over the years. I used to think of choices like paths that led to good or bad places. I don't think that anymore. You did what you did. That's over and done with, and I don't think it's put you in a wholly good or bad place. The only thing left for you to do is to accept the fate you had a hand in creating, and to make the next choice the best you can."

"Is that where you are, with the fate you made?"

"If fate wants anything else out of me, it can come to Malibu like everyone else. It'll find me sitting on the beach, content, and ready to tell the truth."

Donut Delivery

An early morning knock at the Lint Detective Agency sends the animals into hysterics.

Ralph rolls off the couch and trudges through the sunlight blasting though the front window. Steeling himself for his daily dose of David West, he opens the door to find someone he doesn't expect.

Andie holds out a pink box of Chim Chim donuts. "Hope you like Long Johns."

"What do you want, Andie?"

"Did Teddy talk to you? About me?"

"I heard all about the great kidney hunt. I'll add it to my list of reasons to hate your guts. Anything else?"

There's no quick retort from Andie, only a sheepish silence that says she's not going to defend herself.

Ralph is surprised to find his chat with Vivian Mojica come to mind. According to her, his soul's journey, his perennial lesson to learn, whatever, is one of forgiveness.

He takes the box from Andie and moves aside.

Unable to hide an excited smile, Andie steps into the Lint Detective Agency.

"Oh *wow*, this place is amazing, it's like an actual business! And who are these guys?"

She drops onto one of the couches to pet an excited Chicken and Dog.

"New arrivals." Ralph sits on the couch opposite her and bites into a sprinkle donut. "You sure don't act like someone who's dying."

"I've been told dying people shouldn't. I'm trying to make the most of the time I have left."

"By delivering donuts?"

"Seeing you and Teddy again is the best thing that's happened to me in a long time, and I'm so glad—"

Ralph angrily tosses his donut aside, sending both animals scrambling for the crumbs. "Stop assuming forgiveness, Andie."

"What?"

"Teddy not hating you doesn't mean anything. He doesn't hate anyone."

Andie holds up her hands in peace. "I wasn't assuming forgiveness, I just wanted to—"

"Without me looking after him, Teddy would've been picked apart by strangers a long time ago. Everybody wants a piece of him, and he's too damn Teddy to say no."

"I don't want a piece of him."

Ralph gives a tired sigh. "If you want to spend your last days playing detective with us, I guess I'd be a bastard to tell you no. So, here's how it's going to work. You don't ask Teddy for anything. No kidneys. No favors. Not even 'pass the salt.' Got it?"

"I didn't ask him, Ralph."

Through the front window, Ralph sees Teddy leave Raoul's Pawn 'n' More and head toward the Agency.

"Give me your word, Andie."

"What?"

"That you'll never ask him. Promise me."

"I promise."

She shucks a tear a second before Teddy comes in.

"Andie, you're here! You look great, how are you feeling?"

"Never better."

Teddy pets the animals as they both vie for his attention. "This is going to be a good day, I can tell. Raoul finally sold his Wild West gun safe, Maggie's youngest aced his geometry quiz, and the Chims were very excited about a charming young lady who bought a dozen donuts."

"Andie's going to help us out on the case," Ralph says.

Teddy's face shows cautious optimism. When he's sure there's no gotcha, he says, "Never before in the history of good days—"

The tender moment is interrupted by a ringing phone.

It's Ousmane Ba. He asks them to please come to the West Company building and provides the address.

He asks them to hurry.

King of Nothing

Talk on the ride over centers on West.

Since it seems unlikely that he'll try to maintain the Woodbine alias in a building branded with his real name, he's apparently decided to retire the persona. Why the charade was necessary in the first place is still unclear, but Teddy is more concerned with its sudden end. This, plus West's involuntary breakdown at the end of the propaganda lesson, has Teddy wondering if the man's entire identity is collapsing in real time.

In the West Company lobby, Gerry Weinstein makes a phone call to announce their arrival. He looks a touch nervous, maybe wondering if he played one cruel, hypothetical game too many, and Teddy ratted him out to upper management.

Ousmane Ba enters through the green door. After a polite welcome to Andie, he escorts his guests through the privacy airlock and into the Plaza of Midnight Oil.

Ralph and Andie gawk at the space, especially the neon obelisk of TV screens and its dizzying sequence of advertisements.

"Mr. West is non-responsive in his office," Ousmane says.

"*Dead?*" Teddy asks.

"Perhaps I should have said non-communicative, except to request an audience with you and your brother. I would appreciate your assistance in peaceably removing him from his current mindset as he has a rather important appointment this evening."

"How come he isn't Woodbine anymore?" Ralph asks.

"That is for him to explain if he so desires."

The activity in the plaza is even heavier than the day before, the espresso and sushi bars at max capacity, serving stressed-to-the-gills employees who shout at each other about private jet ETAs and last-minute catering emergencies. Event planning seems to be the topic of the day.

Ousmane reads a message on his phone and frowns.

"Something wrong?" Teddy says.

"Everybody in this town, what do you call it, *flakes*."

"Can I help?"

"Who is the most affecting celebrity you've met?"

"Most affecting celebrity? Well, Royce Janus makes an impression, that's for sure."

"Royce Janus." Ousmane thinks. Nods. "Thank you. Here we are. Good luck."

Through the glass walls of his office, West can be seen slouched in a velveteen armchair isolated at the center of the room. He wears a herringbone suit so wrinkled it's almost guaranteed he slept in it, though the deep lines in his face suggest he hasn't slept in some time.

With his dead eyes and complete absence of posture, he looks like a king on the throne of a ruining empire, one who's been weighed down by unthinkably grim news.

The Zero Hour Approaches

"Mr. Woodbine?" Teddy says gently.

No reply.

"Hey, West!" Ralph shouts.

"It's a casino," West whispers.

Teddy kneels next to the chair. "A casino, Mr. West?"

"Carefully assembled, invisible if you're not looking for it, maintained by some of the brightest people on the planet. Before your feet even touch the ground in the morning, you're in the crosshairs of the evergreen promise: buy the thing and be made whole."

His voice thins into nothing.

Seeing a pitcher of water on West's desk, Teddy crosses the expanse of navy blue carpet and pours a glass.

He takes stock of the other objects adorning the desktop: a rotary phone lacking a '9' button, a slew of Clios, a shoebox with 'David' scrawled along one side in a child's script. The contents of the shoebox have been dumped out; tin wind-up toys, aged ticket stubs, and other childhood ephemera lie around a pile of pictures. The one on top, an enlistment photo, shows a late-teens West, just recognizable with a military-issue haircut and thick eyeglasses.

Teddy gently fans out the rest of the stack.

Most of the photos seem to be from Vietnam. A shirtless West flexing on the banks of a brown river. West standing next to a yoked water buffalo in a field. West grinning with his arm around another soldier whose face has been scratched out. West hunched over a typewriter in a tent, looking like he'd rather be anywhere else in the world.

The man gains a dimension in Teddy's mind.

Up until now, David West has felt more like an idea of a person, a pastiche of words and ideas crammed into a suit. This time, there's a heartbeat.

"Teddy," Andie says. "He's saying something."

Teddy hurries back with the glass of water.

"They found it," West mumbles. "They found it and took it away."

Teddy looks at Ralph and Andie, then kneels close to the chair again. "They found it?"

West suddenly grabs Teddy's wrist, spilling the water.

Ralph moves to break the connection but Teddy holds up a hand. "It's alright. We're alright."

Ralph eases back, watching closely as West pushes up the sleeve of Teddy's yellow cardigan. On the dark canvas of Teddy's forearm, he writes two numbers with a hollow-dot superscript.

"At these coordinates there is a hole in the ground. A hole slightly larger than the dimensions of a shipping container. The Lint Detective Agency has failed in its task of locating the Royal Jelly first. The zero-hour approaches."

He slackens back into the chair wearing the same tragic expression Teddy saw in the typewriter photo, one that suggests he's spending a fortune in neurological capital just to outpace his own thoughts. It's the kind of accelerated burn rate that won't last forever.

"There's still time, Mr. West," Teddy hears himself say. "We won't let you down."

In Beauchamp We Trust

Back in the Celery Express, Andie punches the coordinates into her phone. The map shows a coastal lot in Rancho Palos Verdes, about an hour south of Los Angeles.

Ralph gives a tired shrug. "What's one more wild goose chase?"

"Hold on," Teddy says. "I don't know how many moves we have left to make."

"What do you mean?"

"This could be another wild goose chase, or there really could be a hole in the ground. I don't know what we gain either way."

"What if West is trying to get us out of town?" Andie says. "Didn't that big dude say he has an important appointment tonight?"

"A good point," Ralph admits. "Okay, so we stay in town, and do what?"

"Easy," Teddy says. "We do what we do when we don't know what to do."

"Come again?" Andie says.

"In the latter stages of a case, we usually have the information we need, we just haven't recognized the solution yet. And it just so happens that the Lint Detective Agency employs the world's foremost context architect, an accredited research librarian who is, at this very moment, hunkered down at the main branch of the Los Angeles Library, working her magic with the card catalogue like a Dewey Decimalesque Merlin—"

Ralph shifts into drive and sums things up. "In Beauchamp we trust."

To the Library!

Several times a year, Teddy tries to change Ms. Beauchamp's job title to Partner and rename the business the Lint, Lint, & Beauchamp Detective Agency. And, several times a year, Ms. Beauchamp refuses, saying the proposed name sounds like an abortion of a law firm no one in their right mind would hire and that she could give a damn about job titles.

So, it's the Lint brothers and a few repeat clients alone who understand that while the boys may go out into the field and get dirt under their nails, the reinforced steel spine of the whole operation is a one hundred fifty-pound Jamaican ex-pat who's partial to cheap pantyhose, coco bread, and the hyper-scandalized crises of a fictionalized Providence.

Currently holed up in a study room in the back corner of the lowest level of the Los Angeles Central Library, Ms. Beauchamp has taken the lack of progress on the West case personally. She's pulling out all the stops to ensure that even if progress can't be made on the research end of things, it won't be from a lack of trying.

The room's conference table is bricked with banker's boxes of microfiche she's had routed in from sister branches. A cumbersome microfiche reader in the corner is still cooling down from the paces she's put it through so far that morning. A Thermos of strong coffee—surely safe from Hurricane West down here—means she isn't slowing down anytime soon.

Teddy and Ralph arrive. They're with a girl named Andie, who Ms. Beauchamp greets, then hugs upon discovering she's one of their sisters from the cult. The research team grows even bigger when a strange man named Randall J. Pipp arrives. He's apparently an associate of Andie's and wastes no time in enthusiastically pledging his willingness to die for the cause.

With one contoured cheekbone and a pair of mismatched earrings, Ms. Beauchamp demands more informational coal for her red-hot research furnace; no bit of fuel is too small.

The detectives start shoveling.

Royal Jelly. Agent Orange. The Vietnam War. The Sisters in Sync. The Janusian Order. Rolls Royce *Fantomo*. Edward Bernays. Ousmane Ba. Endangerously Tasty. The Plaza of Midnight Oil. Omission of the number nine. Scary theater masks. Hourglasses married to reproductive organs. It all goes up on a blackboard. Everyone is invited to pick a topic, research it down to the bone, then go back to the board for more.

Andie gets started on the room's desktop computer. It's a few decades behind the cutting edge (there's a Y2K reminder sticker on the housing), but with noisy effort it can load Google, so off she goes. Ralph disappears in the stacks, while Teddy, hoping the breakthrough lies in one of his beloved face-to-face interactions, chats with any library patrons willing to talk to a stranger about Royal Jelly. Pipp posts himself outside the study room, determined to prevent disturbances by the roaming unhoused and nosy grad students alike. As for herself, Ms. Beauchamp fires the microfiche reader back up and resumes her infinite scroll of the printed word.

An hour goes by.

Teddy makes a few new friends, none of whom have the Royal Jelly.

Two hours.

Ralph gets a nasty papercut.

Three hours.

Andie's nearly in tears from pop-up ads.

Four hours.

Pipp uses legalese to scare off a "suspicious" tween after she browses the YA section a little too long for his liking.

Five hours.

Ms. Beauchamp's Thermos of coffee is long since drained, but she refuses to slow down. When she catches Ralph and Andie taking a break to play catch with a congealed clump of shredded paper, she swats the dirty white ball straight into Pipp's left temple. Andie's dizzy attorney staggers around in a circle before regaining his balance and saluting no one in particular. Ms. Beauchamp is about to apologize when she sees the offending ball of paper has cracked in half like an egg, revealing a yolk of still-readable papers inside.

She licks her lips. "New data."

Your Ad Here

They divvy up the hidden trove of letters and numbers, and, as expected, find most of it worthless. Then Pipp finds a piece that went into the West Company shredders at a nearly horizontal angle, leaving a single line of text with its syntax intact.

"The language looks familiar," Teddy says. "It's the same as Ousmane's tattoo."

"Ousmane's what?" Ms. Beauchamp asks.

"Yesterday I saw a tattoo on Ousmane Ba's neck."

"Teddy, when I tell you I need all the information you have, I need *all* the information you have."

"Sorry, sorry." Teddy searches his notebook until he finds the page where he wrote down the sneeze-revealed tattoo. "*La lupo protektas la safojn de si mem.* I meant to look up what language it was, but I forgot."

After guesses of Italian and Portuguese, Andie convinces the ancient library computer to pull up an online translator, but Ms. Beauchamp, who correctly guessed the language to be Esperanto at the outset, John Henry's her with a hard copy English/Esperanto dictionary.

"The wolf protects the sheep from itself," she says.

Barring an unlikely scenario in which Ousmane Ba and David West are the world's worst shepherds, the phrase is assumed to be some kind of flowery, pro-propaganda manifesto, maybe an unofficial slogan for the West Company. Having worked with all manner of industry for several decades, the West Company is well-documented, but the group can find no links to the sheep phrase, in Esperanto or otherwise.

"What about the thing from the ball?" Andie says.

Ms. Beauchamp translates the strip of paper.

Kore invitata al la kvardek-oka ĉiujara Market, esti tenis ĉe la California Club Country Club is revealed as "cordially invited to the Forty-Eighth Annual Market, to be held at the California Club Country Club."

The room full of locals all look at one another. No one's ever heard of an event called Market, nor the tragically named California Club Country Club.

"We've got the inaugural year," Ms. Beauchamp says. "It might be secret now, but most things have a humble beginning. Maybe they had to advertise."

She slots in newspapers from 1976.

An hour of eye-straining scrutiny produces nothing except a blow to morale.

Ms. Beauchamp studies the blackboard.

"I wonder . . ."

She rifles through the boxes of microfiche.

"What is it?" Teddy asks.

"If these people are the type to use a language no one uses, they might do the same with their numbers. If they have an allergy to nines, that suggests base-9."

"Base what?" says the partially concussed Pipp.

"The base-10 number system we use is well-established but technically arbitrary."

Pipp looks panicked. "Numbers are made up?"

"There's no law of the universe insisting 1, 2, 3, 4, 5, 6, 7, 8, 9, 10 is the sole counting mechanism. It probably only came to prominence because we have ten fingers."

"I like the sound of this base-9," says the nine-fingered Andie. "How's it work?"

"Somewhat confusingly, base-9 omits the number nine itself. Forty-eight in base-9 would be . . . forty-four in base-10. We don't need papers from 1976, we need 1980."

New spools are loaded into the microfiche reader. With preternatural speed Ms. Beauchamp scans headlines about Mount St. Helens and Voyager 1. The debut of Post-It Notes and Pac-Man. America loses Alfred Hitchcock and Colonel Sanders, but gains Macaulay Culkin and Venus Williams (causality not necessarily implied).

Suddenly Ms. Beauchamp freezes the scroll. Her finger zeroes in on a 3x5" ad near the bottom of the page.

> Business bad? It doesn't have to be. Reach more customers. Eliminate sales resistance. Let the West Company help you tell a better truth. Leaders of industry are invited to attend the First Annual Market, to be held tomorrow evening at The California Club Country Club.

Below the text is a crude map with a starred location. Below the map is a sequence of numbers that reads 1 2 3 4 5 6 7 8 10. Below the numbers are the words *La lupo protektas la safojn de si mem.*

A cheer goes up from the researchers.

Ms. Beauchamp leans back in her chair and basks in the warmth of a job well done.

Second Star on the Right

Harpreet Singh gives a clap of excitement as Teddy, Ralph, and Andie enter the Hollywood Costume Emporium. "My friends! How did your toga party work out?"

Since they have places to be, Teddy skips a recap of his near bris at the Henhouse.

"It was an interesting evening, Harpreet, that's for sure. Tonight, we're looking for something in the way of service outfits. Line cook, groundskeeper, anything like that."

"Line cook, groundskeeper . . ." Harpreet pulls at his mustache in thought. "Not exactly popular Halloween costumes, but I'll see what I can do."

When all attempts to locate information on The California Club Country Club failed, the best and only plan available became following the newspaper ad's crude map, showing up in golf course-related disguises, and hoping for the best.

Harpreet comes through as he always does, and minutes later Teddy and Ralph are both wearing a Fidel Castro, the pale olive fatigues misidentifiable as custodial at a casual glance. Andie's been given a Jesus of Nazareth, which might pass for chef's whites, again assuming it's not closely scrutinized. All three of them turn down the accompanying beards.

The Celery Express cruises along the winding, tree-lined portion of Sunset Boulevard west of the Strip, where supercars with paid-for respiratory problems angrily make the most of the fifty yards between stoplights.

Ralph and Andie polish off the box of Chim Chim donuts (2640 cal.), plus a bacon-wrapped street dog (310 cal.) and chili-lime fruit cup (110 cal.) bought back in Hollywood. They crack their windows like thoughtful smokers because thanks to a walnut (26 cal.) in the research room, some roti (69 cal.) from Harpreet, and a dinner of celery (4 cal.), Teddy has met his max calories for the day.

Andie turns around in the front seat to face him. "I think you're going about this whole calorie thing wrong. You should be exploring Antarctica or hopping in a rocket. It's a superpower, not a wound."

"You're eating donuts for dinner; I'm eating celery."

"Okay, it's a superpower *and* a wound."

Teddy shrugs. "I just wish I could do something more positive with it like, I dunno, cure cancer, or end world hunger."

"Ooh, that's your Royal Jelly."

"My Royal Jelly?"

"You guys said everyone you ask sorta has their own definition. Whatever suits them best. Affecting good on a mass scale is your Royal Jelly."

"Yeah, that sounds pretty nice."

Teddy traces his finger along the 1980 map.

"It looks like we take a right here."

Ralph turns into a neighborhood of tall driveway gates and dense foliage. The streets were apparently designed by a fan of recursion, because at the end of each road, a smaller one branches off, and a smaller one off that, and so on, until tree branches are grabbing at the Crown Vic's side mirrors like it's driven straight into a haunted forest.

"Dead end," Ralph announces.

Teddy squints at the map. "It says we go straight."

Ralph inches the front bumper toward a wall of trees.

A collision that seems inevitable never comes. Instead, they pass into a tunnel hidden by a clever marriage of forced perspective and careful horticulture. The leafy construction is impressive, generations of branches persuaded to braid and arch in just the right ways. An ivy-snarled street sign dangling from the canopy reads Second Star Lane.

"Cute," Andie decides.

Exiting the tunnel, they drive onto the grounds of a pastoral country club whose edges are defined by an almost solid wall of eucalyptus trees. The trunks are intertwined with hedgerows of English holly, a formidable bush whose razor-sharp leaves and toxic berries made it the barbed wire of yore. A guard booth—the bane of the Lint Detective Agency—halts the Celery Express's progress.

"Ideas?" Ralph whispers as a tuxedoed guard emerges, surveying the pale green sedan with naked skepticism.

"He's trying to look tougher than he is," Andie says. "I can buffalo him."

"I can buffalo just fine."

"No offense, Ralph, but a good buffalo requires you to charm, *then* bully, and you're only good at the second part. Just sit there and look unsuspicious."

Andie rolls down her window and squints at the guard's nametag. "Evening, Milburn. How's traffic tonight?"

Milburn frowns at their uniforms. "Second Star Lane is a members only entrance."

"Swarovski delivery truck was blocking the service entrance, must be a chandelier-related emergency in the clubhouse," Andie says with an eye roll. "We didn't see any cars back at the ol' forest mirage and figured this was the best way to get to work on time."

Milburn's face still looks like he smells a rotten egg. "Why are you all driving together?"

Andie flips from charm to bully. "Because gas is expensive, Milburn, and busses don't stop here in fairyland."

"But why—"

"Milburn, I'm sure I don't need to tell you what kind of assholes run this place. Last Easter I missed a congresswoman's peanut allergy and *whack!*" Andie holds up her pinkyless left hand, then gestures to Teddy. "One-Eye in the backseat pooched a valet park job, and our lovely driver here lost functioning testicles after he overstarched a shirt. I hope you don't need a visual for that one."

"No but—"

"So you can understand why we would absolutely *love* to not find out the punishment for being late on Market night of all nights."

It's a good performance, and a black Maybach idling at the mouth of the tunnel behind them with an air of irritation doesn't hurt their case.

"Straight to the service lot," Milburn says. "Don't let any members see this piece of shit on the way."

Andie gives him a wink. "I don't care what everyone else says, Milburn, you're alright by me."

Judge Hot Dog's Warning

The Celery Express snakes its way through a pristine, nine-hole golf course Teddy wasn't sure they'd actually find.

He opens a map on his phone to see where they are. The blue dot indicating their position is stuck at the entrance of Second Star Lane, which, on Teddy's phone, connects directly to another twisty neighborhood. In actuality, the second neighborhood is on the other side of the golf course. Teddy takes a Thomas Guide from the seat pocket in front of him and finds the same omission.

Someone has defied cartography at large by deleting a portion of latitude and longitude, pulling the adjacent pieces of land together and stitching them up, effectively disappearing a small sliver of metropolitan Los Angeles.

It's an impressive feat in the age of satellite photography, not to mention the dozens of houses flanking the course's thorny border. Are the homeowners all club members, or did the propaganda wizards at the West Company convince people who are living so close to a golf course they're fishing Titleists out of their bird baths that they in fact live next to a null space that isn't worth thinking about?

It's a shame in either case, because boy is the California Club a sight to see.

Fairways clean enough to deliver a baby on. Sand imported—or so claimed at the time of sale—from the beaches of Plymouth Rock. Shallow streams of Evian-grade water trickle over artisan masonry, all the finery culminating in a dazzling Spanish Colonial clubhouse whose lawns are grazed by a family of iridescent peacocks.

Ralph drives past a Member's Only lot loaded with every make of luxury car and even a few of those cool diplomat limos with tiny flags mounted on the hoods. After parking in the much less limo-y employee lot, the detectives scurry through a service entrance that, thankfully, doesn't have a guard booth.

Despite Harpreet's efforts, the best camouflage turns out to be an understaffed workforce, as the employees feverishly cooking and laundering in the bowels of the clubhouse are far too busy to notice, let alone care about, the newcomers wearing slightly non-regulation clothing.

Teddy, Ralph, and Andie pass with relative ease into the staff locker room where they ditch their costumes for authentic server outfits hanging on a wheeled clothing rack. The evening's uniform is black slacks, black button up, black bowtie, and a money-green dinner jacket with gold epaulettes on the shoulders.

Teddy gets dressed the quickest and steps out to see if he can find some drink trays.

Andie watches Ralph fumble with the silken strands of his bowtie.

"Need a hand?"

Ralph battles the tie a few seconds longer, then gives a reluctant nod.

"Nervous?" Andie asks.

"Very."

"I didn't know you got nervous."

Ralph holds out his phone, showing a text from Ms. Beauchamp.

> **Irma**: Nota Bene: WRT the *Propaganda* book: Said Supreme Court Justice Frankfurter to FDR, cautioning him against allowing Bernays to play a leadership role in WW2: "[Admen like Bernays are] professional poisoners of the public mind, exploiters of foolishness, fanaticism, and self-interest."
>
> **Irma**: I think Judge Hotdog is spot on. There was an advertising executive on *Lighthouse* one season, and he tried to shoot Mayor Becksdale with a poison-tipped harpoon during the St. Patrick's Day Parade. If these are the types you're up against, please be careful.

"We've been in a situation or two over the years," Ralph says. "And not once has Ms. Beauchamp told us to be careful. Aside from the dangers of capable propagandists, there's a lot of nice hardware out there in the Member's Only lot."

Andie cinches his bow tie. "Meaning?"

"It's an elite crowd. The kind that tends not to be enthused when uninvited guests sneak into their private parties on their hidden golf courses. The kind that doesn't call the cops because they prefer to handle things internally."

"Are you saying we shouldn't go in?"

"We've come too far in this bullshit case to turn around now. It's just like Ms. Beauchamp said, we have to be careful."

Weaving Spiders

Eddie Mannheim, barely twenty-four hours out of major dental surgery, wipes a tear from his eye as he admires the California Club Country Club Ballroom.

The overhead lights are off, leaving the cavernous space lit only by a hundred or so banker's lamps on a hundred or so cocktail tables, creating islands of green light around which men—and all are indeed men—transact.

Market is precisely the kind of thing tin-foil hats have feared and fetishized since time immemorial: a black-tie swap meet of major economic powers behind closed doors. No watchdog groups or regulatory buzzkills to spoil the evening, just an alphabet soup of CEOs, CFOs, and so on, representing the biggest conglomerates on the planet. Anyone with a taste for conspiracy would experience an orgasmic sense of validation that, by God, they were right all along, seconds before they're bashed over the head with a bag of gold coins, force-fed a quart of credibility-killing booze, and chucked out of a limo in a bad part of town.

Eddie surveys the room like a Terminator with an econ degree, targeting as many big spenders and untapped opportunities as he can.

Corporate heavies strut from deal to deal, trailed closely by assistants speaking at lullaby-volume into burner phones that, by Market rule, don't have cameras. Generals Electric, Dynamics, and Mills are having a laugh. Standard Oil is hob knobbing with so many members of the Saudi Royal Family it technically qualifies as a reunion. Cufflinks heavily favor bulls to bears, and no less than three IMF tie-clips are visible. And let's not forget the savvy entrepreneurs of Silicon Valley who, despite their hoodies and facial hair, throw elbows with the best of them at the cash trough. The sums of money being discussed around the green lamps are so large, they're inconvenient to imagine; what does twenty-three billion dollars even *look* like?

The conversation topics are music to Eddie's ears. Caveat emptor. Monopolistic synergies and sweetheart deals. Economies of scale, tragedies of the commons. Union busting, regulatory capture, product placement. Profit margins, media buys, focus groups, tax loopholes. Junk mailing, price fixing, spam calling, and always just a little more air in the potato chip bag.

Eddie runs his tongue along the serrated triangles lining his gums. Shark teeth were all Doctor Scanlan had on hand, but Eddie had no complaints when he came to, other than he wished he'd made the change years ago.

He spots a few of his classmates doing their best to stay afloat, nervously checking crib sheets as they sidle up to cocktail tables.

Pathetic. Eddie's already off-book with the West Company's extensive suite of services.

With a predator's grace, he jumps off the bench and gets in the game.

Gliding from table to table, he confidently offers everything from prefab ad campaigns to complex blueprints capable of achieving levels of influence that should scare even the company buying them. He peddles reputation enhancement and crisis management, scalable from the micro of start-ups to the macro of countries. Hostile takeovers, M&A consultation, gross market manipulation; it's all legal or so loosely regulated that it might as well be.

What's that? You're in politics? The West Company offers solutions in any party flavor you like. Need a synthetic grassroots movement? How about fifteen hundred people with handmade cardboard signs anywhere in the continental US in under thirty-six hours (Alaska and Hawaii in forty-eight). Wanna lobby the Legislative Branch? Choose Senate or House, pick a name, sign a check, and enjoy your meeting. You'll even get a box of M&Ms with the Congressional Seal on it for your grandkids.

And if any Market virgins dare to doubt the prowess of propaganda, well, Eddie won't punch their teeth out, but he'll damn sure educate them.

What increased cigarette sales *after* the Surgeon General tried to rain on everyone's parade? What got Texaco out of the doghouse for selling oil to the Nazis? What gave Pinochet a much-needed a coat of political polish on his military dictatorship?

As long as your money's green, the big P will get you what you want, when you want it, and won't judge you for a nanosecond.

There's no need to be scared. There's no need to be embarrassed. It's just good business.

Bernays à la Janus

Teddy loiters at the end of a monstrous charcuterie board that spans the length of the ballroom. The half-ton slab of butcher's block is practically invisible under a cornucopia of meats, cheeses, breads, fruits, nuts, and enough fish eggs to overcrowd the Caspian.

He's overheard a good deal of chatter so far, none of it Royal Jelly-related and all of it disturbing. What McDonalds and North America's largest donkey breeder have to talk about, Teddy's sure he doesn't want to know.

Then he hears something he recognizes, the superlatively pleasant voice of Royce Janus, holding court over a table of corporate brass. Royce's words are familiar too, ripped straight from the pages of *Propaganda,* delivered in the tenor of a stuffy, Parliamentary address.

"Public opinion is no longer inclined to be unfavorable to the large business merger. It resents the censorship of business by the Federal Trade Commission. It has broken down the anti-trust laws where it thinks they hinder economic development. It backs great trusts and mergers which it excoriated a decade ago. Public opinion itself fosters the growth of mammoth industrial enterprises."

Applause from Union Carbide and Kraft as Royce flips seamlessly into a sweat-drenched Tennessee Williams affect.

"The public relations counsel should anticipate trends of public opinion and advise on how to avert them, either by convincing the public that its fears or prejudices are unjustified, or in certain cases, by modifying the action of the client to the extent necessary to remove the cause of complaint."

"Hear, hear!" from the Boston Consulting Group.

Royce holds his hands up for silence, inhales, and in a General-Washington-rallying-his-troops bravado, delivers the finale:

"No matter how favorably disposed the public be toward big business in general, the utilities are always fair game for public discontent, and need to maintain good will with the greatest care and watchfulness. These and other corporations of a semi-public character will always have to face a demand for government or municipal ownership. That's where the West Company comes in. Enjoy your evening, gentlemen."

The men clap until it hurts.

Royce bows and steps aside. He's perusing the buffet when he spots Teddy, who he immediately puts in a friendly headlock.

"Freddy! How the hell are ya?"

"Royce? Royce, knock it off, I'm undercover."

"Oh, cool." Royce lets go of his hold. "In the Order all of twenty-four hours and already trying to take down a mastodon. I admire the ambition."

"Something like that."

Royce slathers caviar onto a cracker. "Look, Freddy, I want to apologize for that silly mix-up on the diving board last night. My blood sugar was low and, well, I feel just terrible about the whole thing. At least we can look back at it now and laugh."

"Um."

"I'll tell you something, that pool flush did the Order good. Place was getting lousy with hacks. The real ones stuck around and might be closer than you think."

"What are you doing here?"

"Hired entertainment. Got a call from these weirdos out of the blue. All I have to do is sign a Bible-length NDA, shake a few hands, recite a few quotes from some guy I've never heard of, and I'll collect a paycheck that will fund the Order for the next three years. Like Cosimo de Medici wooing his Florentine sculptor, they have choked me with gold. No sign of bullion just yet, but they gave me a horse for a signing bonus. A horse!"

"That's great, Royce." Teddy looks around. "You said there are Order members here?"

"You won't see 'em yet." Royce smirks. "By the way, best to not mention Silence is Golden in this crowd. They're still trying to scrape The Reef clean and lots of these Mont Pelerin creeps are the advertisers."

"No problem."

"Good! Now I think I'll go meet my horse. They got her hitched to a golf cart out back."

Royce slaps Teddy on the back.

"I owe you one for the diving board thing, Freddy, I won't forget."

Lechery Be Gone!

A grandfather clock once owned by John Pierpont Morgan strikes ten. At this point in the night, the biggest deals have long been closed and the booze is starting to kick in. Priorities begin their irreversible shift from business to pleasure.

No one is more aware of the change than Andie. She doesn't know any of the men here personally, but knows them pretty well just the same.

They're the type who, when they find out she prefers women, take it as a personal challenge to prove her wrong, often times under the mistaken impression that happy hour at Chateau Marmont and a milquetoast dick are going to rewire her libido. Not in this lifetime, buster, but the Chateau's got a decent negroni, so she usually lets them give it a shot.

Andie's done her best to strafe the right conversations at the right moments, but so far, no buzzwords of interest. No sign of that bigshot, West, either. This means she's basically worked as an actual waitress for the last few hours, a profession that invites lechery like few others.

Enduring unwanted sexual attention is no picnic when one is healthy. When one is fresh off dialysis and forced to fill drink orders for people used to getting their way, it's downright unpleasant. With each new wink or pinch, Andie gets closer to slapping every face in the room, blown cover be damned. Or maybe she'll just outright collapse on the pristine Berber carpet, because a human being can only take so much.

She leans up against a cocktail table to catch her breath.

Unfortunately, this display of vulnerability acts as a signal flare for the nearby sales teams from Vanguard and BlackRock, and the well-dressed walls close in. Andie's quickly surrounded by arching eyebrows and a collective stink of Jim Beam. Voices ask if she's ever been to happy hour at the Chateau. How about it? Would she like that?

As a wave of latent dialysis-induced nausea rears its head, what Andie would like is to find the nearest toilet or potted plant she can puke into, but her new friends are making escape difficult.

One guy blows a kiss.

Another puts his fingers in her hair.

Shouts of pain come from one side of the mob a moment before Ralph freestyle swims his way through the barrier of suit jackets. Without hesitation, he punches the hair-toucher in the stomach.

The guy doubles over with a surprised whimper of pain. His colleagues are drunk enough that most of them laugh, but a few swear revenge and grab at Ralph's green dinner jacket.

The commotion pulls the attention of the California Club's private security. All around the room, fingers raise to earpieces as a clarion call spreads on the radio: troublemaking server in section three, neutralize with extreme prejudice, etc.

The circumstance Ralph and Andie feared most has occurred: they've invited the ire of the wealthy, or more specifically, the wealthy's ex-military security team who are bored to tears and looking for some action.

Ralph puts an arm around Andie and shoves through the crowd. A glass of bourbon soaks the back of his jacket. A sloppily thrown haymaker finds his left ear. He ignores both attacks, his only focus the service elevator at the other end of the ballroom.

Slaloming through the hundred or so cocktail tables, he and Andie reach the elevator just in time, the outstretched fingers of security squeaking along the doors as they shut.

Andie puts her hands on her knees, breathing hard. As soon as the elevator opens on the kitchen, she runs for the nearest sink and lets it rip.

Ralph puts a hand on her back, unsure what to say.

"Take your time. No one's going to bother you."

She retches a few more times.

"I seem to have a thing for throwing up in front of you and Teddy."

Ralph puts a towel on the edge of the sink. "It's alright."

"I have to say, I'm usually on the receiving end of your wrath." Andie wipes her mouth with the towel. "It's nice being the beneficiary for once."

Ralph searches for the right words.

"That last day, when you put Maw onto Teddy . . . We didn't understand anything then. It could just as easily been me who did it, and then I would've had to carry what you've been carrying all these years. I wouldn't have been able to do it. I'm sorry you're sick, Andie, and I'm sorry I haven't been better to you."

Andie gives a tired smile. "Such a nice moment. Kinda wish I didn't smell like puke."

"Do you need to go to the hospital?"

"No, but I can't be here anymore. I need rest."

Ralph helps his sister up, and is glad when she rests her weight on him.

Vertically Integrated Truffle Bacon

Eddie Mannheim's quest to secure any loose change that might be better spent by the West Company continues. His current angle is a political one.

By saying the word "President" followed by the last name of whoever he's talking to with the inflection of a question, he subtly introduces the notion that a little more spending might better clear political inroads that, who knows, could theoretically end at 1600 Pennsylvania Avenue. And even though the response is most often a chuckle, damned if each mark doesn't get the smallest partisan murmur in his heart as he privately entertains the suggestion, reasoning, "Now hold on, just why *shouldn't* I be president?"

Eddie's all but got the media buyer from Bayer AG committed to a campaign run when the man's attention wanders to the buffet.

"Vat is this?"

"That's bacon, sir. But as I was saying—"

The media buyer picks up a piece of bacon and nibbles. "Ah! Truffle!"

Eddie gives an annoyed, internal sigh. Unnecessary detours are generally a sales no-no, but Mr. Bayer is yet to be hooked and the bacon at Market has a halfway decent backstory. Best to keep the conversation alive.

"You have quite the refined palette. You're currently enjoying a slice of Vertically Integrated Truffle Bacon, a proprietary delicacy produced exclusively by the West Company. Would you like to know how it's made?"

Mr. Bayer chews and nods.

"Take a truffle-sniffing pig and allow it to eat the truffles it finds. Repeat the process for several months, allowing the fungus to manifest in the flesh. Most of these pigs are in Europe, so you'll have to extricate the animal with the proper permits or bribes, and since pigs somewhat famously can't fly, transport will have to be done in a private jet or otherwise first-class steerage. Congratulations, your truffle-infused swine is now strafing cumulonimbus at near supersonic speeds, which is good, because you're hungry. But air travel causes stress in pigs, which is bad, because stress toughens meat. So it's critical that a world-class masseuse be hard at work smoothing things out. It's also important at this point to project on the inside of the fuselage—and there's no polite way to say it— pig pornography, because an elusive, one percent flavor bump can be achieved if the animal has been stimulated prior to slaughter. Your jet lands. Your relaxed and randy cargo is rushed by police escort to a highly-trained butcher waiting on-site to kill and cook a—in some cases—still-aroused pig who has no clue what continent it's on, and probably the craziest thing about all of this is the fact that there's some guy out there whose job it is to film, edit, and distribute in-flight porcine erotica."

"Wonderful!" Mr. Bayer roars. He presses a business card into Eddie's hands. "I am being tapped out for this evenings, but call me first thing tomorrow and we will make business."

Eddie gives a deep-sea grin. "Yes, *sir.*"

He adds the man's card to a deck that's already bulging his blazer pocket.

Employee of the Month? He's all but locked up Employee of the Century, all without breaking a sweat. And why is he dedicating his once in a generation talent to an ad agency? Two words: David West. Yes, the man is an industry magnate, iconoclast, blah blah blah. He's also quite possibly Eddie's only conduit to an opportunity larger than the West Company. Larger than any company . . .

Then Eddie makes a mistake: he helps himself to a piece of Vertically Integrated Truffle Bacon.

While his shark teeth are a massive hit with the men of Market, sharks rarely eat bacon. The greasy morsel of pig slips around Eddie's mouth before lodging firmly in his throat, drawing immediate attention to the design flaw that put ingestion and respiration in the same pipeline.

Eddie's eyes cross.

His knees buckle.

He crawls across the carpet clawing at pant legs and maybe his situation doesn't look as serious as it is, because nobody's offering so much as a slap on the back. Some are even cackling as they take bets on what color his face will turn next. His only hope is that someone in the ballroom has stayed current on their CPR training.

Given the pervasive self-interest of Market, things aren't looking too good for Eddie Mannheim.

Fist Above Navel, Thrust

"Mercy, is she okay?" Teddy whispers into his phone from the privacy of the clubhouse coat check.

"I think so," Ralph says. "She's asleep already. She didn't want to stay in that mansion tonight so we're on our way back to the Agency. I'll come back as soon as I get her settled in."

"No," Teddy says. "She shouldn't be alone."

"Neither should you."

"I'll be alright, but listen, I'm not going to leave until I have something. We're close, I can feel it."

"That's why you shouldn't be on your own."

"If things turn bad, I'll call you."

"I don't like it. But okay."

"Ralph. I'm proud of you. For taking care of her."

"Don't mention it."

Teddy pockets his phone and heads back into the ballroom.

As much as he hates to do it in a place like this, he listens.

"All I'm saying is, if you're unwilling to cold call, you deserve EBT."

"Yep. It all comes down to personal discipline. My equestrian instructor told me that when I was seven and I never forgot it."

And:

"My kid told me insect populations have declined by a third in the last fifty years."

"That's bad, right?"

"Sure, but I can control my toaster from my phone. You give a little, you get a little."

Then, in between two separate conversations in which the men genuinely believe they're the first to apply *The Art of War* to business, Teddy hears a strange sound.

It's coming from a group of men gathered around the buffet table.

It's the sound of a person dying.

Eddie Mannheim's on his last gasps of air when Teddy wraps him in a reverse hug and begins a textbook-perfect Heimlich maneuver. After three hearty pumps, a mangled hunk of bacon launches out of Eddie's mouth and splashes into the martini glass of an onlooker.

The Market men applaud, thoroughly entertained.

No Such Thing as Good Press

With the live asphyxiation canceled, the crowd at the end of the buffet dissipates, leaving Teddy and Eddie alone at a cocktail table.

Eddie's face desaturates back to a weak pink.

"*Whoo*! Guess I'd better stick to seafood for a while. Thanks for that, Zhou."

"Of course. What are you doing here?"

"What do you mean? The whole class is here. West dropped us in the deep end to see who can swim. Why the hell are you dressed like a waiter?"

Teddy tries not to think about how much easier finding Market would have been if he'd simply gotten onto the class email list.

"This is my, uh, second job. Couldn't get the night off."

"Nothing more American than a second job, I've got three myself. Look at us, me, the sales leader for the night, you, getting in some good, clean service work. Here's hoping the Big Cheese takes note."

"Mr. West? I haven't seen him yet."

"Oh, he's here. Always meet your heroes. Even if they punch you in the mouth, it's worth it. You don't look so hot, Zhou. You coming down with something?"

"It's been a long week."

"Nothing a little sustenance can't fix. Not to worry, Eddie's here."

In characteristic overconfidence, Eddie attempts to remedy the situation in the worst way possible, shoving three strips of Vertically Integrated Truffle Bacon into Teddy's mouth and articulating his jaw until he swallows.

"Down the hatch, there we go, that'll cure what ails ya."

Except it won't. What it'll do is catapult Teddy miles past a caloric threshold he normally doesn't dare put a toe over.

Teddy wobbles. "Eddie . . . I . . ."

"No need to thank me, Zhou. Millionaires like us gotta stick together."

"I'm not a millionaire," Teddy gets out as he plummets down a high-calorie waterslide, headed for the untested boundaries of Post-Traumatic Hypometabolic Magnification Syndrome.

"You're not?" Eddie says in surprise. "Don't worry, that'll pass. Two questions have come to matter in this country. How do you justify what you have, and how do you explain what you don't? You ask me, poverty is nothing more than a meting of cosmic judgement . . ."

While Eddie explains the tenets of economic morality, the decadent bits of bacon are hard at work disassembling Teddy's senses. His vision goes into double exposure. Every inch of skin begins to tingle. Reasoning skills are deeply impaired, evidenced by what he says next.

"I need advice."

Eddie is unbothered at the interruption. "I love giving advice. Shoot."

"Andie needs help. I want to help her, but I don't know if I can."

"I don't know who Andie is, but what are we talking here? Risk arbitrage, hostile takeover?"

"She's my sister. She needs a kidney. She'll die if she doesn't get one."

"You seem like a straight shooter, Zhou, so I won't sugarcoat it. In every relationship, it's always just a matter of time before the ol' kidney ask. I've dealt with a lot of people on this planet—good, bad, and ugly—and I've yet to meet anyone worth living a half-life for."

"But it's the right thing to do," Teddy slurs.

"Says who? Shit, man, you're all banged up and missing an eyeball. You'll be nothing but an empty pair of tennis shoes by the time the world's done with you. Least you can do is not speed things along."

He claps a hand on the back of Teddy's neck and pulls him close.

"More for them, less for you. Always get yours, Zhou, and remember, there's always more to be gotten."

Even in his stupor, Teddy recoils from the advice. He wants to tell Eddie that he's mistaken, that it doesn't have to be that way, that thinking that way is what makes things so bad.

This is what Teddy thinks. What he says is, "*La lupo protektas—*"

Eddie's eyes go wide. "*La šafojn de si mem.* I knew you were worth knowing, Zhou!"

"Huh?"

Eddie lowers his voice. "You're vying for Lich membership too, you coy son of a bitch!"

The blast of an ancient war horn fills the air, announcing a procession of white-gloved California Club attendants who stride in unison through the ballroom to open a pair of double doors, revealing the exquisite golf course beyond.

With cheers of ecstasy, the men of Market stampede for the sacred grasses outside, carrying Teddy in a surge of manic energy toward the remarkable conclusion of an already remarkable evening.

Better Living Through Hedonism

One of the many foes night-shift nurses must contend with is the phenomenon known as "sundowning," whereby patients on their best behavior in the daytime hours become erratic, violent, and downright squirrely after sunset. True Jekyll and Hyde-type stuff.

This may partially explain the near insanity that is Market's final act.

The mask of décor slips with vigor as businessmen in various states of sudden undress run riot across fairway and green alike, issuing guttural cries of revelry into the night.

One group chases after a golf cart loaded with barnacle-acned chests of wine from a Bermudan ship wreck. Whether these ancient elixirs will send the drinkers to blissful delirium or the emergency room is a toss-up, but the gamble is apparently worth it, because the cart is quickly overtaken, its cargo zealously consumed.

On the green of the 9th Hole, men fence with putters around a layer cake the size of a small house. A series of antique, upright pianos have been set up along the fairway of the 7th, decidedly non-musical players aiming for Mozart before settling for Chopsticks.

Flags are urinated upon, ball washers defiled. Frantic requests are made for everything from Schedule 1 psychedelics to strawberry milkshakes, everything post haste.

Tattoos once concealed by dress shirts are on full display. One guy's got the Friedman Doctrine inked over his heart, the bit absolving business of all social responsibility spiraling around an unreasonably hairy nipple.

In his bacon-induced delirium, Teddy is having trouble discerning what's real as he staggers across the acres of greenery. Gravity finally takes a run at him somewhere around the 4th Hole, landing him in a sand trap. Peeking over the rim of the pit, he watches as a parade emerges from behind the clubhouse.

The first float crawling along the cart path is a 1/8th replica of a Dutch East India Trading Company freighter. Next is a Standard Oil derrick, spurting chocolate syrup onto the onlookers. Then a tribute to the first Ford assembly line, its tiny conveyor belt spitting out take-home Model-T Matchbox cars. The float trailing close behind is crowded with literal straw men, their sashes bearing the names of scourges like 'org. labor,' 'age of consent,' and 'alimony.'

Armed with sand wedges, the Bermudan wine zombies set to brutalizing these apparent societal demons, cheered by onlookers who offer their full-throated support.

Then comes the final float.

Attacks on the straw men stop. A reverent silence falls over the golf course.

David West stands alone on an unadorned platform, dressed in a perfectly pressed black suit. Hair combed and eyes clear, his entire appearance is a clean-cut rebuke to Teddy's theory of mental deterioration.

The Market men keep pace with the float like children hoping to catch a piece of candy, hysterical with adoration for a man whose company has gifted them unsustainable but fun-in-the-meantime prosperity.

The float stops.

Teddy watches helplessly as West raises his arms, summoning several hundred white drones from the roof of the clubhouse.

The Climax

Keeping a low altitude—no sense in erasing your golf course from the map only to give it away with an aerial show—the drones, each equipped with a color-changing LED screen, fly at sixty miles per hour along the dogleg of the 4th Hole, zipping over Teddy's head to a chorus of "tally-ho!s" from the half-naked businessmen.

West crests his arms upward with conductor-like gusto and the drones respond, segmenting into a slideshow of logos: the Swoosh, the Marlboro Man, the Golden Arches, each holding its shape long enough to be recognized before melting into the next, giving every Market attendee the thrill of seeing their child on stage.

Arms are slung around shoulders. Tears dribble down cheeks. This is as close to religious ecstasy as most of these men will get.

West spreads his arms to their full wingspan.

The drones divide into two chaotic orbs whose internal vectors appear random, though no two nodes ever collide. One resolves into a phallic constellation, the other a yonic. As the concave shape turns to face the convex, it's not hard to guess what comes next. The genital clouds converge and scatter in a climactic explosion of color.

Teddy staggers onto the main fairway in the hopes of staying upwind of any Agent Orange.

The skies, however, remain clear. The end of the light show isn't death, it's a starter pistol for something else entirely.

On the green of the 9th Hole, the house-sized cake bursts open, releasing dozens of nearly-suffocated sex workers—male and female—who shed dollops of buttercream as they sprint toward the Market men. The Market men, in turn, sprint toward the sex workers.

A cry comes from the thorny bushes to the east.

Teddy watches as fifty Janusian Order artists, each armed with a bucket of tar and sack of Monopoly money, spill onto the course.

A second, nearly simultaneous cry issues from the western perimeter.

Teddy spins around in time to see fifty Sisters in Sync, each clad head to toe in Valkyrie riot gear, storm out of the bramble.

All four groups—the businessmen, the sex workers, the Janusians, and the gynarchists—show surprise at seeing the others, but none slow down. The unstoppable collision comes on the main fairway, right where a disoriented private investigator happens to be standing.

An impossible pressure squeezes the breath out of Teddy's lungs. The crush seems to go on forever, but eventually accordions back out, dropping Teddy to the grass, gasping but alive as a violent and lusty chaos consumes the California Club Country Club.

A shirtless exec to Teddy's left is willfully overtaken by a trio of professional Adonises moments before a screaming Janusian douses all five of them with a bucket of warm tar. A second Janusian unleashes a flurry of Monopoly money that immediately sticks to the tar. Teddy wipes his face in time to see a fast-approaching phalanx of SIS warriors chasing a VP who's leg-shackled by his own underwear. Rolling hard to his right, Teddy narrowly avoids being trampled, and begins a long crawl through the mayhem.

A group of resourceful Market men armed with champagne bottles unleash a cannonade of cork and foam. Drones fall like neon meteorites as their propellers clog with tar and cake frosting. Screams of pain intermingle with cries of ecstasy and stern reminders not to kiss on the mouth.

Teddy takes cover under a dropped SIS shield. He has no clue where the exit is, and wonders if he'll be stuck in the hostile orgy for all eternity.

Then he sees an angelic sight. It's a mirage, it has to be.

But no, the golden horse galloping down the main fairway doesn't waver as it jumps over steeplechases of writhing bodies and hand-to-hand combat.

As the Palomino passes by, a toned forearm reaches out from behind the flaxen mane. Teddy's shoulder is nearly pulled out of its socket, but he lands safely on the horse's back behind none other than Mayor Becksdale.

"Hold tight, Freddy!" Royce Janus shouts.

Teddy wraps his arms around the Movie Star as he heels the mighty steed.

"Hyah!"

Risking sights that can't be unseen, Teddy looks over his shoulder to see if he can spot David West. The parade float is empty; the chief propagandist has fled the scene.

Royce's horse clears the battlefield and makes quick work of the remaining stretch of golf course. As they reach the mouth of Second Star Lane, he pulls up on the reins. "This should do it."

Teddy slides off the Palomino. Gazing up at Royce Janus, he once again tries to parse the real from the unreal.

"I don't understand what's happening," he says.

"Said I owed you, didn't I?" Royce adjusts a SIS helmet that ended up on his head. "Now we're even, eh?"

"No, I mean . . . I don't understand what's happening in general."

"Oh boy, I've had nights like those. That's the kind of question you have to answer for yourself. Good luck to you, Freddy."

Royce tips his winged helmet in goodbye and gallops off.

Teddy limps past the now-empty guardhouse and into the leafy tunnel of Second Star Lane. About halfway through he realizes his phone is gone, probably buried in the sand trap of the 4th Hole. He heads for Sunset

Boulevard on foot in the hopes of hailing a ride from a friendly Angeleno.

A VW Bug idling by the entrance of the neighborhood looks like a good candidate.

Teddy's approaching the car when a white van swoops in from behind him and screeches to a halt.

He has just enough time to read a "Can Do!" sticker on the van's bumper before the side door slides open and a pair of powerful hands pull him inside.

Yoinked

Big Sue sets Teddy down with surprising gentleness.

"You're the Seabee," he says in dreamy confusion.

"Belt him, Sue!" Mario yells from the front passenger seat, his mustache fluttering with the force of the command.

"I don't think I have to. He looks drunk." Big Sue gives Teddy a curious sniff. "He smells like truffles."

Waldo Vaughn turns around in the driver's seat. "Don't fuckin' 'it 'im yet. Not 'til we've 'ad our question. If 'e doesn't answer, *then* ya 'it 'im. He still doesn't answer, then I 'ave my go…"

Out comes the WASP knife, reflecting a spooky teal in the light of the speedometer.

Big Sue gives Teddy a soft shake. "Hey, buddy? Where's the Royal Jelly? We know you know. Save yourself some grief and just tell us where it's at."

"I don't know where it is."

"Butcher's hook aft why don't ya," says Vaughn.

Nobody moves.

"'Ave 'im look to the back!"

Big Sue turns Teddy's head to the back of the van where two rope-bound figures sit with burlap sacks cinched over their heads.

The sight gives Teddy an adrenaline dump that sobers him up a touch. "Ralph? Andie?"

The gagged figures murmur underneath the burlap.

"Nabbed your mates," Vaughn giggles. "All trussed up, ready for the drum 'n fife."

"Hey," Big Sue says. "There's something written on his arm."

Mario leans back as much as his short stature will allow and studies the numbers West wrote on Teddy's arm that morning. "Coordinates for the Jelly?" he barks at Teddy.

"Yes," Teddy says. "Go get it if you want, just please let us go."

"No, no. We're going to go together. One big, happy family."

Vaughn pulls the location up on his phone. "Down the frog an' toad we go."

The Coordinates

The van putters south to a coastal town famous for slow-pulled taffy and Joan Didion. Just as the Hollywood Hills punished the Celery Express, the steep grades of Rancho Palos Verdes seem determined to put the van's drivetrain into early retirement, giving Teddy time to game escape scenarios in his head.

If he can land a punch or two and overpower Vaughn before that big knife . . . No. Teddy's never hit anyone in his life and Big Sue could probably snap him in half without even trying.

Everything depends on what's at the mysterious address. Since it came from West, Teddy isn't feeling overly optimistic about his chances.

Vaughn eventually pulls onto a road marked 'PRI-VATE' that dips down toward the coast. He points at an isolated property just visible in the darkness. "Voila. Cat an' mouse."

Big Sue helps Teddy out of the van. The two of them watch as Vaughn throws open the back doors, spilling the captives to the dirt with grunts of pain. Vaughn giddily prods them to their feet with his knife.

Now that Teddy can see the captives' body shapes more clearly, he knows they could be just about anybody in the world *except* for Ralph and Andie.

Big Sue pulls the hoods off, revealing Virginia Ham and Blue Joe.

Mario stares at them. "Who the fuck are these two?"

"Oo's 'oo?" Vaughn asks. "Fridge freezer's cheese and kisses—"

Mario pulls out a small, silver .22 pistol. "One more word of Cockney and I'll put you down. Got it? I told you to get his brother and the girl they've been running around with. I don't know who the fuck these people are."

"I went to the strip mall," Vaughn says. "Ralph wasn't there so I got a replacement. And this bird was in the mansion at the address you gave me. Nothing to worry about though. I know our friend Teddy here better than you do. Soft as a dropped peach, he is. Observe."

He holds the knife up to Ham's neck.

"Don't!" Teddy yells.

Vaughn smiles. "With this one, any warm body'll do."

A scowling Mario motions into the darkness with his gun. "Walk."

Teddy leads the way, followed by the bound prisoners and their captors. He squeezes through a simple gate at the bottom of a gravel driveway. The gate itself is ancient, but the padlock securing it might have been bought yesterday.

Up the driveway, they come to a dilapidated ranch house that looks like it hasn't been inhabited by anything human for decades. It's strange to see a large piece of coastal property, undoubtedly worth a good chunk of money, left in such disrepair.

Vaughn sweeps his phone's flashlight across the front of the house. The light startles a nested family of mockingbirds before illuminating a hand-painted sign leaned against one end of the porch. The paint has paled to near illegibility, but it's just possible to make out an illustration of lemons above the words *Karrr Citrus*.

Teddy stares at his father's name and waits for an understanding that never comes. With each passing second, the words become more shocking, and less comprehensible.

To the rest of the group, the sign means nothing.

"Looks like the coordinates are in the backyard," Vaughn says, squinting at his phone.

Mario jams his gun barrel into Teddy's spine. "Go."

Teddy walks numbly past the sign and into the overgrown grass of the backyard. The swaying greenery ends abruptly thirty or so feet ahead, the noisy crash of unseen waves suggesting an oceanside cliff.

There's nothing here.

West's coordinates are a dead end.

He was lying about the Royal Jelly, is more than likely insane, and has for some reason constructed the most elaborate death ever for a perfect stranger.

Teddy wishes he'd given Andie one of his kidneys while he had the chance.

He wishes he'd had a conversation with his sick father.

Ralph's going to lose all three of them, and he'll never forgive himself.

On Teddy's next step, the ground is gone. Strangely, he only falls a few feet before landing hard on broken concrete.

Picking himself up, he feels around with his hands and finds the walls around him are concrete as well.

Vaughn's flashlight appears somewhere above.

Teddy looks up at the others from a rectangular cavity roughly the size of a shipping container.

Mouthful of Dirt

The light from Vaughn's phone reveals a yellow backhoe and a pile of excavated dirt next to the hole.

Mario slaps one of the machine's large treads. He starts to laugh.

"Just couldn't resist, could ya? Had to rub it in our faces one last time, didn't you?"

He paces the edge of the hole.

"Come into my bar and brag about finding the Jelly, run me all over town, and top it off with a snipe hunt in Palos *fucking* Verdes!"

Teddy wipes blood from his nose. "I just want to understand," he says to no one in particular. "I just want to help."

Mario spits on him. "At least we won't have to dig a grave. And look at that, it's big enough for three. Toss 'em in."

Vaughn grabs Blue Joe by the shoulder and pushes him toward the pit.

Catatonic up to this point, Blue Joe suddenly animates, sinking one of his few remaining teeth into the nearest target, which turns out to be Mario's clavicle. Mario screams and pulls away, dragging the tooth sideways like a can opener, splitting the skin across the bottom of his neck. He collapses by the treads of the excavator with a gurgle of pain.

Big Sue moves to pull Blue Joe's head off but finds herself intercepted by someone her own size.

With a guttural cry last heard on the ringwormed mats of Iowa State, Virginia Ham pulls her restraints apart like gauze. She grapples Big Sue, and the two giantesses begin wrestling along the edge of the pit.

Seeing an opportunity to fulfill his lifelong murder fantasy, Vaughn gleefully charges Blue Joe with the WASP knife. Before he can reach his target, the knife inexplicably sparks and spins into the air, falling into the pit where it wedges blade up in the cracked concrete. The report of a rifle crack wavers down the coast as Vaughn cradles what remains of his hand.

The battle between Big Sue and Virginia Ham—veering away from anger into another emotion entirely—inadvertently knocks both Blue Joe and Vaughn into the hole.

Blue Joe lands on top of Teddy.

Vaughn lands on the WASP knife.

His weight activates the nitrogen release in the weapon's hilt, sending a slurry of vital organs geysering into the moonlight like the breaching of an eldritch whale.

So ends the tale of Waldo Vaughn.

And so begins the tale of Virginia Ham and Big Sue, who, having discovered something between them more meaningful than death, run off together in the direction of the van.

Blue Joe climbs off of Teddy and uses a jagged break of concrete to saw through his restraints.

Partially concussed, Teddy tries to sit up. "Joe? . . . Joe are you okay?"

But Blue Joe isn't interested in talking. His focus is on the corner of the hole where the concrete is most fractured. Chucking the loose chunks aside, he begins to claw madly at the soil beneath.

Light and sound ignite up above. A shadow sweeps the hole as the backhoe's long arm swings over to the pile of dirt.

The blood-soaked Mario is briefly visible, slumped in the cab in a way that suggests he won't get out of it again. An oath of vengeance bubbles the blood in his mouth as he dumps a full load of soil into the hole.

The dirt lands hard and heavy, flattening Teddy and Blue Joe against the concrete. Blue Joe gets right back up and resumes his digging.

This time, Teddy joins him.

They work until they're knocked down by another deluge from the backhoe.

Spitting out a mouthful of dirt, Teddy digs.

The next load of dirt buries them so deep they can't climb out again. They dig side by side in total darkness, the air thick and spoiling. Buried alive, a bad way to go.

Then something changes.

The earth gets strangely lighter, and suddenly its racing away from their fingers all on its own.

The next thing Teddy knows, he's siphoned out into nothingness.

Down But Not Out

Something cold touches Teddy's cheek.

His eye opens to a flat curtain of foam receding across the sand.

Crawling away from the surf, he lies on his back. About halfway up the cliff face, he can see the spot where he and Blue Joe tunneled out, just low enough not to be killed by the fall.

A trail of footprints in the sand suggest Blue Joe has already left for Lorenzo Dunes.

Climbing slowly to his feet, Teddy follows the tracks north, any euphoria at his improbable survival made syrupy by fatigue.

Waldo Vaughn is dead. Likely the Seabee in the backhoe, too. Teddy cares, or thinks he should, but he can't muster the energy to do anything other than put one foot in front of the other and walk to the rhythm of crashing waves.

A sharp whistle comes from his right.

Teddy looks up the gentle slope of beach to see two figures backlit by the headlights of a car.

"You're welcome," one of them calls out.

Unsure if he's walking into more danger, Teddy trudges toward the headlights until he recognizes a familiar face.

"Ms. Ortega?"

Felicity Ortega holds her hands up in a gesture of peace. "I'm here as an act of contrition. For what I did, or tried to do to you in the Henhouse."

"Oh."

"You remember Ruth." Ortega nods to Ruth Dice, sitting on the VW Bug's bumper with her Olympic sniper rifle. "A knife at two hundred yards. I'd say she's still got it."

"Thanks for that," Teddy manages.

Ruth nods.

"How did you know where I was?" Teddy asks Ortega.

"Ruth's been following you for two days. Sometimes tailing the white van that was tailing you. She lost track of you last night but picked you up again this morning. When I heard you'd found the California Club, I got the girls suited up and there in time for the finale. Those bastards were long overdue, and damned if it didn't galvanize the girls once and for all. You helped solve my problem. I suspect you do that for a lot of people."

"I try."

Ortega smiles. "Looks like you could use a lift. Where you headed?"

Teddy realizes where he needs to go as he says it. "Malibu."

The Waning Karrr

Teddy steps into the sand of Karrr's backyard.

His father is right where he expects: sitting in a chair, gazing at the ocean. A floodlight on the back of the house casts a flat yellow glare that hits Malibu Marx at an angle, hiding the inscrutable eyes in depths of shadow.

"Dad?"

Karrr starts, then relaxes when he sees Teddy.

"Teddy. You're here."

"I'm here. How are you feeling?"

"Something of a peculiar night but—" Karrr notices the gash across Teddy's nose and his torn clothes. "My god, what happened?"

"I've had something of a peculiar night myself." Teddy sits in the other chair. "We took a new case on Monday."

"Ralph mentioned it. Something about a strange client."

"The man introduced himself to us as Dixon Woodbine, but we've since come to know him by the name David West."

Karrr goes perfectly still.

"He asked us to find something," Teddy says.

"Royal Jelly," Karrr breathes.

"Tonight, I was at an old house in Rancho Palos Verdes, and I saw a sign with your name on it."

"Good god. Good god, David, what did you do?"

"Dad, I'll listen to whatever you have to say, but you have to say it."

Phù XIII rubs past Karrr's shins, but he ignores her.

"I don't want you to think less of me."

"I won't."

"You don't know that."

"Tell me the story you need to tell."

Karrr stares at the sand for a long time.

"Back in my Army days, David West and I were in the same unit. 6th Battalion, Psychological Operations. That made us friends. Then we went to war together. That made us brothers."

"Keep going."

"We were good at what we did, proved ourselves on the usual leaflet campaigns and earned a little free reign. David had the idea to make audio recordings of dead Vietnamese soldiers persuading those still alive to defect and go home. We played the tapes in the jungle at night. Manipulative, but a lot more forgiving than a machine gun. That's what we told ourselves.

"We were assigned to work with the Air Force and Chemical Corps on Ranch Hand. They were spraying Agent Orange around the clock by then, wiping out the crop yields of entire villages on the off chance they might be helping feed the Viet Cong. Starving children are something of a bad look, even in war, so we were asked to soften the blow. So we did. Narratives that recontextualized any leaked reports or photographs deemed unsavory. We even made a cartoon in Vietnamese. *Brother Nam*. He promised the chemicals being sprayed were harmless."

Karrr looks nervously at Teddy.

"I'm listening," Teddy says.

"One afternoon, a new assignment came in. A spraying had drifted into a hamlet and killed some people. We were given the usual secondhand stats and figures, and told to write a digestible account by 0700.

"In our earlier days, David and I would've done the job, no problem. But we were different by then. We'd seen too many things we couldn't forget. Things we'd helped hide and excuse. Our enthusiasm had been replaced by disgust. With our orders, and the war, and ourselves.

"The hamlet was close enough to get to in a Jeep. We gave a motorpool guy a case of PBR to drive us out. He was a chatty kid who knew all about the hamlet. Apparently, it had been driving the higher-ups nuts. No matter how many times they cleared the place out, shot the livestock, Zippo'd the roofs, enemy activity would start up again."

Karrr puts his gaze back on the ocean.

"We came to a ghost town. Brown jungle. Livestock bloating in the fields. No movement, no sound. At the center of the hamlet, we found the people. They'd gathered around a well, maybe trying to wash off the thick film that coated every inch of the place. This wasn't drift from a nearby mission; the village had been sprayed directly and repeatedly, until everything was dead.

"Back at our typewriters, we tried to come up with the right words, but found that normally reliable phrases like 'containment policy' felt somehow inadequate to explain what we'd seen. For the first time ever, I couldn't do it. Neither could David. 'People back home think we're over here planting Old Glory in the hearts of rabid Commies,' he said to me. 'That's what they want to think, and we're the ones who let them do it. The truth is, we crossed an ocean to kill people who've never even heard of us. We can't change that now, but we *can* stop lying about it.'

"I agreed with him. We couldn't end the war we were in, but maybe we could help stop the next one from starting. The only question was how. That's when the Royal Jelly arrived."

Razing of the Lemon Grove

"This shipping container wasn't like all the others. The munitions guys who handled it kept getting sick, so it was moved to the edge of the base and fenced off. People whispered about it. Kept their distance. Someone painted a snake on the outside and there it sat, a box that killed people if they got too close.

"Ranch Hand was discontinued soon after. The war was winding down. The only thing left to do was tie up loose ends. Operation Pacer HO. All remaining Agent Orange was sent to Johnston Atoll, a tiny island a thousand miles west of Hawaii where we'd been testing nukes for decades. Somehow it fell to a cargo ship from the Netherlands to burn up the surplus chemicals using retrofitted incinerators. They'd preheat the oven to two thousand degrees, slide in the Agent Orange, and cook until it floated away in the sky. The ugly truths we'd helped conceal for years were being vaporized on a Dutch junker in the middle of the Pacific, like none of it ever even happened. It was David's idea to save the Royal Jelly.

"'We dump it on front lawns and city streets,' he said. 'Spill a few barrels on the National Mall. A waterfall down Mount Rushmore, if that's what it takes.' The point wasn't to kill anyone, but to make a mess so big, no one could look away. We intercepted some paperwork, doctored the destination fields, and watched as the Jelly was loaded onto a ship bound for the Port of Long Beach.

"I rotated back to the States before David. I stayed at my late aunt's place. She had a house with a small lemon grove, not too far from the port. Every day, I drove from Rancho Palos Verdes to Long Beach with a ham sandwich, a Thermos of lemonade, and a pair of binoculars. Then I'd sit and watch the containers come and go by the thousands. I was starting to worry the Jelly had been discovered in transit, when I saw it: the snake eating its own tail, coiled around a payload of death.

"I rented a flatbed truck and showed the port guards a fake ID that matched the doctored paperwork. I paid a crane operator ten bucks to lift the Jelly onto the truck, hid the container in the lemon grove, and waited for David to come back. That's when something happened I didn't expect."

Karrr goes quiet.

"What happened?" Teddy asks.

"For the first time in years, my life was quiet. I could think, I mean really think and feel. As I watched the lemons wither and fall from their branches, the obvious occurred to me: if David and I went through with our plan, people would get hurt, probably killed. We'd have to accomplish our goal some other way. I dug a hole in the lemon grove, lined it with concrete, and buried the container. Then I chopped down the last of the trees, burned the trunks, and salted the earth.

"When David came stateside a few weeks later, I met him in Los Angeles. He had a thousand ideas about how we were going to use the Jelly, wouldn't talk about anything else. I asked him to listen. I told him we couldn't go through with the original plan, and told him why.

"He asked where the Jelly was. I told him it was safely hidden, and that as long as I was around, it was going to stay that way. He accused me of siding with the government and conspiring to keep its secrets. I told him some time over here would change his mind, but he didn't want to hear it. Our years of friendship, our brotherhood, ended.

"We'd both come back, but only I'd come home. David was angrier every time I saw him. Given our skillsets, I guess it isn't a surprise he went into advertising, but he wasn't airtight as a person, and it changed him. I'd known him as a kid from Virginia, someone with a big heart and a big mouth who wanted to change things for the better. He became instead a person who used clever words to say clever things, all without ever moving the needle on anything meaningful. The middle-of-the-night phone calls begging me to give him the Royal Jelly slowed, then stopped entirely. I thought he'd moved on. I guess I was wrong."

Karrr looks at Teddy.

"A man visited me earlier today. Big Black guy with tiny glasses, very polite. There was something different about him, the clothes he wore or the way he carried himself. He said he represented a group that had acquired the Royal Jelly. He showed me pictures of the excavation. I asked what they were going to do with it. He said they were going to destroy it, but that they thought I'd want to know."

"Do you believe him?"

Karrr thinks for a moment. "I do. But now I'd like to hear a few things from you. Like what in God's name happened this week?"

Big Bag of Gratitude

Teddy tells his father everything. Tom Hanks on the client couch. The not-so-friendly Seabees. The dead ends of SIS and the Janusian Order. Market and the deadly excursion to Rancho Palos Verdes. David West's dissolving mental state and a nebulous something that may or may not be called Lich.

"The man who came to visit you is named Ousmane Ba," Teddy says. "It seemed at first like he worked for West, but I don't think that's right exactly. They're involved in something, something bigger than the West Company."

"That's Lich?"

"Maybe."

"I can't believe he brought you into this." Karrr has a short coughing spell. "After all this time, I really thought he'd moved on."

"It seems like he found out about the excavation after the fact, like he wasn't a part of it."

"Which could mean he's been cut loose by whatever Lich is."

"Right. He's in a bad place, Dad. He needs help."

"Teddy."

"If we can talk to him, sit him down and agree on the truth—"

Karrr shakes his head. "Truth was a junction in the tracks a long time ago. Before Vietnam and a whole lot else. West is a man to be pitied, but he's also dangerous. With the Jelly gone for good, after a lifetime of refusing to let it go . . . there's no telling what he'll do."

"Dad." Teddy looks down at his lap. "I'm sorry I haven't been here for you. I should've come around more—"

"Forget it."

"But—"

"*Forget* it."

Phù XIII jumps onto Karrr's lap. He scratches her behind the ears.

"I understand, and it's okay. Now that you know my whole story, maybe you'll agree that I'm not entitled to anything more than the bounty life's already given me. I kept the Jelly safe from David. I was blessed with you and your brother. I sit before you a big bag of gratitude, free from want or expectation, ready for whatever comes next."

"What do I do next?" Teddy asks.

"You do what you think is right."

No Place Like Lorenzo Dunes

The VW Bug pulls away from Lorenzo Dunes, its taillights briefly tinting Blue Joe red.

Teddy watches him kick cigarette filters around the bus stop and growl the usual non-sequiturs. If the man's been changed by the mortal perils he survived that night, he gives no outward indication.

The rest of Lorenzo Dunes' nocturnal activity appears similarly unchanged.

Stinney's Scouts are hitting each other with dried out palm husks while the dryers in SUDS! churn late night loads. Inside Chim Chim Donut, Mony rolls dough while Phirum sleeps at her elbow, dusted in flour. A customer knocks hopefully on the window of Raoul's Pawn 'n' More, desperation knowing no set hours.

Inside the Lint Detective Agency, Teddy quietly greets an excited Chicken and Dog. The animals calm down and follow him back to the apartment in a silent parade.

Asleep in the bottom bunk, her breathing soft and shallow, is Andie. Ralph snores on the floor close by, half leaned against the bed with an empty garbage can in his arms. Teddy watches his siblings sleep a while longer, then gently closes the door.

He sits at Ms. Beauchamp's desk, feeling like he knows less about the world than he did on Monday, and not for lack of trying.

Still, he's still got a job to do.

Grain by grain, he sifts through the chaos of West's case, the irrelevant bits slowly falling away until only a few pebbles of actual substance remain. Pairing these facts with his perspective when appropriate, Teddy organizes a coherent analysis that's hopeful without cheating.

When the case report is finished, he seals it in an envelope and writes the West Company's address on the front.

That was the easy one. There's still has a far more important decision to make. One in which Teddy's head says no, but his heart says yes.

Tie goes to the heart.

He writes a second note. Once it's finished, he slips it under the bedroom door and goes back down to the parking lot.

"It's four thirty in the morning," he says to the Stinney's Scouts loitering outside. "You guys should be in bed."

"Future's uncertain, boss," one of them says. "We're getting in all the living we can while we can. You just . . . you never really know."

The others echo the mantra.

Teddy holds out the case summary. "Feel like running an errand?"

Without a word, the boys snatch the envelope and take off, running serpentine around spots of streetlight.

As Teddy watches them go, he notices a man and a woman leaned up against a sleek white coupe parked halfway down the block. It's the same car he saw Monday night. The same square button at the top of each shirt. The same calm disposition. If Teddy had to guess, he'd say Lich is closing in.

They're welcome to try, but he's got somewhere to be.

Walking into Chim Chim Donut, Teddy gives a wink to Mony, who's still rolling dough. She winks back. An unseen departure has been necessary once or twice before, and she knows the drill. Slapping her hands onto the table, she kicks up a cloud of flour that briefly obscures the area.

"Thanks, Mony."

Teddy passes into the cloud, and out the back door.

FRIDAY

-Edward Bernays

Scanlan at the Bat

Dressed in his pajamas, Doctor Scanlan washes his hands in the operating room sink.

"An amateur sword swallower in a canoe," he says. "A blind proprietor of a scorpion farm. A dissident Muscovite whistling on a third story windowsill."

"What about them?" Teddy asks.

"They all have a better survival rate than you if you go through with this."

"Does that mean you won't do it?"

"A surgery request made under significant emotional duress? Most doctors wouldn't." Scanlan dries his hands. "I, however, recognize that moments of crisis are tailor-made for great leaps forward. Just wanted to make sure you understand the risk."

"I understand."

"Okay then." Scanlan knocks on two tanks of anesthesia. "Peanut butter or chicken flavor?"

"Whichever has less calories."

"I assume there's a recipient nearby? We can put the organ on ice but this is a sooner-the-better type deal."

"They'll be here soon," Teddy says, wondering if Ralph and Andie have found the note yet. "Any chance you can hurry?"

Scanlan snaps on a latex glove. "Surgery on a deadline. How exciting."

Minutes later, Teddy is lying on the operating table, a clear rubber mask strapped over his nose and mouth. He makes eye contact with a family of Panamanian fruit bats hanging upside down in a cage. Then he tastes peanut butter.

"A nephrectomy begins with a small incision in your lower abdomen," Scanlan says. "After pulling aside the curtains of fascia, I'll secure the spermatic cord."

Scanlan's voice adopts a long tunnel quality as the anesthesia begins to take hold.

"From there, it's a simple matter of clipping some arteries, snipping some veins, and you, my friend, will be one hundred and forty-five grams lighter."

The world gets heavy and dim.

The passage of time loses meaning.

Teddy feels a dull ache near the bottom of his ribs and wonders if Scanlan is making the incision. Then he realizes the procedure is already over. Then he forgets and falls asleep.

The sound of a door closing.

Teddy's eye opens. Through the frosted glass of the recovery room door, he sees a figure walk away. He thinks it might have been Ralph. Sleep comes again.

The sensation of being moved. It feels wrong somehow, unstable.

He's not on a bed anymore. He's on a gurney.

Fluorescent lights flash in and out of Teddy's vision, and he understands he's being wheeled down a hallway.

The nurse pushing him is tall, the sleeves of the man's scrubs reaching only halfway down his forearms. A jolt as the gurney makes contact with a door.

Blinding sunlight.

Teddy feels an eruption of pain as he's picked up. "No," he says.

Mercifully he's quickly laid down again, this time onto soft leather in the backseat of a car. A very nice car.

The engine starts, and a gentle push of inertia lulls Teddy back to sleep.

The Plaza of Refined Oil

Teddy comes to, his nostrils filled with a sweet, fiery smell he can't quite place.

He's sitting in West's velveteen armchair, which has been dragged from the central office onto the spacious floor outside.

The Plaza of Midnight Oil is wrongly quiet.

No steam whistles out of the brass cappuccino machines, no canisters shoop along the pneumatic tubes. Below the obelisk of blank TV screens, West's office looks like it was hit by a concussion grenade, each wall of curved glass shattered outward in energetic patterns across the plaza's marble floor.

Teddy tries to move, inviting a stab of pain in his lower abdomen. His left leg feels strangely stuck. Leaning forward with difficulty, he sees it's been haphazardly tied to one of the chair legs with an orange extension cord.

He gets another whiff of the smell that woke him up, a sweetly corrosive scent he loves and hates at the same time. Still, he can't name it.

Motion draws Teddy's attention to the center of the plaza.

He watches as David West dumps a banker's box filled with glossy pages onto the floor of his office. He's apparently been at it for a while because the blue carpet is almost completely obscured with paper.

West tosses the box aside and notices Teddy is awake.

"Good, no need for the smelling salts."

He crunches across broken glass and crouches down in front of Teddy's chair.

"Question for you, Mr. Lint. How do you drop a C-123's worth of Agent Orange onto a farmer's head and have it be nobody's fault? I'll tell you. The politician is just creating jobs. The manufacturer is just filling an order. The munitions guy's just loading the plane, and the pilot's just flying it. Nobody's responsible, so nobody's guilty, which means we can keep on doing what we've always done, provided there's men like me to tell the right story."

The synthetic smile and Newmanesque good looks are long gone. For the first time since he met him, Teddy sees the real David West.

"Mr. West," Teddy says through a dizzying wave of pain. "I spoke with my father. He told me what happened."

This gives West only a second of pause. "Then you know what he took from me. We were going to tell the truth for once. Just once. You'll say he had his reasons, that he was worried about what the Jelly would do. But it *had* to be the Jelly."

West's footsteps echo as he walks back to the central office.

"I was going to do this alone," he says, kicking the glossy papers into a kind of nest. "But then, early this morning, a couple Boy Scouts pushed an envelope through the front doors of this building. Your case summary. I had you wade through the slime of this town and you came back with a glowing review. Good intentions and miscommunications, the benefit of the doubt given to every undeserving soul. That's when I knew you had to be the one to bear witness."

West's back arches spasmodically, like he's stuck in a werewolf transformation he can't finish. Teddy watches helplessly as a mind that's been bending for fifty years finally breaks.

In the Snick of Time

"Stack the meat!" West screams. "That's how you win a war of attrition, you slaughter the enemy like animals and stack the bodies until they block the sun."

West dumps more boxes onto the floor of his office.

"Your father and I were going to wage a war of attrition for the soul of this country, drive out the barbarism hidden in the chambers of the American heart by any means necessary. You are pure of heart, Lint. That's why you have to be the one to tell my story."

West slaps the lid off another box and hurls its glossy contents across the plaza floor.

"Instant coffee!" he yells, picking up the ads one by one. "Video doorbells, shaving cream, canned pork. Cigarettes for stress, milk for bones. And look at this," he holds up a sunny travel ad. "Vietnam: *Gateway to the Orient*!"

He adds them to the ring of papers on the floor of his office.

"I don't have the stomach for mass murder, but I *can* deliver spectacle. Since I can't do it with the Jelly, I'll use the next best thing." He picks up a red canister. "Nothing to be scared of, Lint. Ninety-three octane. I'll go fast and clean."

West showers himself in gasoline, completely soaking his body and the kindling of ads below.

"Mr. West, please don't do this."

Teddy strains against the extension cord binding his leg. The effort threatens to black him out, but he continues to struggle.

"This is for your benefit," West says, gas dripping from his lips. "Don't look away."

"David, please don't burn yourself!"

But West is done talking. Pulling a Zippo from his suit pocket, he thumbs at the wheel.

The first try fails to summon a flame.

Teddy pulls at the cord harder than ever. Spots pop in his vision, but something in the knot gives and his bare foot slips free.

He could sprint out of the plaza, could get clear of the building before West self-immolates. He could pretend what's happening, isn't.

Teddy looks through the fast-talking ad executive with an answer for everything and sees someone else: a heartbroken idealist convinced he missed his one chance at redemption, one terrified beyond all rational thought, fast on his way to a horrific and lonely death.

Glass cuts into Teddy's feet as he runs into the office. Wrapping West in a hug, he grabs at the lighter.

West tries to shake him off, but Teddy only clings tighter.

The reek of gasoline makes Teddy's head swim. The pain in his abdomen burns white hot. He grabs again for the lighter without success, then waits for the snick of a flame that will erase them both.

Instead, he hears footsteps, echoing across the plaza.

Teddy looks up in time to see Ralph slug West across the jaw.

The Zippo summons a flame a second before it leaves West's fingers and cartwheels onto the carpet just beyond the gas-soaked papers.

Ralph yanks Teddy and West out of the office. He's about to cave in West's face when people, calm and square-buttoned, pull them apart.

Teddy collapses toward the plaza floor but he's caught by a strong pair of arms.

"Don't worry," Ousmane Ba says. "It's over."

West's dropped Zippo catches on the carpet. The flame reaches the gasoline and a hollow boom echoes through the Plaza of Midnight Oil. Burning paper sails through the air as West's office turns into a yellow and orange inferno.

"Everybody out," Ousmane orders.

The other people haul West and Ralph in the direction of the green door.

From Ousmane's arms, Teddy watches as the TV pillar is consumed by long licks of fire. It sags to one side and collapses, pushing out a shockwave of scalding air.

Before unconsciousness takes him, Teddy says one last thing to Ousmane Ba.

"Lich."

Ousmane nods.

TIME UNCERTAIN

> "Propaganda is the executive arm of the invisible government."
>
> -Edward Bernays

Scenes from an Ethereal Lobbie's

"I don't want no ODs during the lunch rush, understand?"

The no-nonsense voice of a seasoned waitress fills Teddy's head.

"I wanna see the whites of those eyeballs or you're both out of here."

"Quite right, Madame," a posh voice replies. "Teddy, rouse yourself."

Teddy wakes inside a Lobbie's restaurant. He's sitting in a booth across from a well-dressed skeleton whose top button is square.

"Apologies," the skeleton says. "I'd hoped to let you rouse naturally but the Lobbie's corporation had other plans. Presumably you know who I am, but perhaps a non-threatening show of power is appropriate."

The skeleton bangs a fork on the table.

In the next booth over, Tom Hanks, Percival Maw, Ms. Beauchamp, Big Sue, and Blue Joe look up from a shared plate of celery stacked bonfire high. In perfect unison, they recite, "This is a non-threatening show of power."

Teddy has the notion he's dreaming, but the notion floats away.

"Nice to see you again, Mr. Hanks," he says.

"Under optimal conditions," Tom Hanks replies, "celery can be stored for up to seven weeks between thirty-two and thirty-six degrees Fahrenheit."

Small and anxious Percival Maw pushes thick spectacles up his nose. "Inner stalks may continue growing if kept at temperatures above thirty-two degrees."

Ms. Beauchamp goes next: "Shelf life can be extended by packaging with anti-fogging, micro-perforated shrink wrap."

"Freshly cut petioles are prone to decay," Big Sue warns.

Finally, Blue Joe: "Decay can be reduced or prevented through the use of sharp blades, gentle handling, and proper sanitation."

The skeleton bangs his fork again, and the group goes back to eating their celery.

"You've been grasping at my cloak, young man," the skeleton says to Teddy. "Well, here I sit. What would you like to know?"

"Who are you?"

"I am the glue that holds everything together."

"How?"

"By any means necessary."

"That doesn't sound so good."

"That's because you don't yet understand. Now if you don't mind, I'd like something from you."

"What?"

"Your bones."

"But I'm not done with them yet."

"Oh, you can keep them close, I'll just tell them where to go."

"How?"

"Like this."

The skeleton clears its non-existent throat. It opens its jaw to speak again, but here comes Dan Karrr running out of the kitchen—healthy and strong as the day he broke the cult—to deliver a thundering right hook that cleaves the skeleton's jaw from its skull.

The Lich feels at its jawless head, and, realizing its capacity for speech is gone, collapses.

Welcome to Elsewhere

A long blur of time peppered by EKG beeps and the gentle touch of nurses comes to an end as Teddy wakes in a hospital room.

While the machines around his bed are state of the art, the room itself is rustic: an arched stone window showing the vibrant colors of an early dawn sky. Birdsong and the soft crash of waves carry in on air that smells clean, herbaceous, and not the least bit automotive.

Teddy's not in Los Angeles anymore.

Ralph jolts out of a chair in the corner. A crick in his posture suggests he's been sleeping there for some time.

"Teddy, you're awake!"

It takes Teddy a moment to find his voice. "Ralph."

"You're safe."

"Andie?"

"She's here."

"Where's here?"

"An island somewhere. I'm not sure."

"Andie," Teddy says again.

"She got your kidney. She's recovering down the hall. Jesus, Teddy. You scared the hell out of me."

"I'm sorry, but you would've tried to stop me."

"You're damn right. But you're both okay now. You made the right call. You're good at that."

"I'm a little fuzzy on what happened that morning."

Ralph sits on the bed. "After Andie and I found your note, I ran every light on the way to Scanlan's to try and stop you, but by the time we got there, you were already in recovery. Scanlan gave Andie the transplant, and when we brought her to the recovery room, you were gone. One of the other patients mentioned seeing a very tall nurse wheel you out. When Ousmane Ba showed up looking for West, it didn't take much to figure out who'd taken you. We decided West's office was a good bet and got lucky, pulled you out just before the whole building caught fire. Ousmane put us in a car and we got the hell out of there, passed about fifty fire trucks on our way to LAX. They drove us straight onto the tarmac and put us on a private jet without windows. Andie was already on board. Then they flew us to wherever this island is. The doctors here seem to know what they're doing. They say Scanlan did a great job with both procedures, but that West's kidnapping has slowed your recovery. You've been out for four days."

"Mercy." Teddy struggles to sit up. "Where's West?"

"I don't know. But I'm looking forward to finishing what I started back in the plaza."

"You know what I'm going to say."

"I'm not forgiving him, Teddy. Don't let the idea into your head because it's not gonna happen."

"I'm sure we'll talk about it." Teddy smiles. "For now, I just want to watch the sunrise. I wasn't sure I'd get another one."

Ralph nods. He puts an arm around his brother and they watch as the sun patiently climbs over an unknown sea.

Ping Pong & Pie

The medical facility is staffed by a crew of international doctors and nurses who really know their stuff. The food is tailored to Teddy's metabolic anomaly, and the flower arrangements are refreshed twice daily. An antique sign hanging from the corner of the building reads *Hospitalo*.

The *hospitalo* is in a small town. The small town is on an island. There are no flags to spoil a specific country, but everything feels vaguely Mediterranean. A Maltese runt maybe, suspended in watery limbo between Italy and Tunisia? Who's to say. Not the *hospitalo* staff, that's for sure. They're warmly polite, but respond to any pointed questions with deferments of, "In time, in time . . ."

The Esperanto used on the island is a touch tricky, but there are just enough English cognates to get by. You don't drink coffee, you sip *kafo*. The man on the cobblestone corner doesn't play the guitar, he strums the *gitaro*. The island's base-9 number system takes some getting used to as well, thermostats going from sixty-eight degrees straight to seventy, cats wandering the town's old-world alleys a bit more carefully than their nine-lived counterparts elsewhere in the world.

Teddy calls his father and promises he's alive and well. He can't say much about his situation, other than it doesn't feel explicitly dangerous, and that he doesn't know when he'll be back. Karrr, for his part, reassures Teddy that he too is alive and well. His voice has firmed up some since Teddy's visit. It's a wonderful sound to hear.

Next, Teddy calls Ms. Beauchamp. Once she's confirmed his good health, she fills him in on happenings at the Lint Detective Agency. Their portion of the Lorenzo Dunes rent has been paid, depleting the company's coffers entirely because West's second payment never materialized, something Ms. Beauchamp finds "frankly, unsurprising." She pledges that Chicken and Dog will be fed, coffee will be available for any new clients, and Blue Joe won't go hungry on her watch. She's confused as to why Mayor Becksdale suddenly has a horse on *The Lighthouse at Providence*, but she doesn't exactly hate how he looks in the saddle.

The doctors allow Teddy to move into the same room as Andie. After a series of tearful hugs and a comparing of scars, attention turns to the situation at hand. Andie and Ralph listen as Teddy recounts the horrors of Rancho Palos Verdes, and the revelations from Malibu. He confesses his suspicions about something called Lich, which he believes is responsible for their being on the island, even if he doesn't yet know what it is.

Teddy and Andie graduate from bedrest to shuffling around the hospital grounds, first with Ralph's help, then on their own. Andie teaches the boys how to play Hearts. Teddy dominates the ping pong table, and Ralph raves about the key lime pie (though Teddy and Andie don't have enough of an appetite to try it).

No news from the outside world reaches the island's rocky shores. If it doesn't happen here, it might as well not happen at all.

More Hearts. More ping pong and pie.

One afternoon, Andie and Teddy are sitting on the *hospitalo*'s veranda, watching sheets of rain darken the town's tile roofs when Andie says, "Thank you."

"For what?"

"For risking your life to save mine, Teddy. I'll never forget it. And I'll never be able to repay you, though I'll sure as hell try. I'm going to start by trying to be more like you. We could do worse than a world populated by Teddy's."

"Just promise you don't forget about Andie. The world needs her, too."

"I knew you were gonna say something like that. Teddy. Thank you."

"You're welcome."

The Moonlit Stroll

The three of them are playing a late-night game of Hearts when Ousmane Ba appears in the doorway.

"Hello, everyone. I'm glad to see you've recovered well. If convenient, your presence has been requested elsewhere on the island. I can escort you."

They follow Ousmane into town. Other than a group of old men drinking wine and the odd stray cat peering down from behind a chimney, the cozy streets are empty, the island's inhabitants asleep.

By the light of a half moon, they walk along the coast before turning inland. Ousmane keeps a slow pace through rolling hills, stopping every few minutes for Teddy and Andie to catch their breath. Eventually, the island's fragrant meadows of wild sage and rosemary descend into a shallow glen.

They walk for a while in the cold shadow of the valley as it gradually narrows, ending at two, almost-touching rock formations. In between the rocks, the scant moonlight reflects dully on a shipping container.

"Is that?" Teddy breathes.

"Yes," Ousmane says. "Come, it is on our path."

The doors of the weathered container are open on both ends, creating a passage to a peninsula beyond.

"It's empty," Ralph says.

Ousmane steps into the container. "The contents have been destroyed, and the container has been sanitized. It's perfectly safe."

Teddy runs his fingers along the corrugated steel and the snake's peeling paint. The mighty Royal Jelly, once a concentration of so much death and fear, is now nothing more than a benign shell, left to rust in the salt air of a nameless valley.

Teddy shakes his head. "I still don't understand what West was thinking."

"We aren't certain," Ousmane says, "though I can offer a possible explanation."

"Please."

"It's possible notoriety won from your Jocular Beef case put you into David West's mind at the same moment he was losing a battle to personal demons, demons related to untreated trauma sustained during his service in Vietnam. David perceived the persistence of that trauma to be, in part, the fault of your father. Hiring you and your brother then, was a punitive action with the aim of damaging what your father considered his greatest achievement. His sons. The risk of injury, corporeal as well as spiritual, would be greatly increased during the course of your investigation. David believed the more you saw of the world, the more likely your resilience would fail, a resilience he came to envy and loathe. In essence, he showed you a sequence without a pattern, asked a question without an answer. You were meant to fall apart inside his riddle, and when you didn't, he did. All of this, of course, is a rational assessment of irrational thinking, and as such, may contain little value."

Andie raps a knuckle on the side of the container. "Why did you guys keep the box?"

"As a reminder," Ousmane says.

"Of what?"

"Of what we're up against. Now, if you please, time must be considered."

He gestures to the peninsula that extends out beyond the other end of the container. Its grassy slope tapers gently down from the hills, ending at a shoreline where a pinprick of firelight winks in the darkness.

"That is your destination. I wish you luck."

Ousmane turns and heads back the way they came.

Teddy looks at the others. "Well. We've come this far."

For almost an hour they walk a dirt path through more fields of herbs. The short greenery is littered with pieces of sculpted white stone: ruins left over from some long-vanished civilization. The night air cools with each step, and they're glad when they reach the end of the peninsula.

A woman sitting next to a small fire stands to greet them.

"*Bonvenon, miaj amikoj.*" She speaks softly, with an accent unknown to the visitors. "My name is Maia. I would enjoy a conversation."

Maia's Story

Maia returns to the fallen white pillar she was sitting on.

She wears a cream-colored garment held together by a square button of cracked leather near the neck. Teddy puts her age anywhere from twenty-five to sixty-five, and even then, he's not sure.

"It is my privilege to host you all. Please." Maia gestures to another horizontal pillar on the opposite side of the fire.

As they sit, Teddy notices a small rowboat beached on the shore nearby. Farther out in the water, an island sits off the tip of the peninsula like the dot of an exclamation point. There seems to be some kind of structure on its shore, but it's mostly obscured by darkness.

"May I ask after your health?" Maia says to Teddy and Andie.

"Better since we came to this island," Teddy says. "Do we have you to thank for that?"

"Your Doctor Scanlan was quite capable. Our staff had little more to do than maintain your recoveries. Please allow me to offer an apology for your abduction by Mr. West. Ousmane Ba is one of our premiere security liaisons. He was tasked with monitoring Mr. West, whose erratic behavior has, as you know, lately increased. Mr. Ba temporarily lost contact with Mr. West following Market, which allowed a brief window of uncertainty. Now, I imagine you have questions."

Andie doesn't hesitate. "How did you find the Jelly?"

"Our methods will remain unspecified at this point in the conversation, but I can say that the acquisition and destruction of the Royal Jelly was determined to be an action of value."

Her mention of this impressive accomplishment comes without a hint of gravitas, as if the effort involved was on par with swatting a fly.

"Who is David West to you?" Ralph asks.

"Mr. West is a member of our organization. He is a talented propagandist whose assigned purview was the city of Los Angeles. He contributed to our mission through his company and events such as Market, though the contributions were mostly monetary."

As before, her mention of Market, an event where they witnessed transactions worth billions of dollars, is given all the weight of an elementary school bake sale.

"What is Lich?" Teddy asks.

Maia gives a gentle nod. "This, perhaps, is the question of greatest consequence."

She pulls a stick from the fire and uses it to draw a circle in the dirt.

"In the world of old, hearty people did everything they could to survive, just like those that had come before. At a certain point, some of these people decided it was unwise to let things continue in such a reckless manner. Violent revolution can bring change, but more often than not, brings along with it a revolving door of opportunistic leaders who are only too happy to exploit the confusion. Change, therefore, would have to be accomplished another way. Through temperate planning. Through patience and foresight on a timeline incompatible with ego. The practitioners of such an ethos would rarely, if ever, live to see the fruits of their labors. However," she draws a square around the circle in the dirt, "their reward would be great: a measure of control over the world."

Teddy, Ralph, and Andie exchange looks of uncertainty.

"Without fanfare or credit, we rise each morning with clear intention to shape new nodes of influence. We use techniques so faint and slow they defy identification. Pressure on this principality, or that military alliance. The subtle editing of a holy text. Delaying one technology while accelerating another. By massaging the global mind, we can nudge paradigms of thought one percent in a direction of our choosing. The agents of chaos are relentlessly creative. So, too, must be our efforts in keeping the shared enchantment of society from fading."

"Let me get this straight," Ralph says. "You're telling me if I look up photos of the biggest historical events since the invention of the camera, I'm going to see Lich operatives milling around in the background?"

"Exactly the opposite, Mr. Lint. Our presence is the last thing you would see, though adjustments may have been made."

"What adjustments?"

"Power pools in different ways in different eras. The church, the state, the market, it doesn't much matter in the end; we are a mechanism through which change is realized regardless of the instrument."

Maia pauses, giving her audience time to process.

"How does it work?" Andie asks. "Specifically, I mean."

"Our agents are given oversight of a fief, usually the size of a city. Broadly speaking, the agent's obligation is to cultivate conditions within their fief as to be concentric with our overarching goals. One aspect of this cultivation involves identifying ascendant groups, assessing the values they hold, and ultimately positioning them for acquisition or destruction. We attempt to do this in the natal stages of an idea, because tomorrow is today, if you take my meaning. Mr. West's fief was Los Angeles, and two groups of recent interest were the Janusian Order and Sisters in Sync."

"And you call yourself Lich?" Teddy says.

"Our organization retains no official title, for named things are vulnerable things, and vulnerable things end. From time to time however, we are given a name by those who feel or even suspect our influence. One such example of late, is indeed Lich."

"Mercy," Teddy breathes.

In Maia's tone, he finds none of the righteous frustration of Sisters in Sync, none of the mischief of the Janusians, and certainly none of the perverse greed of Market. She speaks with unbothered confidence, a godlike certainty that every word out of her mouth is a letter-perfect encapsulation of all available truth.

"The agent position is a delicate one," she continues. "As such, we take a great deal of precaution in selecting prospective candidates. While all three of you have displayed courage, ingenuity, and many other admirable qualities during Mr. West's imposed ordeal, you, Teddy, have done so with a functional empathy we find exceedingly rare."

A compliment of this magnitude, punctuating a speech on the true machinations of the world, leaves Teddy momentarily speechless. He looks at Andie and Ralph, then back to Maia. "Oh, well, sure . . . always happy to help."

"You misunderstand." Maia gives a warm smile. "We would like to make you an offer."

The Pitch

It might just be the chilly sea breeze blowing ashore, but a full-body shiver runs through Teddy's body. "An offer?"

"An offer to join an organization that, in a sea of impulse and mania, soberly designs information and reframes truth for more optimal outcomes."

"When you say design information and reframe truth, you mean lying."

"In a sense, but there's no need for such a rigid connotation. You're familiar with our work already. The media you see, the food you eat, the hierarchies of control you accept or don't accept in your daily life. It all comes from the maintenance of a superculture resistant to germination from unvetted ideas. Individual actions and events can't be predicted, but habits and behavior can. We deal in averages, macro perspectives on a relaxed timeline. Cultivating fruit. Fabricating distraction. Fomenting unrest. Perhaps you've noticed the ruins of this peninsula. There is no consolation prize for a failed civilization. You, Mr. Lint, can have a rare vote on the future of our species."

Teddy looks again at Ralph and Andie, who seem just as stunned as he is.

"I . . . don't know," he says.

Maia nods in understanding. "In my opinion, the work you do for your clients and your community seeks the same end goals, albeit on a reduced scale."

"I guess."

"And your rewards, most often, are frustration and fatigue."

"Sometimes."

"We can relieve you of these undue burdens. After an extensive period of study and training, you would be made an agent and assigned a fief. You would participate in international efforts as well. Your capacity to affect the lives of others will increase exponentially."

"What about the people in my life? What about Ralph and Andie?"

"Given the volume of power involved, any favoritism or corruption would be fatal to our aims. As such, acceptance of the offer necessitates an end to the life you lived before. Know that there is precious little we cannot accomplish. We can show you a better world, starting this very evening."

Braziers of fire come to life on the small island in the distance, giving border and dimension to a black acropolis set among the rocks.

"Whoa," Andie says.

In response to the lit braziers, a fleet of yachts anchored offshore turn on their underwater lamps, creating halos of light in the water. Figures from the yachts climb into rowboats identical to the one beached behind Maia. With a lantern hanging from the bow of each tiny boat, they converge on the island. Upon landing, the figures carry the lanterns in a silent procession toward the acropolis where they pass between the black pillars and vanish down a staircase at the floor's center.

"What happens down there?" Teddy hears himself ask.

Maia shakes her head. "To know the answer to that question, you must bear witness yourself. All that will be conveyed, has now been conveyed. Only your decision remains."

One Foot Out the Door

Teddy thinks.

The question before him feels a bit like one of Gerry Weinstein's impossible riddles. He can have turnkey power beyond imagination, quasi-omnipotence, and an infinite bank of resources to do the most good possible. The cost is the people he loves.

Teddy finds his head is again at odds with his heart, except this time, he can't tell which is which.

"We were raised in a cult," he says. "Of course, you probably know that already. The man in charge was named Percival Maw. Maw told us what the world looked like and how it worked. Our universe was the size of a warehouse, and he was the all-knowing god that controlled it. I think he believed in that constructed reality even more than we did. He had to, otherwise it would all fall apart. It sounds to me like you're offering to put me in that same position."

He looks at Ralph and Andie, then back at Maia.

"I can't say there's no merit in sitting around tables and drawing up blueprints for the future, but if we can trade good intentions for good deeds, keep the focus on today instead of tomorrow, a thing like Lich might not have to exist. Your offer is generous, and makes a certain amount of sense, but I don't think it's for me."

Maia's dedication to neutrality wavers only slightly in a mild look of surprise. Probably no one's ever turned Lich down before. But her expression quickly moves to one of acceptance.

"I understand, and I thank you for your consideration. We will see to your safe return. *Adiaŭ.*" She begins to push the rowboat into the water.

"Let's get the hell out of here," Ralph says.

He and Andie start back up the peninsula's path.

Teddy follows them for a few steps, then stops. "Maia."

Maia pauses launching the boat. "Yes?"

"What will happen to David West?"

"Mr. West's fate is one he has invited upon himself."

"That may be true but . . . please don't put him in a box somewhere."

"He is guilty of one of our worst offenses. He risked our exposure, and we cannot allow our anonymity to be compromised. His punishment will be consummate with his indiscretion."

"What if we look after him? Act as his advocates. You can hold me personally responsible for anything he does in the future."

Maia considers the offer, then shakes her head.

"I'm sorry. His offenses are too great."

"What if I say yes?"

Ralph is standing perfectly still, but Andie runs back and grabs Teddy's arm.

"Teddy, what are you doing?"

"If you were to accept our offer," Maia says, "and Mr. West was released into the care of your siblings . . . Yes, that would be an acceptable arrangement."

Teddy turns to Andie, numb to the massive swing of fate he's just orchestrated. "Andie."

"Teddy, no. Come with us. You don't need to throw away your life for his."

"I'm not," Teddy says quietly. "I'm helping him. Him and everyone else. That's what I've always wanted. I didn't think it would be like this, but this is it."

"Ralph," Andie pleads. "Say something to him."

Ralph doesn't move.

"I'm sorry," Maia says, "but we must be on our way."

Teddy brushes a tear from Andie's cheek. "Please help Ralph look after my dad. And West too. Can you do that?"

Andie gives a reluctant nod. Teddy wraps her in a hug.

"Goodbye, Andie."

"Goodbye."

Teddy looks at his brother. "Ralph? I have to go."

Ralph still doesn't move, except to take a step back when Teddy reaches out.

"I understand," Teddy says. "I hope you will too."

Half in a daze, Teddy helps Maia push the boat out into the choppy water and climbs inside.

They row toward the small island, the black rotunda growing larger and larger, plumes of incense and weird music floating up from the staircase at its center.

"Ralph!" Andie shouts.

Teddy turns to see his brother swimming through the water.

"Wait!" he says to Maia.

Ralph fights through the waves until he reaches the boat. Teddy helps him get his arms over the gunwale, and for a moment, they just look at each other.

"I'll do my best," Teddy says.

"You'll do well. And you'll do good."

Ralph kisses the top of his brother's hand, then slides back into the sea.

He treads water as the boat pulls away. When he can no longer make out Teddy's face, he swims back to the peninsula where Andie is waiting.

They stand together by the fire, watching as Teddy and Maia walk by the light of a lantern to the black rotunda.

At the last moment, Teddy turns to face the peninsula.

He holds up a hand in fond farewell, then follows Maia down the staircase, leaving this world for another.

FROM HERE ON OUT

"The great enemy of any attempt to change men's habits is inertia. Civilization is limited by inertia."

-Edward Bernays

Back to Reality

Ralph and Andie are flown back to Los Angeles in the windowless airplane.

They're told West will be delivered soon and are given a list of plausible cover stories for Teddy's absence.

Ralph crumples the note and tosses it on the tarmac. He's not one to litter, but emotions are running high.

Gearing down to re-enter life-as-usual proves more challenging than he expects. When the question inevitably comes, from Ms. Beauchamp, and the tenants of Lorenzo Dunes, and a large network of concerned well-wishers,

Ralph can only offer the unsatisfactory explanation that Teddy made a difficult decision and won't be coming back. Having already been visited by Lich, Dan Karrr alone is told the whole truth. Everyone else wants more, but given that Ralph also vanished and clearly isn't sleeping well, a temporary moratorium on curiosity seems to be in effect.

Ralph's never been big on dreaming, but every night that week he has the same nightmare.

Far off in the universe, a towering cosmic antagonist bigger than a planet is cooking something in a stellar furnace. The figure is a lich, of course, its tattered rags waving nonsensically in the vacuum of space. Starlight ripples across the lich's smiling, skeletal face as it withdraws invisible springs long enough to connect galaxies. Coiling the springs impossibly small, the lich floats to Earth, where it carefully places the springs, watching with infinite patience as they exert their constant and measured pressure.

Then something changes.

Teddy appears, drifting into the lich's eyeline and spoiling the view.

A showdown brews between Teddy and the lich, but Ralph doesn't get to see who comes out on top, because that's when he always wakes up. He supposes it's because he doesn't know what comes next.

Andie's return is similarly tricky. She doesn't have bad dreams, but with the fresh perspective a vacation provides (not to mention a life-saving surgery), she finds she can't live her life the way she did before.

Her first act is to fire Randall J. Pipp. She doesn't think the man's heart can stand the constant exertion of defending the Lesko estate much longer. Pipp expectantly protests her decision with a filibuster worthy argument that lasts two days, but at the end of it, Andie senses her attorney is secretly relieved to be retired.

As expected, the undefended Lesko empire collapses in a hurry. The unseizable mansion is finally seized.

When Ralph gets word, he insists that Andie come stay at the Agency for as long as she likes.

She takes him up on the offer.

The two of them are seated in the lobby on Friday afternoon, talking about Teddy for the ten thousandth time, going back and forth on what to do next. Today, Andie is on the offensive.

"We find the island, don't ask me how, and raise hell until, I don't know . . . something happens."

"If there was any hope of going back, I'd be the first one at the airport," Ralph says. "I'd fly the damn plane if I had to. But Lich Island won't be in any atlas available to the public. Even if we did somehow find it, they'd be long gone the second our feet hit the shore. They'll always be elsewhere."

"I know."

"And this is what he wanted."

"I know."

Ms. Beauchamp shuffles in the front door carrying two bulging paper bags.

"No," Ralph says.

"Yes," she fires back.

"Do we have to?"

"That's a ridiculous question, and I make a habit of not answering ridiculous questions."

"What's going on?" Andie asks.

Ms. Beauchamp sets the bags down on her desk. "On the last Friday of every month, the Lint Detective Agency holds a party for its clients and friends. It's a tradition of Teddy's, an effort to get people talking who might otherwise not."

"That sounds . . . nice actually."

"It certainly is." Ms. Beauchamp surveys the lobby. "And there's still lots to be done. You look lovely already, Andie, you're welcome to help. Ralph, please get yourself cleaned up, the guests will be arriving soon."

Since there's rarely any point in arguing with Ms. Beauchamp, Ralph accepts that the party is happening.

He showers, throws on a clean shirt, combs his hair, and re-enters a lobby that looks similarly spruced up.

The front window's been Windexed to bird-killing levels of clarity. An assortment of pretzels, ginger ale, and other party fare lies spread across the coffee table. Streamers adorn the walls and the Beauchamp Family crystal punch bowl, used on only the most special of occasions, gleams impressively atop Ms. Beauchamp's desk.

Andie is putting small black neckties on Chicken and Dog, while Ms. Beauchamp finishes removing the anti-West defenses from the coffee pot (filled with decaf, given the late hour).

Ralph gently hangs a cardigan and eyepatch on the lobby's ill-used coatrack. He hopes it will bring a hint of his brother's presence into the room, but finds it only highlights the lack.

Is this the way things are going to be from now on? Will everything Teddy touched be hollow, his only legacy one of painful absence?

It's a troubling thought, one Ralph doesn't have to entertain for long because that's when the guests arrive.

The Party

Worlds collide perhaps most famously at weddings, wherein the friend known for gravity bongs and streaking somehow gets seated next to ultra-prim Grandma Whoever. Still, no table arrangement in the history of matrimony has come close to the pair currently hashing it out on one of the Lint Detective Agency couches.

Felicity Ortega, replete with a jet-black pantsuit and smoldering cigarette, listens with great interest to minute twenty-six of Eddie Mannheim's pitch for bringing the underleveraged concept of a gynarchy into the mainstream. A man fostering Sisters in Sync's goals might not be dynamite optics, but Eddie qualifies more as a force of nature than anything else, so Ortega seems surprisingly game.

The rare couplings don't stop there.

Mark Acevedo, the Scallop Czar himself, swaps shrimp scampi recipes with Harpreet Singh, who's dressed in a Hannibal costume (complete with papier-mâché elephant).

Doctor Scanlan regales Ruth Dice with a story about a fight between an elderly appendectomy patient and a rabid sugar glider.

Violet, the once lonely grandmother, pales the punch bowl while her neighbor Tyronica actually gets Gerry Weinstein to smile.

An overalled Vivian Mojica reads Randall J. Pipp's restless palms ("You're a man of caution and restraint."), and newly single Brian from the lumber yard hits it off with Alexandra the Great near the pretzel bowl.

Mnemonic Magicians mingle with gynarchists to the tune of a keyboard played by Nelson, of Lobbie's waiter fame.

Dressed in his finest Hawaiian shirt, Dan Karrr teaches Stinney's Scouts the secret to picking a perfectly ripe cantaloupe.

Mony, Maggie, and Raoul are treated like minor celebrities, peppered with endless questions about what it's like to share a strip mall with the Lints. Perched on Maggie's shoulder, Belfast the parakeet screeches "You're plenty" at everyone who passes.

Royce Janus, who left Ms. Beauchamp temporarily speechless by saying "Enchanted" as he kissed her hand, is now being grilled by the same woman as to why in the hell Mayor Becksdale didn't start his search for the Town Hall arsonist with the obviously pyromaniacal Fire Chief O'Shaughnessy.

The ginger ale hits the collective bloodstream. Interactions bloom and merge as the partygoers unearth more common ground than any would have previously thought possible.

Ralph savors the sight a while longer, then clears his throat. The time has come to say what he has to say.

"Excuse me everyone."

Conversations around the lobby pause.

"My brother usually does these speeches but, well, you're all aware by now that he isn't here. This will sound strange, but for those who don't know, Teddy won't be around anymore, and I can't say much about why. I've had a hard time accepting his decision, but I also know that when it comes to things like this, he almost always ends up being right. He saw the world as being full of people who didn't ask to be here. People who are confused, and hopeful, and maybe a little bit scared as they try to figure things out. He said that these people have good days and bad, and that they deserve love on both. I can't replace my brother, no one can. But I'm going to do my best to see the world as he did, and to treat the people in it accordingly, good days and bad."

Ralph holds his ginger ale high.

"To Teddy."

Breakfast for Dinner

With the party still going on upstairs, Ralph and Andie slide into a booth in Chim Chim Donut.

Karrr joins them a moment later with a freshly purchased box of a dozen assorted. He bites into a jelly donut, and offers another to Andie.

She shakes her head. "Thanks, but I'm good."

"Still not much of an appetite, huh?"

"The doctors said it should've come back by now. It's weird, I feel fine, just not very hungry."

A young gynarchist and Janusian walk in. They buy an orange juice and slip into the next booth over, giving a nod of hello to Andie and the others.

"They're adorable," Andie says.

Ralph nods. "I'd say Teddy bridged a gap or two tonight. Dad? What's wrong?"

Karrr's gaze is trained on the parking lot, where Ousmane Ba and David West stand next to an idling *Fantomo*.

Ousmane faces Chim Chim Donut and gives a nod of acknowledgement. Then he shakes West's hand and gets into the backseat of the car.

The *Fantomo* leaves Lorenzo Dunes, never to return.

David West stands alone in front of Lorenzo Dunes, looking like he's just crash landed on Earth and has no idea how anything works.

Ralph looks at Karrr. "You okay?"

"Sure," Karrr says, not taking his eyes off West. "Just . . . deciding."

He abruptly stands and heads for the door.

Ralph isn't sure if he should restrain his father or run outside and hit West as hard as possible. He's still weighing his options when he feels Andie's hand on his shoulder.

"Let's wait and see."

They watch through the window as Karrr approaches West.

The two men stand facing each other.

Karrr says something.

West says something back.

This goes on for some time, until suddenly: a handshake.

"I'll be damned," Ralph says. "Forgiveness."

Strong, Conflicting Signals

While Karrr orders a coffee from Phirum Chim, West joins Ralph and Andie in the booth.

His jaw is still lightly shaded with a bruise from Ralph's punch. He looks a touch uneasy about sitting so close to his assailant.

"Don't worry," Andie says, "He hated me at first, too. I'd say he's worth the wait, more or less."

Karrr sits next to West and slides over a styrofoam cup of coffee. "There's still a good deal to be discussed, but quite the crew we have here. I have to say, I didn't see it coming, but I suppose that's what it means to be alive."

"I'm alive because of Teddy," West says. "You all probably know that, but I want to say it out loud. I'm here because of Teddy."

The others nod.

"C'mon," Andie says to Karrr. "Let's put these to better use."

She picks up the pink box and heads for the door. Karrr follows her out into the parking lot.

Ralph watches as they share the donuts with Blue Joe and Stinney's Scouts.

He gives a half smile and his gaze wanders over to the next booth, where the young Janusian and gynarchist are scrolling through social media on the gynarchist's phone. Post after post flies by, mostly ads disguised as content, the whole enterprise dictated by proprietary metrics that are good and getting better. The gynarchist slows on a video of Richard Nixon giving a national address from the Oval Office.

"Fate has ordained that the men who went to the moon to explore in peace will stay on the moon to rest in peace," a somber Nixon says. "These brave men, Neil Armstrong and Edwin Aldrin, know that there is no hope for their recovery. But they also know that there is hope for mankind in their sacrifice. These two men are laying down their lives in mankind's most noble goal: the search for truth and understanding."

Ralph's vaguely familiar with the speech. He thinks it was prepared for the event of a fatal anomaly with the Apollo 11 lunar lander, but as far as he can recall, Nixon never actually recorded it. An actor maybe? No. This looks and sounds like the actual Nixon. Something else then, a new take on an old trick in which fragments of truth are stitched together into something decidedly less true. Tapped by the magic wand of AI, the seams are getting harder to spot.

"The astronauts died?" the Janusian asks.

The gynarchist shrugs, unsure. "I guess."

There's no consensus of understanding, only strong, conflicting signals. The confusion is uncomfortable, and the couple quickly scrolls on, passing an ad for Lobbie's that shows the doomed crustacean smiling from his pot of boiling water.

Ralph looks at West.

"Is there any chance Teddy can do there what he did here? Can he actually make a difference?"

West takes a reasonable sip of his coffee.

"I'm certain he'll try."

A strange precipitation feathers against the window.

Ralph and West watch as Lorenzo Dunes is slowly coated in the ash of a distant forest fire.

Andie, Karrr, and Blue Joe take refuge under the bus stop overhang while Stinney's Scouts run around the parking lot, catching the black snow on their tongues.

Feeling like he has no other choice, Ralph gives another half smile. For any of this to make sense, one must imagine Lobbie happy.

Patrick Canning is the author of the novels *Hawthorn Woods*, *The Colonel and the Bee*, *Cryptofauna*, and *Cryptonalia*. He currently lives in Chicago with his dog, Hank. You can find him online at patrickcanningbooks.com and on Instagram @catpanning.

9 781737 878452